FOUR PLAY

TRIUNE ALLIANCE BRIDES BOOK 4

BY
HOLLY BARGO

HEN HOUSE PUBLISHING
Springfield, Ohio USA
www.henhousepublishing.com

This is a work of fiction. Any resemblance to actual people, places, or events is strictly coincidental.

ISBN: 979-8-9998797-2-1 (paperback)
ISBN: 979-8-9998797-3-8 (e-book)

Edited by Cindy Draughon
Cover designed by E-Django

For Kimmy, my daughter-in-law.
Welcome to the family.

PROLOGUE

U rsula woke up alone. That wasn't unexpected, at least for the next ten days or so, but it didn't stop her from resenting the loneliness. She preferred to be awakened on the precipice of an orgasm with a tongue, fingers, or a prehensile tail between her thighs and calloused hands caressing everywhere else with surprising gentleness. Bran and Gil always took care not to abrade her delicate skin.

Her mates, elite warriors of Uribern, served their frequent and increasingly dangerous military rotations with both stoicism and patriotic pride, fighting against the insectoid Sivuul and the even more horrific Ogranox. Uribern's alliance with Kaan and Ahn'hudin meant they did not fight alone against two ravenous species spreading across the universe in an endless quest to consume everything they encountered. At least the Sivuul only ate the species they conquered. The Ogranox ate them, too, but they took those considered prime specimens as captives and used them as involuntary hosts for their eggs, much like parasitoid wasps. The thought of Bran and Gil battling against them frightened her and inspired her to pray for their safe return.

Not for the first time, she sighed over the loss of her third mate, Crow, the berserker for whom her young son had been named. Being a Urib-human hybrid physically and emotionally bonded to her triad, Ursula could no longer produce offspring because one of her beloved triad was gone. *Dead.* So, the Urib government sent Gil and Bran out on dangerous missions as often as legally possible in the hope that they might *both* be killed and that she could be given to another triad who would bond with her, open her womb, and sire more children upon her.

The perfidy of the Urib government's intentions infuriated her, but there was nothing she could do about it. Females in Urib society enjoyed privileges, not rights. It was great good fortune that Urib males generally doted upon their precious mates.

Shoving her worries aside, Ursula performed her morning ablutions and dressed in the long, flowing garb Urib culture deemed appropriate for females in the planet's the harsh desert climate. After checking her reflection in the mirror—finely scaled, mother-of-pearl skin, emerald eyes, long white hair confined in a tidy braid—she joined her son, Crow, in the light and airy room she'd designated as the morning room.

"Mama!" he greeted her with a sharp-toothed smile. He pulled away from his nanny and raced into her embrace.

Ursula pressed a kiss to his bald pate between the buds where his horns had begun to grow. "Good morning, pumpkin. Are you ready for breakfast?"

"Yes!" he shouted. Crow seldom remembered to use his "indoor voice."

Ursula looked at his nanny, one of the many castrati who had sacrificed his breeding potential for the honor of serving the Fangrys Triad, their mate, and their son. "How is he this morning, Suvesh?"

The nanny averted his gaze so as not to look directly into the Prima's eyes and reported, "He rose at dawn and has already eaten once this morning."

"Thank you, Suvesh," she said and gave her son another hug.

The boy wriggled impatiently, so she released him. He bounded to the table and climbed into his chair. "Hungry!"

"Younglings are always hungry," Suvesh murmured as he passed her on his way to the table where the Lady of Fangrys had established the scandalous custom of dining with a trusted and beloved servant in the mornings.

Two more castrati entered the morning room bearing trays heaped with food, most of which the child would devour. Growing warrior breed males required lots of calories. Ursula filled Crow's bowl.

"More! More, Mama!"

She paused in the transfer of food to her own plate, knowing Suvesh preferred to serve himself. She leveled a sober look at the child and said, "Finish what I gave you and you may have more."

Suvesh said nothing, but she felt his approval.

"Yes, Mama." The boy pouted.

Ursula smiled at her son, keeping her lips closed so as not to expose her teeth. Bared teeth indicated animosity and threat.

As they ate, Ursula informed Suvesh of her plans for the day. The other two servants, lingering nearby to clear empty dishes and take care of any mishaps, as there tended to be with any toddler mastering the use of eating utensils, would no doubt spread the word of those plans. She hadn't actually witnessed them gossiping, but did not discount the possibility they had the same ability as she had with her mates to communicate mind to mind over short distances.

"I've got some new pieces to stock in the shop," she told Suvesh. "If you don't mind, I could use some help keeping an eye on Mr. Yells-at-the-Top-of-His-Lungs while I integrate them into inventory."

Suvesh nodded, the corners of his eyes crinkling in silent amusement as he set down his knife and two-pronged fork. "Of course, my lady. It is my honor."

The castratus took a sip of *ti'chal* and looked away for a second as he gathered his thoughts. Setting the mug down, Suvesh took a breath as though to speak further, then pressed his lips together and focused his gaze on his plate.

Ursula knew his stalling tactic well. "Spit it out."

The servant cringed, keeping his eyes averted.

"Tell me," Ursula commanded, having learned that the servants navigated a fine line between protecting her and *not* telling her what to do. As per Bran, the Fangrys Prime, *she* gave the orders.

"There is word …"

Ursula sighed and set a crumpled napkin on the table beside her plate. "Suvesh, just tell me what's going on."

"There is word of rosvoi in the area."

"*Rosvoi?*"

"Yes, Prima."

She sighed again. "Explain, please."

With a small nod, Suvesh complied. "Every species of intelligent life has individuals who prey upon their own kind. Uribern, too. Rosvoi are savages, low criminals who—"

"I get it," Ursula interrupted to forestall a lecture. Males were predisposed to "mansplaining," even on distant planets. "Are they in Fangrys? Have they actually been sighted?"

Suvesh nodded. "Not in Fangrys, but in Omari. The Omari Prime sent a personal caution at the behest of their mate. They request you postpone your scheduled visit. The Omari Triad bids us to not risk your safety nor the young master's."

She nodded, appreciating the servant's caution, even while she chafed at the restrictions he and the rest of the planet's overwhelmingly male population attempted to impose upon her. Although she'd been assimilated into Urib culture for four Urib years—after she'd been claimed by a warrior triad and physically transmogrified on a cellular level into a human-Urib hybrid— Ursula retained her human memories, human perceptions, human values, and human thoughts. The dichotomy frustrated her mates more often than not, although she never doubted their fierce devotion to her and their son.

"I'm still heading out to the shop," she declared, earning Suvesh's frown of concern. "I've got a lot more inventory for the shelves."

The servant again tried to forestall her. "Prima, Fangrys does not require the income from your business—"

"I know that," she said, cutting him off. "But *you* know that I'm not one to twiddle my thumbs and do nothing with my time."

Suvesh sighed, his resignation audible. "Yes, Prima."

Ursula smiled, a human expression, not a Urib threat. "See? That wasn't so difficult. I'll take four castrati with us. They'll keep you, Crow, me, and our driver safe and still be of use in loading and unloading the wagon."

"Yes, Prima."

She clapped her hands. "Terrific. As soon as I get Crow ready, we'll head out. Have someone load the wagon, would you? I've got all the new inventory already packed for transportation."

"Yes, Prima." The servant bowed and backed away three steps before turning to carry out her instructions.

An hour later, Ursula held Crow's small hand in hers while the beast-drawn hoverwagon lumbered down the road. The local reliance upon low-tech conveyances in a technologically advanced society never ceased to astonish her, but she'd learned to accept it. Out in the hinterlands like Fangrys and Omari, people prized a slower lifestyle. The hoverwagon, a finely crafted amalgam of wood, metal, and some sort of artificial composite, floated above the ground and was drawn at the speed determined by the team of animals pulling it. She thought the numpties looked like a weird composite of rhinoceros, llama, and iguana. The phlegmatic animals spooked at little, could move at a steady pace for several days without ever tiring or stopping to eat or drink, and were incredibly surefooted. Their one major draw-back: numpties reeked. That the Urib name for the species and the same word had a much different meaning in Scottish slang never failed to make her giggle.

Although progress was slow, particularly compared to the modern motorized vehicles on Earth and Urib's planet-wide, long-distance transportation system, the ride was smooth. Hoverwagons floated on a cushion of air, reducing the drag of the weight the numpties pulled. Suvesh himself held the reins, unwilling to delegate supervision of his lords' precious mate and their son to anyone else. The coachman sat in the back of the hoverwagon and enjoyed gossiping with the other four castrati who walked beside the open-air vehicle.

CHAPTER 1

A puff of dust and a low grunt drew Zul's attention away from the small band of rosvoi he was following. The bandits paused, too. He refocused his attention. A quartet of castrati traveled along the dusty road toward the Fangrys village, escorting a hoverwagon. Two of the castrati carried pikes, the glowing blue tips indicating the blades could do a lot more than merely jab and stab. That extra capability made them either additionally lethal in the hands of an experienced warrior or foolishly dangerous if wielded by an amateur. Because lesser breeds who served as castrati typically weren't warriors, Zul assumed they carried the weapons more for show than anything else.

He wondered what they guarded that was so precious. His eyes narrowed, as his ears caught the light, sweet voice of a female and the high-pitched laughter of a youngling. Zul revised his assumption of the castrati's inexperience with weapons. He couldn't believe that the female was the Fangrys Triad's mate. He shook his head in disbelief. *No, the female and her youngling must belong to a merchant dyad who are too cheap to hire proper protection.*

He'd heard of the Fangrys Triad; their fierce reputation commanded respect. Zul, along with all of Uribern, had mourned when their berserker perished from grievous wounds sustained in battle. The Urib would not have won that momentous battle without the mighty warrior's unflagging courage, vicious skill, and sacrifice. The Ogranox had retreated from the galaxy in humiliation.

Uribern, however, did not rest secure in that victory. All knew the Ogranox would return in larger numbers sooner rather than later.

Zul assumed the remaining warriors of the famous triad would not allow their mate to travel unprotected and thought it strange they would allow her to travel unaccompanied by at least one of them. Rumor had it their female was uncommonly independent. He attributed that particular character flaw to her human ancestry. Urib-human hybrids, he'd been told, took time to acclimate—if they ever did—to Urib expectations for females. He wanted a closer look; he'd never seen a human before.

It did not occur to him to consider what adjustments the Urib males who mated those hybrid females made to accommodate their prized mates.

A flicker of movement drew his attention. He cursed under his breath. The rosvoi had crept closer while he focused on the female, the youngling, and the castrati. His thigh muscles ached as he held still within a crouched position, ready to charge forward to the rescue. Though the only survivor of his warrior triad and yet to be accepted by another bonded pair, Zul yet held to his honor unlike the bereft rosvoi who had lost their honor along with their blood bonds.

Zul crept forward, careful to avoid stirring up any dust that would alert the rosvoi to his presence and location. He paused, watched the hoverwagon's slow progress, heard the youngling's bright chatter, and inhaled the numpties' stench. It was strong enough that he doubted the rosvoi or the castrati would detect his own scent though the reek, although one of the plodding numpties cocked a long ear in his direction.

He calculated the moment when the rosvoi would leap from cover, their ululating war cries cutting through the air to startle their victims. He charged, too, claws and blade at the ready, teeth bared in a ferocious snarl. The castratus driving the team slapped the reins on the numpties' backs, but the stolid beasts stumbled to a halt rather than leap forward into a lumbering gallop. The animals jigged and danced in their harness, bellowing their fear. The two castrati with pikes leveled their weapons at the bandits. The other two castrati leaped onto the wagon and, with the two already riding, surrounded the female and youngling, forming what was intended to be a protective circle.

Zul ran, dry air sawing in and out of his lungs while the thick, heavy muscles of his legs propelled him across the hot, arid land. The telltale sizzle of a laser striking flesh informed him that at least one of the pike-wielding castrati managed a hit. Zul's blade swiped in a broad arc that took the head off another bandit. Twisting to one side, he leaped, avoiding the heavy swipe of a tail while twisting midair to whip his own tail at his opponent. The castrati shrilled and snapped, small predators courageously defending against much larger ones. They darted in and out, bit and slashed. Their distraction sufficed to enable Zul to drive his sword into two more rosvoi, giving them a warrior's end rather than the ignominy they deserved. Unfortunately both of the pike-wielding castrati were the first among their number to die. Three more followed in all too quick succession in defense of their Prima and her son.

The remaining three rosvoi turned their collective attention to Zul. Keeping to a coiled stance and ready to dart in any direction to attack, parry, or retreat, Zul nonetheless kept one eye focused on the female and the youngling who quite sensibly crouched behind the remaining castratus for protection. He noted her small size, barely larger than a half-grown purebred Urib. Something sizzled low in his gut and twinged in his broad chest. He ignored the sensations, preferring to survive and deal with them later.

"Get them to safety!" he snarled at the driver.

"Suvesh, please!" the female hissed. She picked up an item from the back of the wagon—Zul could not see what it was—and flung it at the jigging numpties. The item struck one numpty's hindquarters and shattered. The beast bellowed and lurched forward. The other numpty immediately matched its pace. The hoverwagon floated smoothly behind the racing beasts, leaving behind five dead castrati on the dusty earth. The driver shoved the reins in the female's hands and leaped from the wagon. As soon as his feet touched ground, he scrambled to retrieve one of the fallen pikes.

"I will fight with you," the castratus promised, his voice surprisingly deep and mellifluous.

"Protect my back," Zul ordered.

"With my life."

The remaining three rosvoi charged. The castratus aimed the pike with surprising accuracy and wielded it with unexpected skill as he defended Zul's blind side while the berserker thrusted and parried and lunged and dodged. When one of the better skilled rosvoi knocked the sword from his hand, he drew the dagger at his hip and swiped with his claws, horns, and tail. Using every tool at his command, he finally unleashed the deep rage that burned inside every berserker.

A red film glazed his eyes, giving him access to the infrared spectrum that made blood glow and illuminated weak points with lethal accuracy. His muscles felt the sizzle of new energy and increased strength, enabling him to move with enhanced speed and precision. The base of his horns turned cold and hardened, lending additional strength where they were anchored in his skull and contracting the tips to deadly, extra-sharp points. With a bestial roar pitched to concuss brains and liquefy bowels, he slaughtered the three remaining rosvoi.

The berserker rage retreated when he no longer had a target. He took deep breaths and blinked away the red haze. After a moment, he found himself looming over the castratus huddled on the ground in a submissive pose beneath the threat of his dagger. Zul shook his head to dispel the lingering effects of the berserker rage. He sheathed the dagger and stepped away to retrieve his sword from the dusty earth.

"You are safe," he grunted at the shivering castratus.

The hoverwagon's driver slowly picked himself off the ground and, when standing, dusted himself off with grave dignity despite the spreading stains of blood on his clothes. His green eyes narrowed as he focused on the ruddy-skinned, black-horned berserker. He looked around, and what he observed distressed him. He made a low keening sound in the back of his throat then said, "Fangrys owes you a great debt of gratitude."

"Where are her mates?" Zul demanded. "How can they allow a female to travel without protection?"

"Prima cen'Vyr does as she wills," the servant replied.

"*Prima?*" Zul was appalled.

The servant bowed. "As I said, Fangrys owes you a debt."

Zul huffed. "That debt will grow, as *I* will protect the Prima if her warriors will not."

The driver averted his gaze then said, "They *cannot.*"

Zul leaned forward, a growl building in his throat. "Has the loss of their Third so besmirched their honor?"

The castratus met his gaze without flinching, a bold and unexpected response. "They are deployed."

He hissed in disbelief. "Does the government not know—"

"Of course, they know," the driver snapped. "But it was deemed more important to Uribern to have them fighting on the front lines than to remain here to protect their mate."

"I don't understand," Zul admitted. "The Ogranox retreated."

"And the Sivuul attacked."

"What is the date?" Zul demanded. At the castratus' answer, he clenched his jaws. He'd definitely lost track of time.

"Who are you?" the castratus asked.

"I am Zullar cen'Gyrah, Third of the Uk'khadir Triad."

The castratus's eyes widened in recognition then narrowed in suspicion. "The Uk'khadir Triad was killed sixty years ago."

"I am all that remains," Zul admitted.

The castratus remained unconvinced, but said nothing of the sort. Instead, he bowed then began walking toward the village.

"Where are you going?" Zul asked as he fell into step beside the castratus.

"To the village. The Prima conducts business there."

Surprise again compelled Zul to blurt in disbelief and astonishment. "The *Prima* conducts *business*?"

With cool dignity and quiet pride, the servant explained, "The *Prima* is a skilled potter. She sells her ceramics in the village. Her wares are much sought-after."

Zul then realized what she had thrown at the numpty's hindquarters and blinked in a weird mixture of admiration and fury. How *dared* the Prima ignore her safety and jeopardize the youngling? His mouth opened, but the words of objection and condemnation remained stuck in his throat. He decided he would admonish the foolish female himself, because she obviously needed a stronger hand to guide her than the indulgent Fangrys Prime or Second applied. The idea that, perhaps, it was not his place to scold and chastise another's mate flashed into his mind and dissipated like a wisp of smoke.

"Return to inform the Fangrys household of what has happened," Zul declared. "Your wounds must be treated." He thumped his chest with a massive fist. "*I* will protect the Prima until her mates return. She and the youngling will come to no danger while I guard them."

The castratus leveled a speculative gaze at him as the warrior broke into a ground-covering trot and quickly put distance between them. Zul almost thought he heard the servant mutter something insolent like, "Good luck."

CHAPTER 2

Ursula hauled on the reins to stop the numpties. The great beasts' sides heaved as they panted, heads lowered in weariness. A stolid plod expended far less energy than a panicked gallop. A neighboring entrepreneur, who owned and operated a restaurant exited his storefront, glanced at the hoverwagon and turned a querying eye to her.

"Where are your guards, Prima cen'Vyr?"

Before answering, she checked to make sure Crow had come to no harm. Rather than being frightened by the flight into town, the boy's eyes sparkled with excitement. She turned to her neighbor and replied, "We were attacked on the road from the manor." She bit her lip, blinked watery eyes, inhaled deeply, and took a moment to muster the necessary calm before she succumbed to fright and grief. "I do not know who, if any of my people, survived."

The restaurateur's tail lashed. He extended a hand toward her. "Disembark now, Prima cen'Vyr. You and the youngling must be kept safe."

She smiled at him. "Thank you, Mr. Gallik. Your concern for our safety does you credit and honors us."

The restaurateur frowned. Ursula wondered if he thought she mocked him, despite the polite words. Nonetheless, she took his hand and descended from the hoverwagon. She held up her arms, and Crow leaped into them. The restaurateur steadied her as she began to topple over. Crow seemed to get larger and heavier every day.

Ursula set her son on the ground and turned to her fellow businessman. "Mr. Gallik, I must speak with the mayor and sheriff to send assistance. May I borrow your staff to unload my wares?"

He raised his chin and blinked his yellow eyes slowly. "*I* will alert the mayor and sheriff, but only if you retreat to the safety of your shop. Sifgul and our mate will keep you company."

She knew he meant for his mate and his dyad bond, a slender, bookish male, to keep an eye on her and report back to him, a report he would then gladly relay to Bran and Gil when they finally returned from their latest deployment. Ursula also knew the mayor and sheriff likely would refuse to speak with her; neither approved of a female running her own business, but they would grant audience to Gallik.

Bowing to him, she said, "You are most gracious, sir. I thank you."

Gallik nodded. He aimed a pointed gaze at the door to her shop and waited, making clear without speaking that he would do nothing until her safety was assured. Taking Crow's hand in hers, Ursula complied with the unspoken order to retreat. When the glass-fronted door closed behind them, she looked through it and met the male's gaze. He nodded in approval before ducking into his own store to summon his staff, his dyad bond, and mate.

Moments later, Addilli and Sifgul entered the pottery shop accompanied by two males of the same small, nimble breed as the castrati servants who managed and maintained the Fangrys manor. Addilli's servant saw his mistress seated on a stool in the storeroom where she would be expected to stay out of sight while keeping the Fangrys Prima company. Sifgul positioned himself near the door. Ursula sniffled and wiped her tears with her sleeve.

"Thank you for keeping me company, Addilli," Ursula greeted her friend with a warm if watery smile. She ignored Sifgul who would have taken affront if she'd acknowledged him. "Would you like some tea?"

The restaurateur's mate gave her a nervous smile and nodded. "Gallick says there was trouble on the road from Fangrys. Are you and your youngling unharmed, Prima?"

"We're fine," Ursula said and sniffled.

Addilli gave the boy a fond smile as he rummaged through the toy box Ursula kept at the shop for his amusement. He had yet to understand the gravity of what had just happened.

"I worry for the castrati, though," Ursula added. "At least one of the rosvoi who attacked us was warrior breed."

Addilli nodded. "Yes. Gallick will see that the authorities are notified of this crime in lieu of your mates. He has already assigned two of our staff to unload your merchandise and care for the numpties." She paused then leaned forward. "How did you get them to run? I could not believe I witnessed numpties actually galloping!"

Ursula shook her head and let Addilli's comment distract her from her grief. "I'm not sure what really happened. One moment we were traveling as usual, the next a gang of thugs attacked." She shook her head again and rubbed the back of her neck. "The castrati fought back, defended us as well as they could but—" Her voice cracked and she sobbed. A moment later, she again mustered her composure before Crow realized she was upset. She sighed and wiped her eyes again. "A warrior came to our defense."

"A warrior?"

"Yes, he… he looked like *Crow*."

Addilli glanced at the child.

Ursula shook her head. "No, not my son, but one of his fathers: Crow cen'Vyr, Third of the Fangrys Triad and the Bridge who connected my First and my Forever."

Addilli's eyes widened. "What did he look like?"

"Big. Massive. Perhaps not as tall as Bran, but… *huge.* Red with black horns."

Addilli nodded. "Ah, a berserker."

"Do *all* berserkers look like that?"

Addilli nodded. "Yes. Gold Urib are high caste: they are leaders. Other Urib castes and vocations range a spectrum of colors, but the mightiest of warriors—the beserkers—they are always *red like blood,* and they are *always* bonded within a warrior triad." Addilli paused. "It is worrisome that you encountered a berserker alone. They are dangerous—unstable—when not bonded."

Ursula pursed her lips, realizing she'd spent too much of the last few years immersed in the minutiae of her life and mourning the loss of her Bridge and *not* learning more about the culture to which she now belonged. *What's done is done.* She took a deep breath and turned her head toward the clatter of merchandise being set upon the floor of her shop. Rising from her own stool, she said, "I should supervise."

Addilli's eyes widened again. "Surely, that would not be wise."

"Why not?"

"What if the rosvoi followed you here?"

"You've heard about them prior to today?"

Addilli nodded. "Yes. My mates hired extra staff to protect me."

Annoyed, Ursula muttered, "Does everyone know about these criminals? Am I the last to know again?"

"Your people do as they must to protect you," Addilli said.

Ursula rubbed her temples, feeling the throb of a headache erupt. "I… I…" She gasped and burst into tears, unable to hold back the horror any longer.

"Mama?" Crow wrapped his arms around her waist and laid his head in her lap.

Ursula stroked his head with a trembling hand while she sobbed. Addilli pulled a handkerchief from her pocket. Handing the potter a clean square of cloth, she rested her hand on the female's shoulder in quiet support as Ursula wept. The slam of the store's front door startled them.

"Prima!"

The two females gasped. Addilli cringed. Sifgul, whose presence Ursula had forgotten, scrambled backward several steps with an awkward squawk. Ursula looked around for something, anything, she could use as a weapon and grabbed a small ceramic pot, thinking she could throw it and hit the intruder with it. If nothing else, it might prove a distraction and give them a few necessary seconds to escape. Standing on trembling knees, she disentangled Crow from her skirts and whispered an order for him to stay with Mistress Addilli. Hefting the pot in her hand, she sidled through the doorway separating the storeroom from the shop.

She gulped at seeing the hulking red warrior standing in the center of the display floor. His broad, muscled shoulders strained the much-mended fabric of his shirt. A torn sleeve revealed the impressive musculature of his arm. Worn leather vambraces encircled his forearms. A wide belt wrapped around powerful hips from which hung a brown kilt of heavy, well-worn fabric. His tail lashed, a sure sign of irritation. A sheathed blade dangled at one hip, the hilt of another, longer blade poked above one shoulder. Heavy boots encased feet which she knew would be tipped with sharp black claws. He was dusty, but otherwise looked clean.

"Prima," he repeated, this time quietly, although she felt the deep rumble of his voice in her bones.

She wiped her eyes again, straightened her spine, and stepped fully into view. "I am Ursula cen'Vyr, Prima of Fangrys." She swallowed and hoped he did not intend to finish what the thugs started. "I owe you a debt of gratitude."

His keen black eyes glanced around her shop. His nostrils flared as he inhaled. "Where are your mates?"

"Deployed," she answered, knowing her candor might well be the death of her and Crow. She glared at the berserker and swallowed a lump of fear. "Where's Suvesh?"

Sifgul frowned at her admission of vulnerability. The berserker nodded, the wicked sweep of his black horns gleaming beneath the overhead lights. "The castratus? I sent him back to your household. He was injured. I will secure your protection until your mates return."

Ursula opened her mouth to object, but closed it without saying a word. She'd learned early of Urib male dominance in a culture that considered its women precious and coddled them. Independence in females was neither common nor condoned. A woman in Urib society lived by privileges, not rights. Although she loved her mates and the son she'd born, Ursula—not for the first time—mentally damned the shifty, weaselly government official on Earth whose deception had exiled her to a galaxy far, far from Earth.

She set the ceramic pot on the counter and said the only thing she could: "Thank you."

He nodded again, accepting her simple expression of gratitude with what might have been a fine shiver of… pleasure?

Ursula figured she might as well be hospitable. He'd defended her and Crow against the rosvoi, so she assumed he harbored no ill intentions toward her or her son. "May I get you something to eat? To drink?"

"That would be welcome."

She nodded and retreated to the storeroom where Addilli waited with eyes widened in fright. "Will you watch Crow for me? Please?"

Addilli pressed her hand to Crow's small body, holding him against her as he squirmed and hissed to be let go. She whispered, "Shall I take him to Gallik?"

"The youngling is safe. I will not harm him," the berserker's deep voice rumbled from the shop.

Ursula's eyes widened and Addilli squeaked. Ursula bustled about, pulling food and drink from the refrigeration unit, food that had been meant to feed the castrati who had perished defending her and Crow. She coughed, the lump of sorrow in her throat swelling.

"Go," she whispered, urging Addilli to return to her mate and the safety of their restaurant. "I'll send Sifgul shortly."

Addilli understood the unspoken request to determine whether Gallik had summoned law enforcement. With a swish of brightly colored skirts, she hurried away, using the connecting door between the storerooms.

Ursula carried out a tray of food and drink, Crow walking beside her, a fold of her skirt clasped in his small fist. She set the tray on the counter and backed away a few steps.

Mustering her courage, she asked, "Who are you?"

The hulking, red-skinned, black-horned warrior thumped his fist against his sternum and said, "I am Zullar cen'Gyrah, Third of the Uk'khadir Triad." His expression turned melancholy without the movement of a single facial muscle. "The Uk'khadir Triad is no more. I am all that remains."

"May your loss be forever honored," she intoned the formal expression of condolences and bowed her head. "I am grateful for your service."

"Sit," he bade her and poured water from the pitcher into a tall glass.

She retrieved her stool and brought it from the storeroom into the shop. Placing it behind the counter, she perched on it. Crow sat on the floor beside her.

"Will you tell me of my people?" she asked after Zullar had quenched his thirst.

"All dead but for the driver," he replied.

Ursula closed her eyes and sent up a heartfelt prayer.

"Mama?" Crow whispered.

She looked at him and gave him a watery smile. He offered her Addilli's handkerchief to wipe her tears. She took it.

CHAPTER 3

Zul ate the food the lovely female brought him, observing her and the youngling who clung to her, his tiny fists clutching the fine fabric of her skirt. His hearts beat in synchronicity, a powerful pulse within his broad chest. His blood, still heated by the glimmering of berserker rage, warmed even more. A seductive little voice seemed to whisper in his ear that this lovely female was unprotected and, therefore, *available*. He could steal her away and imprint his bond upon her.

He shook his head to dispel such dishonorable thoughts. He was not so far gone in his devolution that he would willingly abandon all semblance of honor to become a ravening beast such as one of the rosvoi. He swallowed a long gulp of water and asked, seemingly ignorant of the answers to ensure she was truly who she claimed to be, "Who are your mates, Prima?"

She answered, "I am mated to Gilvane cen'Vyr and Brannal cen'Vyr."

His forehead wrinkled and he lied again, "I was not aware they were the lords of Fangrys." He paused, then asked, "Was there not a third in their triad?"

Ursula nodded. "Crow cen'Vyr. He… he perished before our son was born."

"May your loss be forever honored," he murmured at seeing her genuine grief at the loss of the famed and mighty berserker. He wondered if Crow had died in glory, but did not ask. He aimed a piercing look at her, noting she did not have the same appearance he had seen in other species of females biologically compatible with Urib males. But then, he realized, he had not yet seen a human female, the latest species to offer their females as brides to Uribern. He remarked, "You're a hybrid."

Feeling the tickle of loose strands that had escaped her braid, Ursula smoothed back her white hair. "Yes. I came from Earth."

Zul absorbed the information: *Earth* meant *human*. After a long moment during which he devoured three rolls, he said, "I heard the Council Supreme negotiated a treaty with a new planet and that Uribern was to receive brides."

Ursula nodded. She pursed her lips, a sour expression. "Yes, Earth is that planet. The brides were not informed as to their destination or their purpose."

His eyes narrowed in suspicion. "Do you accuse our governing council of falsehood?"

She shook her head and tried for tact. "No, but the government of *my* homeland concealed their true intentions. Uribern's honor was not besmirched in the importing of brides."

She'd left something unsaid, but Zul ignored the unvoiced accusation because wanted to take her hand in his, to examine her fine skin up close. She was truly exquisite. He refrained because he still considered himself an honorable male. An honorable male did not touch another male's mate, no matter how much he desired to feel her softness. Instead, he asked another question, again concealing what he already knew and hoping to lure her into revealing something he didn't know. "What is your species called?"

"Human." Ursula didn't bother with scientific nomenclature—*Homo sapiens sapiens*—and get into a discussion of Primates and evolution. That was unnecessarily complicated. *I was an event planner, not a biologist.*

"When are your mates expected to return?" Zul asked and popped another chunk of meat into his mouth to chew while he listened to her reply.

She sighed. "Not for another ten days." Before he could ask as she assumed he would, Ursula added, "I don't know where they've been deployed to or any details regarding their mission."

Zul snorted. "Of course, you do not. It is not proper for you to have such knowledge."

A door closed as the last of Gallick's servants departed, having unloaded the contents of Ursula's hoverwagon. She stood and bowed her head, the youngling clinging to her skirt.

"Please excuse me. I have inventory to display," Ursula said.

The berserker set down the large cup he was about to drink from and followed her even though he could have watched her from behind the counter where he sat. Curious as to what this strangely appealing human-Urib hybrid would do, he watched as she opened a crate, pushed aside fibrous packing material, and withdrew a gleaming ceramic vessel. She ran her hands over its surface, ensuring no stray particles of the packing material remained to dull the shiny exterior. She placed it on a shelf and returned to the crate.

"Crow, please fetch me the polishing cloth."

"Yes, Mama," the boy replied and darted behind the counter to retrieve a clean cloth. "Here, Mama."

"Thank you, pumpkin." She took the cloth from his hand and pressed a kiss between the nubs of his horns.

Zul stared as she worked, unsure as to what his reaction should be. He believed her to be the artist who crafted such gorgeous yet functional items—something that made him feel proud, though she was not his to inspire such pride—or appalled that a high caste female demeaned herself with such menial labor as she was now performing. He glanced about, but the neighboring business owner's servants had already departed, and she had none of her own with her. Of course not: they'd been killed by the rosvoi.

"Stop," he ordered.

She looked at him, blinking in surprise, her hands going still.

"I will do that."

She blinked again. "I appreciate the offer, but this is my shop and these are my wares."

"It is not for a Prima to perform such menial labor," he said.

She pressed her lips together and leveled a hard stare at him. After a moment's thought and realizing that "menial labor" wasn't the hill she wanted to die on, Ursula nodded and stepped away from the crate. "All right, then, *you* carefully remove each item from the crate and wipe it clean. *I* will set it where I want it to go."

Zul shook his head. "*You* will direct *me* where to place each piece."

She opened her mouth to protest then changed tactics. "I thought you had assigned yourself to guard duty."

Zul decided he liked her push-back. It showed spirit, something many Urib males did not appreciate and something he figured was a remnant of her of her human nature. Humans, he had heard, were contrary beings. "I can do both."

"Fine," she muttered. She sighed and averted her eyes. "But you'll leave the customers to me."

Zul frowned.

"You'll just scare them," she pointed out. "If you frighten my customers, then I won't be able to sell anything to them, and my shop needs to turn a profit if it's to remain a viable business."

Still frowning, he nodded. She was correct; he *would* frighten them. He also understood the necessity of profit to keep a business open; however, what he did not understand was why the Fangrys Prima needed to earn money. Were her mates careless in their spending? Did they not place limits on her own foolish expenditures?

As though intuiting the direction of his thoughts, Ursula growled, "Don't even think it."

Perhaps, he thought, her mates were lax or overly permissive in what they allowed her to do. Were she his, he would ensure her security from foolishness. *But she is not mine and I have no true authority over her—only her mates do.* The admission convinced him to acquiesce to her terms. He bowed his head and said, "I will not interfere with your interaction with your customers as long as they treat you with respect."

"I'll let you know if I need help," she replied, her tone arid.

Taking her youngling's hand, she murmured to him, and they retreated to the back room only to return a moment later with a small mat and a handful of toys. Zul pulled out a jar, took a second to admire the unusual blue, green, and silver glaze, and wiped it clean.

"Put that one next to the green vase in the window," she said. "Don't forget the lid."

Lid? He rummaged through the packing material to find the lid which had become dislodged during that morning's flight to safety. He pulled it out, wiped it clean, and set it in place.

While he worked, Ursula kept an eye on him, an eye on her son, and an eye on the front door. *Luckily, I'm good at multitasking.* Gallick returned, doing a double-take upon seeing the hulking berserker performing menial work. But he said nothing about that, only solicitously inquiring as to her well-being.

Ursula smiled at him and replied, "Thank you, Mr. Gallick. Crow and I are fine. Have you spoken with the mayor and the sheriff?"

The restaurateur replied that he had, but he did not feel comfortable relating the details of the conversation to her. It wasn't appropriate.

Ursula sighed. "Mr. Gallick, you should know very well by now that I will insist on being informed."

He glanced at the berserker who was quite obviously listening to their conversation. "Prima, I would not cause you worry."

"Mr. Gallick, I will be *excessively* worried if I do not know what the sheriff and mayor have decided."

"Tell her," Zul ordered.

The restaurateur's eyes widened in surprise.

"Please, Mr. Gallick," Ursula added.

Unwilling to confront the hulking berserker, the smaller male acquiesced, his shoulders sagging. "The mayor believes word has gotten out that the Fangrys Prima is not adequately escorted and protected. When you leave town today, you should not be permitted to return without an armed escort and one of your mates."

Ursula ground her molars and reminded herself that her neighbor was only the messenger. He did not deserve her ire, despite his agreement with those who would treat her as weak, stupid, and incompetent. He also had not delivered the answer she sought, namely, the formation of a posse to pursue and take into custody any other rosvoi patrolling the region.

She took a breath to calm herself, then asked, "And how do they expect me to get home if I must always be accompanied?" She wiped the tears that welled up. "I *was* accompanied by an armed escort! They *died* defending us." She paused. "And when was the mayor going to inform me of his decision, since he won't talk to me directly?" She paused again and took a deep breath to calm her frustration. "He *would* have to inform *me*, is that not correct? Because my mates are not here."

Gallick gave her a calm, cool look of offended dignity. "The mayor sent the sheriff to inform the Fangrys household to send another escort to see you and the youngling home." He glanced at Zul. "Warrior, have you seen other rosvoi in the area?"

Zul looked down at Gallick from his greater height. The other male flinched beneath the berserker's silent dominance. Zul replied, "I have not, but I will escort the Prima and her youngling home. I will ensure their safety."

Gallick's gaze flickered to the boy who played quietly on his mat. Zul knew the boy was listening.

Gallick's expression turned suspicious. "You look like a rosvo yourself."

Zul absorbed the implied accusation without anger. He nodded, a single dip of his chin, in acknowledgement of his less than reputable appearance. "My bonded were killed in combat long ago."

"Many rosvoi were once bonded," the restaurateur pointed out.

Zul admired the smaller male for that stubborn, selfless courage and acknowledged the truth of his statement. He pressed his fist to his chest and quietly declared, "I lost my bonded. That does not mean I also lost my honor."

"Well," Ursula interjected herself into the conversation, "as the only available representative of the cen'Vyr triad, I will see that you receive a good meal, a clean bed, coin, and a bath in appreciation."

Zul's nostrils flared. "I do not seek your coin."

"If you've been wandering about for a while—" she let her gaze run over his dusty, much-mended garb, "—and it looks like you have—then you are obviously in need of funds." She jutted her chin at him. "You *will* accept payment."

Gallick groaned.

With cool dignity, Zul replied, "I have adequate funds, Prima. I have simply not accessed them lately."

She huffed and turned away from the two males, muttering, "Stupid, prideful men. They always think they know best."

Gallick threw him a long-suffering glance in a moment of male solidarity. Zul stifled a chuckle. He *was* prideful.

"Prima, I will remain with you until your mates return," he declared. "It was ill done of the Council Supreme to command both your mates to duty and leave you without adequate supervision."

"Supervision?" she echoed, eyes narrowing in outrage. "I am a competent, intelligent adult and fully capable of—"

"Protection," he amended with a small, one-shouldered shrug.

A shiver of pure fury rippled through her. Zul thought it both magnificent and charming. He understood why the cen'Vyr triad had claimed her: she had fire. He wondered if she burned as brightly when being fucked, then shoved that dishonorable thought aside before he succumbed to the urge to find out.

Gallick backed away, apparently familiar with the Prima's temper tantrums.

"If you weren't so damned big …" she hissed, propping her fists on her hips. She wanted to poke him in the chest, but the heated gleam in his black eyes stayed her hand.

Zul's hand itched to touch her, to cup her cheek in his palm. He clenched both hands into fists.

The door opened and two males entered, one tall, slender, and officious looking and the other obviously a servant. Still fulminating, Ursula turned her attention toward them and forced herself to speak in a polite tone, "Welcome, Mayor. How may I help you?"

The male in charge turned his thin face to her, frowning at her for having the audacity to speak to him directly.

Ursula sniffed. "Get over yourself. Gil and Bran aren't here, so you'll just have to speak to me directly."

Zul stepped forward, drawing himself as tall and imposing as possible, which was *very*. While he'd enjoyed tweaking the lovely female's temper, the mayor's dismissive attitude toward her irritated him. So, he took charge. "In the absence of her mates, I will represent the Prima of Fangrys."

Ursula's indrawn hiss of outrage gratified him. He interposed himself between the female and the mayor.

"And who are you?" the mayor inquired, his gaze taking in Zul's dusty, mended clothes and dismissing him as unimportant.

Once again, Zul identified himself. "I am Zullar cen'Gyrah, Third of the Uk'khadir Triad."

The mayor's eyes widened in surprise even as his servant muttered, "The hero of Horwill'an!"

Zul loathed that appellation. It reminded him of the day his bonded had been killed in battle.

The mayor's expression conveyed his disappointment. He expected more from an illustrious hero than worn boots, clothing near to rags, and scarred horns that needed a good polishing. "And how do we know you speak the truth?"

Zul growled. The menacing sound made Gallick squeak and flee. A sweet bouquet rose in the air from the beauty behind him. His growl lowered, nearly becoming a purr at the fragrance of her arousal. The mayor's expression soured further, although whether at scenting Ursula's physical response to a mighty male equal to her mates or at the warrior's own affront, only he knew.

"The Prima will close this shop and remain home until I am assured no other rosvoi are in the area *and* her mates return to provide proper escort," the mayor intoned.

"This is *my* shop, and you can't close it!" Ursula protested. "I have broken no law!"

The mayor met Zul's black eyes with a supercilious glare. Apparently, he expected an itinerant wanderer to exert authority over a high caste female mated to two highborn warriors. "The female is impertinent."

Zul nodded. He turned to command the female's attention.

"What?" she snapped, upper lip lifting in a sneer.

The contempt in her voice raised his ire, but he forced calm upon himself. "Prima, do you require the income from this business?"

She began to shake her head, then caught herself and protested, "It's *mine*."

The youngling whimpered and buried his face in the folds of her skirts. Zul gave her a steady, unblinking look. A rosy flush brightened her cheeks as she averted her gaze and stroked her son's head. The change of color fascinated him, and he wondered what it meant. Was it a common trait of human-Urib hybrids? Or was it special to humans only? Did her skin flush that wonderful rosy color when she orgasmed? He wanted to find out. Zul clenched his fists again and his tail twitched.

He turned around once again to address the mayor. "We will finish unpacking her wares, then I will escort the Prima and her son home. Contact the sheriff to inform him Fangrys need not send a new escort."

Zul caught the small, inarticulate sound of rage in her throat but knew she would not defy him. Her compliance satisfied something deep within him. It settled him—at least for the moment. He practically heard her consider a delaying tactic: making the unpacking and display of her wares take all day.

"Do not tarry," the mayor said as if he'd heard her thoughts, too. "I will send the sheriff to accompany you and ensure their safe delivery home."

Zul nodded, acknowledging the mayor's distrust. An unbonded warrior, especially a berserker, did not deserve wholehearted trust. They were too unstable, too prone to devolving into mindless violence and brutality.

"Glory to your house, Zullar cen'Gyrah," the mayor intoned with a nod.

"And prosperity to yours," Zul replied politely.

CHAPTER 4

Ursula fumed as she and Zul finished unpacking her pottery and displaying each piece to its best advantage. He silently endured her curt tone and obeyed her snapped instructions. His false meekness made her feel guilty. She'd been ungracious and shown a distressing lack of gratitude for his service, but she was too angry to apologize. Bran and Gil were so solicitous of her preferences and so willing and quick to run interference for her that she'd stupidly forgotten the reality of living in a culture where females had only privileges, not rights. Ursula couldn't deny that she'd grown accustomed to being prized, coddled, and indulged by her mates, but she forced herself to acknowledge that they allowed her a high level of privilege and autonomy few other women received.

It almost made her wish she'd never answered that employment advertisement. Almost. If she hadn't loved her mates so much, then the sacrifice of freedom wouldn't have been worth it.

After displaying her wares, Zul returned the crates to the hoverwagon. He handed Ursula up into the driver's seat. When she settled, he lifted Crow and set him beside her. She slapped the lines against the numpties' broad backs. The lumbering beasts obliged by plodding forward. Addilli, catching sight of the passing hoverwagon as she wiped down a table, waved at them through the window.

Ursula glanced down at Crow cuddled against her, snoring. The excitement of the day had exhausted her baby. After transferring the reins to one hand, she lowered her empty hand to her son's head and stroked it, her fingers pausing to gently rub the base of his pedicels. Crow found the touch soothing. A numpty tossed its head, long ears flopping, so Ursula transferred its reins back to her other hand. The numpty settled back into its customary plod with a grunt.

Zul walked alongside the hoverwagon. He had declined her offer to sit beside her, stating that doing so was neither proper nor advantageous. She argued he'd have a better view of anything threatening coming at them, but he merely replied that he would rely on her keen eyes to alert them of any danger. He'd be best able to defend them on the ground. Ursula opened her mouth to refute that claim, then said nothing and picked up the reins. Having never been permitted to drive the team before that day, she was nervous about it, but the plodding beasts knew the way back home and headed inexorably to their shared destination.

During the ride, Ursula ruminated on her untoward reaction to the hulking berserker. She knew he'd scented her arousal and was mortified. She reasoned that she hadn't acted on it, so she hadn't actually betrayed her mates. However, it puzzled her that she'd felt her core grow slick and heated when she'd had no such response to any male who was not part of her triad since having mated them. Why now, and why this particular male who was obviously a loner, an unbonded berserker? She felt guilty, as though she had actually cheated on Bran and Gil.

She wished Bran and Gil were home so she could talk with them. She dreaded their disappointment in her, but knew that Bran would appreciate her honor in not acting upon that desire and that Gil would explain what was happening. Bran always brought out the best in her, and Gil always took the time to ensure she understood what was going on. A tear gathered in her eye, and she wiped it away, for she still missed her son's namesake, Crow, the burly berserker whose fiery nature brought out the passion in hers. Bran was honor, Gil was intellect, and Crow was emotion. Without him, they all felt bereft, less than whole.

Ursula glanced at Zul, who walked without speaking beside the numpties. The stoic animals plodded inexorably toward the mansion where the lords of Fangrys lived when the Urib government hadn't deployed them on practically suicidal missions. She was glad the Council Supreme hadn't managed to decimate what was left of her beloved warrior triad. She knew if either Gil or Bran died, the Urib government would take her away from her one remaining mate and give her to another intact triad. A fertile female was too valuable to waste.

In defiance of what little she understood of biology, she would not and could not conceive another child except by a bonded triad. Somehow in the process of being converted on a cellular basis into a human-Urib hybrid and mating to a warrior triad, her body had adapted and would only accept the seed of three bonded males. Ursula didn't understand the technicalities of how or why that worked, she simply accepted it. *I'm an event planner, not a biologist.* And she wondered if her attraction to Zul meant her bond to Bran and Gil was weakening. That thought made her worry.

Crow wakened when the hoverwagon eased to a halt, the numpties belching their desire to be unharnessed and fed. The surviving member of the castrati who had accompanied her to town stood waiting, his arm bandaged and confined in a sling and both legs wrapped in bandages.

"Suvesh!" she cried out, hurling herself from the hoverwagon.

Zul dashed around to catch her, making sure she landed gently on her feet before releasing her to greet her servant.

"Are you all right?" she asked, seeing his collection of bandages. Then, to the castratus' mortification, she hugged him. "Oh, I'm so *glad* you're alive!"

The servant closed his eyes and endured the enthusiastic embrace and the subsequent noisy outpouring of grief for those who'd given their lives for her and Crow. He exchanged a pained glance with the stoic berserker who'd escorted their mistress home.

Wiping her teary eyes and runny nose on the already soiled and crumpled handkerchief, Ursula finally stepped back to allow the servant to restore his composure and dignity. "You *must* take time off to heal, Suvesh. I can't have you working when you're injured."

The servant gaped in astonishment. "It is my honor to serve you, Prima. Who shall ensure the operation of the household and the well-being of Master Crow if I am not there to do it?"

She sniffled and wiped her eyes. "Oh, Suvesh, you have everyone so well trained that they can run the household perfectly fine for a few days—or even a few weeks—if you need that long. You know how much I rely on you!"

The castratus bowed his head and clasped his hands in prayerful fashion. With a low bow, he said, "Prima, I shall see you and Master Crow settled then take the rest of the day to recuperate."

Ursula wiped her eyes and sniffled. "You must at least take the rest of the *week*. Have your second-in-command organize a memorial for those castrati lost today. We must honor their memories and ensure their families receive appropriate support."

Suvesh cocked his head to one side. "They were castrati. They did not have mates."

She gave him a gentle smile. "But they were all sons and brothers. Their families must be notified if they haven't been already and given the opportunity to mourn their loss properly."

Suvesh's eyes bugged, then he composed himself again. Bowing his head, he said, "You are most gracious, Prima."

She gave him a watery smile. "It's the least I can do. I'm sure Bran and Gil would do the same if they were here."

The castratus was entirely certain the warriors would not. The harsh world in which they lived did not encourage sentimentality. However, their hybrid Prima had strange notions and equally strange customs that puzzled many of the Urib servants. As none of those notions and customs created true hardship for any of them, the Fangrys Triad's castrati accepted them with an indulgent sort of tolerance.

After reaching out to clasp the servant's hand and give it a quick squeeze of affection, Ursula excused herself and turned back to the hoverwagon to fetch her son who stood beside the hulking wanderer. Zul held the quivering boy in place with a heavy hand on the child's shoulder. Seeing that the Prima was ready to reclaim her son, he lifted his hand. Without casting a glance at the castratus hobbling away, Crow raced to his mother. Zul rather thought the youngster would need to be broken of that habit soon. The son of a warrior triad should not cling to a female for safety and reassurance.

Ursula embraced her child then instructed him to go with the other castratus—ostensibly Suvesh's second-in-command—who lurked nearby. She fixed the servant's gaze with her own and said, "Hurvi will see to your bath and supper. Be good and do as he bids you, sweetheart."

The golden-hued child's eyes flashed with rebellion, then he sighed and said in a quiet voice, "Yes, Mama."

Observing the interaction, Zul approved of the boy's obedience to his mother's instructions. It would be a long time before the golden-hued male earned the rank and respect of leadership.

Ursula pressed a kiss to Crow's head and sent him on his way. Turning again to Hurvi, she said, "Please see that Zul is given every courtesy. He is our honored guest for as long as he wishes to stay. In fact," she added in a louder voice, "I am sure Bran and Gil will wish to speak with him themselves when they return."

Hurvi nodded, understanding the Prima's expectation that the vagrant berserker would be a long-term guest. One hand clasping the boy's, he gestured with the other hand for the berserker to follow yet another servant standing nearby. From the corner of his eye, Zul saw two more servants lead the numpties away, presumably to their stable. He fell into step behind the castratus and, entering the manor, gazed at the magnificence in which the Prima of Fangrys lived.

Beautiful ceramics—obviously the Prima's skilled handiwork—decorated many niches throughout the building. Tapestries, brightly colored and finely woven, dressed the stone walls. Gleaming wood railings and floors contrasted with the smooth stone walls. Cut glass sconces placed at regular intervals complemented the intricate chandeliers hanging from the ceilings, all casting warm light throughout rooms and corridors that would otherwise have been gloomy and dark. Tall, narrow windows cut into the thick stone walls admitted long planks of sunlight. Shutters were thrown open, so a refreshing breeze wafted through the building.

"This suite is yours while you remain with us," the castratus said and bowed. "We are grateful for your assistance and for saving the lives of our Prima and her son. If there is anything you require, simply ask and you shall receive it."

Zul felt heat suffuse him at the catratus' simple and profound gratitude. A second later, he recognized it as embarrassment. He bowed his head in gracious acknowledgement of the servant's words. He felt as though he ought to bow to the servant, but to do so would have shocked the castratus—and the poor male had endured more than enough that day as it was.

"I shall stay to ensure the Prima and her son's safety until her mates return," he stated.

The servant nodded. "Suvesh has already sent word to the Prime of Fangrys about your brave service. He will be eager to honor you."

"It is my privilege to serve the Prima and her son," Zul said, mentally noting that the castratus knew how to contact the Fangrys Prime even if the Prima didn't. *Interesting.*

He barely refrained from glancing down the corridor in a futile effort to see his lovely hostess. He was well aware the guest suite would be properly located far from the Prima's personal quarters. No warrior triad would risk their mate's dishonor by putting her in proximity with other males—males who might be less than honorable or have less than firm control over their instinct to claim a mate.

CHAPTER 5

The idleness of being an honored guest gnawed at Zul's patience. Over the next several days, he dined with the Prima of Fangrys and listened bemused to her lively chatter. He agreed with her as to the perfidy of the human government which had duped her into traveling to Uribern, but decided that he was grateful they had done so. He thoroughly enjoyed looking at her and listening to her, thinking that her mere presence brought peace to his soul. He also enjoyed spending time with Crow, always supervised by lurking castrati who were eager to keep their mistress informed of every interaction or to tattle about any infraction.

Zul used his limited time with Crow to begin instructing him in martial arts. To his surprise—for he'd incorrectly assumed the Fangrys Prime and Second had coddled the young male—the boy already knew some of the basics. Zul was happy to pass the time working with the child on perfecting those basics, exercising a patience he'd not known he possessed.

"Papa Bran!" Crow cried out during an afternoon session, breaking from Zul's light hold positioning his arm for a proper strike.

Zul swiveled around as Crow dashed toward the Fangrys prime. Seeing the hulking, golden-skinned brute, he bowed low to show respect for the dominant male, although his own nature balked at the show of subservience. He straightened and met the prime's golden stare with bold confidence.

A turquoise-scaled male passed through the door into the courtyard to stand beside his prime. His silver horns glinted in the brilliant sunshine. The second offered a gracious nod and said, "You must be Zul. Our mate explained your presence to us."

The golden warrior dipped his chin. "We owe you a great debt of gratitude, Zullar cen'Gyrah. We heard of the demise of the Uk'khadir Triad, but were not aware their Third had survived."

"They died with honor and in glory," Zul replied, the ache of their absence lingering in his heart and the shame of having survived making his gut churn with guilt.

Bran nodded, again a single dip of his chin. "We will speak after dinner of your service to our Prima."

"I would be honored," Zul replied with studied civility. With a lethal race such as theirs, sometimes civility was all that prevented bloodshed over the most trivial of matters. The Urib had adopted and strictly enforced polite behavior to ensure their killing instincts were unleashed against their enemies rather than their own kind.

"Come, Crow," Gil ordered, giving the boy a smile in toothy mimicry of Ursula's friendly expression. "You must tell Papa Bran and me of your adventures while we were gone."

"And we can have a snack, too?" the child pleaded. "Please, Papa Gil?"

Gil chuckled. "Yes, we shall have a snack, too." He looked at Zul, his expression sobering and his whole demeanor changing. "We thank you for furthering our son's training during our absence."

"He will grow to be a fierce warrior," Zul replied, observing how the strangely genial Second quickly turned into a lethal warrior.

The golden and turquoise males departed, their son skipping between them and bubbling over with excited chatter. Zul wasn't sure if he found the boy's loquaciousness charming or annoying and decided it was probably inherited from his hybrid mother. In her, such chatter was definitely charming and one of the many attributes he found appealing about her. Were he not an honorable male, he would have stolen her for himself.

Zul picked up the wooden practice knives and returned them to the armory, then retreated to the library to wallow in his thoughts while pretending to read a book. As he turned the pages with desultory slowness, his hostess entered the room. She moved languidly, and a small, sly smile curled her lips. His nostrils flared as he caught the scents of her mates. Zul's stomach clenched in envy. Prima Ursula had been well and thoroughly ravished by her mates: their scents clung to her skin, though the fine scales gleamed with the dampness of having recently bathed.

"Oh! I did not realize you were in here," Ursula said, stumbling to a halt. "I apologize for intruding and will leave you in peace."

Jealous of the intimacy she had enjoyed with her mates—and not him—but still wanting the pleasure of her company, he said, "You are Prima here; you do not intrude. I shall leave if you wish."

Ursula gracefully settled in an oversized chair, tucking her bare feet under her. Giving him a small smile, she said, "No, no need to leave just because I'm here. I get lonely, you know, so it's lovely to have company. I consider you a friend."

Zul exercised firm control not to pull a sour face at being labeled a friend. He desired so much more. Instead, he nodded and replied, "I am honored."

"Bran and Gill are cautious and protective," she explained, although there was no need. He, too, wanted to coddle her, give her every luxury, and isolate her from all threats. "I told them of your heroics, and you have their gratitude."

Zul did not want their gratitude; he wanted their mate. His honor strained to the cracking point, he gave her a slow nod and said, "I am honored to have been of service."

Ursula sighed, then complained, "Such formality." She rose from the chair and took three steps toward him before he rasped, "*Stop.*"

She halted. "What is wrong, Zul?"

He clenched the arms of the chair, his claws piercing the upholstery and digging into the wooden frame beneath. Through gritted teeth, he said, "You tempt me to abandon my honor, Prima."

Ursula's expression changed from concern to wariness. She took three small steps backward.

"Do *not* run," he warned, knowing if she ran then he would give chase, unable to override the strong, raw instinct of an apex predator.

She nodded and continued to slowly back up. She bumped into a chair and put a hand back to feel her way around the furniture. Slowly, carefully, she continued to retreat until she passed through the door and closed it behind her. Zul took a deep breath to catch and savor the scent of her and eased his claws free of the chair. He'd have to replace it out of the fortune he'd not touched since the demise of his triad.

He thrust himself to his feet and lurched a step toward the door, then stopped. He was committed to dinner with the Fangrys Prime and Second. They would scent his desire for their mate. He could smell it himself, the lust rolling off his skin. Only the absence of his spoor on her skin would prevent them from killing him—or trying to kill him. He was a berserker and unbound: killing him would be no easy task. Only knowing that killing Bran or Gil would harm Ursula restrained the overpowering urge to attack them and annihilate the competition.

Zul lowered himself to the floor and assumed a meditative position. He took long, deep breaths and exhaled slowly, forcing himself to relax one tight muscle at a time. By the time he managed to restore his calm, a servant entered the room to announce his presence was requested for dinner.

He rubbed a hand down his face and replied, "I shall be there momentarily."

The castratus bowed and retreated as silently as he'd entered.

Zul went to his room and quickly washed and changed into clean clothing more appropriate for dining with his hosts. He had received the clothing courtesy of the Prima's order. He would have to leave it behind when he departed, for a vagabond had no need of such a fine or extensive wardrobe. He was glad he'd changed when he entered the dining chamber, as both Bran and Gil wore formal garb. Ursula was not present in the room.

His hosts stood to greet him. Bran gestured toward the table and said, "Welcome, Zullar cen'Gyrah, Third of the Uk'khadir Triad. Please be seated."

Gil's nostrils flared, but he said nothing as Zul walked around the table and seated himself in an empty chair.

"Where is the Prima?" Zul inquired, carefully modulating his tone.

"Safe," Gil replied. "While we are grateful to you, we do not trust you."

"We do not trust any unmated Urib," Bran added, waving his hand to indicate the servants should begin serving. "And we can smell your desire for her."

Gil's nostrils flared again. "It is testimony to your honor and our gratitude that you still live."

Zul met his gaze, his own hard and glittering. "I'm not so easily killed."

Bran nodded. "No, berserker, you are not. But I have controlled a strong berserker before, and I can control you."

Zul almost managed to repress a snort. "Not if I don't allow it."

Gil slid a sideways glance at Bran. "Do you think he's stronger than Crow was?"

Bran shrugged, not caring that their guest overheard their conversation. "Perhaps." He met Zul's eyes, his own expression inscrutable. "Now that we are home, you will not be alone with our mate or son."

"And when you are deployed again?" Zul snapped.

"You will not be here," Gil answered.

Zul bared his teeth.

"Eat," Bran ordered, the heavy weight of his authority thrumming within the space. "We must discuss a boon in reward for your service."

"I need no money," Zul stated. "I am all that is left of the Uk'khadir Triad and sole owner of our accumulated wealth."

"Then what do you want?" Gil asked.

Zul took a breath, paused, then answered slowly, honestly, "Peace. I want peace."

Bran nodded, understanding that he meant peace of mind rather than an absence of violence. "We live with regret and loss. Peace is not ours to give."

Zul took another deep breath and nodded, thinking of another boon, a request he dared not ask. He met the warrior's eye and said with aching candor, "I miss the bond of brotherhood."

Bran nodded again. "As we miss Crow, our Third and the Bridge between our mate's First and Forever."

"We did not have a mate," Zul admitted, not needing to express that his triad had greatly desired a female of their own. Uribern had not yet made contact with Earth when the Uk'khadir Prime and Second were killed in battle. He recalled his astonishment upon learning how quickly the nations on Earth agreed to trade their females for Triune Alliance technology and protection. Humans, apparently, did not properly value their abundance of females as a blessing. "You will treasure yours for the divine gift she is."

"We do," Gil confirmed. He grimaced. "We are aware that our commanders seek to free our mate of a broken triad to give her to a whole one so she might bear more young." He bared his teeth. "We will not permit that."

Zul nodded. "I am not surprised. Politics cares little for well-being, only for victory."

"We sent the Ogranox running again for the time being," Bran said of their latest deployment, his tone matter of fact rather than boasting. "They'll be back after they recoup from this latest defeat. The Kaan are worthy allies."

Zul interpreted the comment to mean the feline warriors were vicious, effective fighters. He'd not met one himself. "I have not battled beside them, but agree that our alliance with Kaan and Ahn'hudin will eventually ensure our triumph over the Sivuul and the Ogranox. They are evils that must be obliterated from existence."

The three warriors fell silent, each remembering their many battles against the implacable and terrifying enemies threatening many planets and civilizations throughout the universe.

The Ogranox and the Sivuul desired meat, hosts, and slaves. Conquered species reduced to mere livestock fulfilled those functions, yet never satisfied the conquerors' rapacious appetites.

"Why do you wander alone as rosvo?" Gil inquired.

Zul wanted to wince, but held on to his composure. He wanted to prevaricate, but his hosts, fellow warriors, deserved truth. "The loss was more than I could bear or bring into a new triad."

"We know of the battle that killed your First and Second," Bran said, not mentioning the humiliating defeat Uribern suffered in that battle. "I lost one of my sires there."

"Shortly after that, the Council Supreme decided it was in Uribern's best interests to deploy broken triads more often," Gil added. "After the battle that killed Crow, we hoped for a reduction in deployments to spare other mated triads; but a broken warrior triad" —he gestured at himself and Gil— "is useful only as cannon fodder. However, we are determined to live and to keep our mate."

Zul nodded in complete understanding. "That is why, before the official mourning period ended, I removed myself from service. I am all who retains the memory and honor of the Uk'khadir Triad."

"And wealth," Gil murmured. "War is expensive. With your death, the Uribern government would be pleased to reclaim your wealth."

Bran sighed. "It pains me to admit that our people's leaders are more conniving and less honorable than they should be."

"Then perhaps you have not received word of the regime change on Ahn'hudin?" Zul was happy to change the subject.

"Regime change?" Gil echoed, expression brightening with interest.

"We have not had time or opportunity to review updates in Alliance news," Bran explained. "We were most eager to return to our mate."

Gil nodded. "Our mate and youngling are our highest priority."

And that, Zul knew, was the Uribern government's true reason for reducing the frequency of deployment of mated, unbroken triads: their highest and strongest instinctual loyalties were to their mates. No amount of training could overcome that. "In my travels, I hear a good deal of news. The emperor of Ahn'hudin perished, and the heir behaved with grave dishonor. As was justified, their general superior—"

"I've seen the brute on the battlefield," Gil muttered under his breath, his tone tinged with respect. "He's a mighty warrior."

"—defeated the heir and assumed the crown," Zul continued, knowing his hosts would understand "defeated" meant "killed."

"General Superior Yas'kihn is reputed a hard and honorable warrior," Bran commented. "With him as emperor, Ahn'hudin will be well-ruled."

"Have you met him?" Zul asked.

Bran shook his head. "No, I only know him by reputation."

Zul shrugged. "I did meet him when my triad was still whole. Your words are accurate: he is a hard and honorable warrior and mated now."

"Mated?" Gil echoed in surprise.

"His bride is like yours, a human hybrid."

"It seems we've been too long out of touch with Alliance news," Bran muttered. Gil nodded in silent agreement. "We will speak with the Omari Prime to see if this lack of information is common. It will not do for Uribern's warriors to be uninformed."

Zul nodded. He wasn't sure what Bran would or *could* do if he learned that the government wasn't keeping its military informed, but the golden warrior's molten gaze promised hellfire on them. He hoped Bran's vengeance wouldn't result in the male's death and Ursula's reassignment beyond his reach.

Not that she wasn't already beyond his reach.

CHAPTER 6

Ursula's flesh quivered in the aftermath of bedsport with her two remaining mates. After only three days of her mates returning home, the Uribern government summoned them back to service. During their short break from warfare, Gil and Bran used every opportunity to lavish her with affection and indulge themselves in her feminine softness before leaving again on another deployment.

She lay between them, one hand stroking Bran's heavily muscled chest while Gil's prehensile tail gently stroked in and out of her wet, slippery vagina. Bran rose over her to press kisses along the elegant sweep of her collar bone. She sighed as Gil's tail gently and inexorably drove her into another shuddering climax. Bran dredged his finger through her swollen, sensitive folds to coat it with her release. He brought the digit to his mouth and sucked it off.

"So sweet," Bran murmured.

"You spoke with the Omari Prime?" Gil asked, rolling over on his side and clasping their mate against his body. Ursula moaned as his tail lifted her leg and his hips rolled to press that long, thick cock inside her body. Bran's tail wound around her raised leg and prodded her anus. She moaned again, deeper, when it penetrated the tight sphincter. Soon, she was panting as another orgasm began to swell within her.

"I did," Bran replied before capturing their mate's mouth with his. After a pause during which he twined his tongue with hers and plucked her reddened, swollen nipples with his fingers, he broke the kiss to take a breath and add, "They did not know of the regime change on Ahn'hudin."

Ursula's breasts jiggled as Gil pumped his cock in and out of her body, the force of his thrusts slapping his hips against her buttocks. Bran's gaze focused on her breasts for a moment, then he palmed them and gently squeezed them in counterpoint to Gil's rhythmic movement. Ursula lifted the one arm not trapped beneath her body to clutch at Bran's muscular upper arm, her short nails digging into his scaled hide. She cried out as another orgasm crashed over her. Gil followed her into the climax a moment later.

He withdrew from her body and rolled Ursula onto her back, unleashing a gush of fluids that Bran eagerly lapped up. He surged up her body and drove his cock into her, his tail still lodged inside her ass. Soon, Ursula's thin whine heralded yet another impending climax.

Her weak, breathless scream of sublime pleasure made both her males bare their teeth in masculine triumph. They had pleasured their mate until she could endure no more. Bran rolled off to the side, one hand gently stroking between their mate's legs, and said, "We must gather a coalition and confront the Council Supreme."

Gil sighed and stroked gentle circles on Ursula's belly. The touch was intended to lure her to sleep, but she focused on remaining awake, trying to stay alert. "I do not wish to leave our mate alone. The risk is too great."

Bran nodded. "I will ask Zul to remain here to guard her and Crow."

Ursula's blood ran cold, then heat suffused her. Her arousal bloomed anew in the sex-saturated air. Bran's nostrils flared, and Gil looked intently at her.

"I feel the quiver in your belly," her silver-horned mate whispered.

Bran's eyes gleamed. "Has he touched you, *elska'adir*?"

Knowing she could not lie to them even if she wanted to, Ursula shook her head, a small movement accompanied by the trickle of a tear leaking from the corner of her eye and running down her temple to be absorbed by her hair. "No, no he has not touched me. He's been most—" her breath caught as Bran's tail drove itself into her channel "—*most* respectful."

"Good," Gil snarled. "I'll not have any male taking advantage of you."

Bran's expression turned thoughtful. He glanced at Gil. "You looked into his background?"

"I did," Gil said as he rolled away. Ursula missed his gentle touch. "He served with utmost honor. He is a worthy warrior." He paused, then added, "Are you thinking what I'm thinking?"

"Do you desire him?" Bran asked.

Feeling ashamed of her attraction to the berserker, Ursula began to sob. "Yes. I'm sorry. I didn't mean to."

However, Bran looked triumphant. "He is the one to restore our bonded triad."

"And then?" Gil growled.

"And then we speak with other triads," Bran replied. "My investigation reveals there is no immediate threat from either the Sivuul or the Ogranox. The Council Supreme acts against the best interests of Uribern. Change is needed."

"I spoke with the Golbyu Second yesterday," Gil said slowly. He rubbed the back of his neck. "Human immigration has been halted. The human governments deceived Ahn'hudin to prevent their brides from conceiving. Ahn'hudin is renegotiating their treaty with Earth."

"The ambassador wasn't all that honest with me," Ursula muttered, reminding them of her failed attempt to escape Uribern and return home. "My government sold me and other women to Uribern, so it's not surprising more were sold to Ahn'hudin and were neither informed nor allowed the opportunity to give consent."

"And are you unhappy?" Gil asked, turning to face her.

She reached across the bed and placed her hand on his heavily muscled thigh. "No, I am not unhappy. In fact, I could not have dreamed of such a wonderful life as I live now. But it remains that my own government treated me like chattel, and your government seeks to do the same."

"There is no longer our government and your government," Bran gently reminded her. "You are Urib now."

Ursula didn't bother to debate him. She knew the physical changes she'd undergone as well as he did—probably better. It was her body, after all. Those changes enabled her to live on Uribern, to endure its harsh climate and the searing radiation of its scorching sun. The plasticity of the human genome never failed to astonish her with the readiness of alien technology to convert human brides into hybrid brides.

"I spoke with Carmen," she said, her words ending in a moan as her hips thrust against the big hand stroking between her thighs. "I can't think when you do that, Bran."

He smiled at her, a pleased expression that showed no teeth. His thick finger penetrated her and began stroking in and out. "I think I like it when you can't think."

Trying to corral her thoughts into some semblance of coherency, Ursula persevered. "She keeps tabs on the embassy."

"And?" Gil prompted, his eyes gleaming as her body began to tremble.

"She thinks brides are being *sold* to the highest bidders," she said in a rush. She squealed, "Ah, Bran!"

Bran's eyes turned molten, and Gil's eyes flinty. The latter met his prime's gaze and said, "They are not allowing for natural matches?"

"This is treachery," Bran growled. "We will *not* deploy."

"That is insubordination," Gil pointed out.

Ursula cried out, breathless as an orgasm shattered her again.

"It's only insubordination if the revolution fails," Bran said and bared his teeth in a vicious smile.

Gil turned to bend over their mate, and he pressed a soft kiss to her open mouth as her breath sawed in and out of her lungs. Rising, he said, "Rest, *elska'adir*. I shall have refreshments brought to you, and then you shall bathe. Join us for supper."

Ursula blinked bleary eyes. Her words slurred, "What time is it?"

"You have plenty of time," Bran reassured her. "Rest, eat, drink, and rest some more. I'll summon you when we're ready."

"Ready for what?"

He smoothed her tangled hair back from her forehead. Her eyes fluttered shut.

"Your warrior triad."

Her eyes snapped open. "Triad?"

"Gil, me, and Zul."

"He looks like Crow," she murmured as her eyes closed again.

"All berserkers are red-skinned and black-horned," Gil said, his voice gentle and quiet. "But you must remember that Zul is *not* Crow."

Bran shook his head and communicated mind to mind with his bonded brother, *No, I believe Zul is stronger than Crow. He will not be so lenient with her as Crow was.*

Gil replied in kind. *Will she love him, too, do you think?*

They rose from the bed and stalked from the room. *She admits attraction, something she has not felt for any Urib male other than us. That is a good indication.*

And will he love her and respect her independent nature? She is not truly Urib, despite how much she now looks like us.

Once bonded with us and mated to her, he will not willingly cause her distress. I am sure of it.

And what about this revolution you seek to launch?

Bolstered by his second-in-command's unstinting support, Bran chuckled. *Do you think the indolent fools who sit on the Council Supreme can withstand an uprising of honorable warriors? We'll have the berserkers on our side.*

A lot of those "indolent fools" are high caste like you, Gil pointed out.

Bran sniffed, a sound of derision, and said aloud, "Honor has been bred out of them. They are weak and will fall before us."

CHAPTER 7

Zul rose from his chair and bowed in respect to his hosts. Garbed in the fine clothing they had given him, he felt awkward and beholden to their generosity while guilty of some crime he had not committed—yet. He ached with the desire to claim their mate as his.

Although Bran and Gil smelled fresh as though having recently bathed, he could still detect the faint, lingering scents of sex and the sweetness of their mate on them. He willed his body not to react.

"Please be seated," Gil invited with a slow sweep of his hand.

Zul reclaimed the chair while Bran and Gil seated themselves, facing him across a low table.

Gil spoke again, "We have been summoned to duty."

Zul showed no outward reaction, but commented, "Surely, it is too soon after your last deployment?" He paused, then asked, although he suspected otherwise, "Is Uribern under threat again so soon?"

Bran leaned forward, his mouth twisted in a sour expression. "The Council Supreme attempts to rid itself of us so they can give our mate to another warrior triad." His golden eyes narrowed. "They will fail."

Gil's answer confirmed their governing leaders' perfidy. "No. But we must go nonetheless."

"However, after the attack on our mate, we cannot leave her unguarded," Bran added. "The castrati are loyal and brave, but they are not warriors."

Zul agreed and suspected the upcoming request. "No, she should not be left unguarded. Nor should the Prima be permitted to wander about."

Bran grinned, showing his teeth. Zul bared his teeth in reaction.

Bran, please do not threaten him, Gil reminded his Prime. Bran closed his lips and hid his sharp, pointed teeth. Aloud the silver-horned Second said, "A mated male will do anything for his mate's happiness."

"Foolishness," Zul declared. He shook his head then beat them to the punch. "If you are going to offer me employment as her guard, I must decline."

"We wish to offer you more than that," Bran said, leaning back in the chair.

Zul held himself still. Hope ignited deep within his body. The words necessary for confirmation came slowly: "What do you mean?"

"Ursula, our lovely mate, needs and desires a bonded triad," Bran said slowly, each word measured and precise. "She'll not conceive again without a triad."

Gil nodded. "You have shown yourself an honorable and skilled warrior, and we know our mate appeals to you."

Zul said nothing, but that flicker of hope grew stronger.

"And you appeal to her," Bran added. He leaned forward again, bracing his elbows on his knees. "Our instincts and hers do not lead us wrong. You are well-suited to become the new Third of our triad."

That tongue of flame, that hope, erupted into a full-scale blaze. The Fangrys Prime and Second offered him what he'd lost decades ago: a home and bonded brotherhood. They also offered him what he'd never had: a mate. They offered him everything he desired, if only …

"I will *not* submit," Zul said, his expression hardening. "I submit to *no one.*"

Gil leaned forward, his posture mimicking his Prime's. "We offer you everything an unbonded warrior wants." He glanced at Bran. "You will not find a better prime than Brannal cen'Vyr."

Zul pressed his lips together and swallowed the words that threatened to spew forth. Gilvane cen'Vyr was far too insightful for comfort. The Second continued speaking. "We know some primes are harsh with their berserkers, chaining them as though they were unthinking beasts. Bran is no tyrant." Gil paused. *Not usually.*

Since when am I a tyrant?

Since you decided to wage war upon the Council Supreme and did not discuss it with me first.

I feel your agreement: the Council needs to be replaced.

They do, but it would have been nice to have been consulted for my opinion and agreement first.

Bran pressed his lips together. *If you object to revolution, tell me now.*

Zul scrutinized their closed expressions as the two communicated directly mind to mind. He wondered what they debated even as he privately acknowledged that he missed such closeness. He missed the deep bond of a triad brotherhood even if he did not necessarily miss his deceased prime.

I agree that revolution is necessary, but I also think we should comply with deployment, Gil replied after a moment, addressing Bran's intention to disobey the Council's orders. *We will be more effective recruiting support from among our fellow warriors if we are with them than if we act without them.*

Then we will add mutiny to our transgressions, Bran agreed. He refocused his gaze on Zul who watched them with the wariness of a seasoned predator. "A berserker who cannot be controlled is a danger to himself and innocents."

"I've managed to control myself for quite some time," Zul replied, his tone stiff with hauteur and his expression icy with obdurate pride. "I will not submit."

"You will not *willingly* submit," Gil corrected. He leaned back in the chair and rubbed his chin. "What if Bran engages you in combat and wins? Will you then submit to him?"

Zul bared his fangs. "Only my former prime was ever able to subdue me." His gaze ran over the golden warrior's tall, muscular form and knew himself to be stronger and heavier. "You won't succeed."

Bran responded with his own bared teeth. "Then let's put it to the test, shall we?"

Zul rose, accepting the challenge.

Gil, also rising, said, "Do *not* kill each other."

Bran snorted. Zul dipped his chin in a curt nod of agreement. All three understood that blood would be shed.

The three males walked to the practice arena, a large outdoor area with a floor of coarse sand to drain spilled blood.

"Weapons?" Zul queried.

"I need none," Bran replied with quiet confidence. He held up a hand and threw the first volley in words of insult. "My claws and teeth and tail will suffice. But *you* may use a weapon if you like."

Zul nodded and his lips curled in a small smile. He knew what Bran attempted to do by needling him like that. His massive shoulders rolled in a shrug. "I do not need to carry a weapon. I *am* a weapon."

Bran nodded and began to strip. Zul followed suit, determined to meet his opponent on honorable terms, for honor was one of the few things remaining to him that he treasured. Bran glanced at Gil and said, "Do not interfere."

Gil blinked. "Of course not."

"Do not permit Ursula to witness this."

Gil snorted. "Of course not."

Bran looked at Zul, noting the hard bulge of muscle beneath the ruddy hide. He was taller than Zul, but the berserker was thicker, broader, and heavier. He walked to the center of the arena, testing the depth and resilience of the sand beneath his bare feet and clawed toes. He rolled his shoulders to loosen them and observed his opponent's coiled, economical movement. Zul would be a fierce fighter, difficult to subdue.

Bran and Zul circled one another, each gauging the other's readiness. Zul found much to admire in the golden warrior facing him: the stillness, the observant readiness, the keen gaze. The high caste male was a seasoned warrior with recent experience in battle, not an pampered commander content to shout orders from behind his troops. Bran would be a fierce fighter, difficult to subdue.

By some unseen, unheard signal, the two males clashed. Fists thudded into flesh. Claws gouged tough, scaled hides. Tails whipped and slashed. Horns crashed and locked. Teeth bit. Grunts and hisses punctuated every strike and parry. Sand rasped and sprayed. Blood dribbled onto the sand.

Gil kept an eye on his Prime and the berserker while constantly checking to ensure their mate did not venture near. The knowledge that she'd been exposed to the rosvoi's violence made his stomach clench with fury mingled with regret. The desire to keep her safe from all violence made him clench his fists. Their sweet female was to be coddled, protected, and indulged. The fact that she called it *spoiled* made him want to smile.

Bran roared as a particularly vicious swipe opened parallel gashes across his abdomen. He retaliated with blurred speed that surprised Zul. Knowing the bleeding would soon diminish his strength, speed, focus, and coordination, Bran resolved to bring this duel to a fast end. He employed every technique and skill he'd ever learned on the battlefield and off—and he'd learned much from the frequent battles against the Ogranox and Sivuul. Minutes passed, and he acquired two more nasty lacerations on his right thigh. He also delivered several punishing blows and left deep gouges in the berserker's upper left arm and back.

The Fangrys Prime felt the shift after he landed a hard kick to his opponent's knees. Zul stumbled and his berserker nature took over. With a deep roar, he morphed into a swollen tornado of pure rage and bloodthirst. Bran was stretched to his physical limits which were failing, but Zul's shift opened his mind to

Bran's dominance. Seizing the opportunity, Bran, too, roared as his consciousness speared into Zul's. His mind fought against the wild wrath of the berserker to impose order and control.

As Bran wrestled for dominance and control, Zul faltered. Like the apex predator he was, Bran lunged as the opportunity opened. A moment later, he had subdued Zul, his teeth sinking into his opponent's red neck.

Hot, dry air seared Zul's lungs as he gasped for breath. The heavy weight of Bran's knee dug into his back as the golden warrior hauled on his arms stretched behind him. Bran's hand wrapped around his throat, claws digging in and ready to tear through flesh, blood vessels, and windpipe. Zul's tail lashed, but it was twined with Bran's tail, imprisoned within a tangle as it were.

"Yield," Bran rasped, his voice hoarse and his respiration heavy.

Zul growled his refusal. The crushing weight of Bran's control closed around his mind and *squeezed*.

"Yield."

Gasping for breath, Zul let his face drop to the sandy floor. The words were wrenched from his pounding hearts as he hissed, "I yield."

Immediately, the knee in his back lifted and the clawed hands holding him at bay released him. The Prime's golden tail unwound from his, but the crushing grip of the Prime's mind remained. Grunting with pain and effort, Zul hauled himself to his feet. His black eyes burned with fury.

"Release me," he snarled.

"Do you submit?" Bran asked.

Zul's shoulders and head drooped. Then he raised his eyes to meet Bran's without flinching. His voice was cold and remote as he replied, "I submit."

Bran's heavy hand landed on his lacerated shoulder as his mind released Zul's. Zul gasped at the relief and took another deep breath. Gil laid a short-bladed knife in Bran's palm. Zul recognized the ceremonial blade and resentment ignited in his belly.

"The triad bond requires blood," Bran said as if they weren't already bleeding profusely.

Zul's lips peeled back from his teeth in silent threat.

Bran gave him a flat look that let him know his retreat from dominating Zul's mind was a courtesy, not a necessity. He had released Zul's mind, not retreated from it, which meant he could exert control again—and would if he saw the need. He quickly drew the blade across one palm then the other, a light slice just deep enough to bring blood to the surface. "I am Brannal, the First of the Fangrys cen'Vyr Triad."

Palms bleeding he handed the knife to Gil who sliced his palms and intoned, "I am Gilvane, the Second of the Fangrys cen'Vyr Triad."

His gaze more intense than Zul would have expected, Gil handed him the knife. Zul glanced at Bran who nodded at him, a gesture of mingled encouragement, approval, and expectation. A flicker of Bran's will in his mind reminded him that coercion remained an option, but one Bran would prefer not to choose.

Zul's upper lip lifted in a silent snarl as he sliced his palms and hissed, "I am Zullar cen'Gyrah, now the Third of the cen'Vyr Triad of Fangrys."

The thrill of acceptance and approval filled Zul's mind as the three males raised their hands and clasped them, palms touching palms, blood mingling with blood. Zul's left palm pressed against Gil's right palm, and his right palm pressed against Bran's left. As the circle of three closed, each of them threw his head back and roared. Fire streaked through their bodies and their horns blazed with heat.

With the bond sealed, they lowered their hands and released their grips. The lacerations crossing their palms had healed, a gold scar on Zul's right palm and a blue-green scar across his left. Bran and Gil each bore a fresh red scar crisscrossing the old bonding marks left by Crow, their former Third.

Zul shook his hands to dispel the tingling in them. Gil rolled his shoulders, which ached from tension. Bran slowly blinked those inscrutable golden eyes, the only sign of his lack of composure, and said, "Bathe. Treat your wounds. We will reconvene at supper."

Zul nodded, resentful of his defeat. He wondered when the chains would come out and vowed he would not offer his wrists to be manacled.

"I am not Borsulvar cen'Gyrah," Bran said in a quiet tone. His invasion and control of Zul's mind had been complete and illuminating. "Your former prime was honorable but harsh. I will not confine you as he did."

"And you will share our mate," Gil said, his tone and words gentle and encouraging. "She will welcome you."

Zul blinked in surprise, unsure as to how Gil had sidled so close without him noticing. His wrists and ankles felt the faint echo of shackles that no longer restrained him. Gil rested a hand on his shoulder. "I am the Second and Forever of the Fangrys Triad and your eternal ally. You will *never* be alone or be chained again."

Zul shuddered as he felt Bran link them together, connecting their minds in a firm and bright bond stronger than he'd ever experienced. He felt Gil's love and admiration for their Prime. Even more amazing to him, he felt Bran's acceptance and welcome. The Fangrys Prime knew what he was, what he'd done, and did not judge him for it. Zul felt the entirely foreign urge to kneel before the high caste warrior and spout words of undying allegiance and fealty.

No need for that. I have no desire to be king.

Gil laughed aloud. *Yes, you do. Sometimes.*

Bran's answering laughter surprised him. Borsulvar would have cuffed his Second for such impertinence.

CHAPTER 8

Ursula's keen eyes did not miss the careful way Zul and Bran moved or the subtle thickness of bandages beneath the fabric of their clothing. Her voice turned thin and suspicious when she demanded, "What happened?"

Gil cupped her cheek and pressed a kiss to her crown. "Sit, *elska'adir*, and we shall explain all."

Ursula waited for Gil to sit and allowed him to draw her onto his lap. Leaning against his chest as he splayed a hand across her belly, she shot a sharp glare at Bran then Zul. "I heard the commotion. The servants barred me from the corridor leading to the arena. Why were you two beating on each other?"

Bran sat down and gave her a toothy smile, a facial expression he'd learned from her. His mate's expression didn't change; she remained suspicious. "Be at ease, *elska'adir*. Your triad is once again whole."

Ursula's eyebrows rose in surprise. "And you had to beat the snot out of him to accomplish that?" Zul grunted in offense. He'd given as well as he'd received. She paused to consider her next words, then said, "Did you do this for me?"

Gil's thumb stroked her, the tip gently rubbing the underside of her breast through the filmy fabric of her dress. His low chuckle rumbled through his chest and soothed her like a cat's purr. "No, my love, Bran did this for *us.*"

"Sit, Zullar cen'Vyr," Bran bade the hulking, red berserker. "You have tonight to heal and adjust to your new triad. Before we depart, we will claim our mate together."

Zul sat, every movement careful. He glanced at Ursula, his black gaze almost sheepish. His velvety baritone filled the room: "Only if she accepts me."

Ursula gasped. Gil said over her soft sound of surprise, "I have registered our triad with the government. Perhaps now they will cease trying to get us killed."

Bran nodded. "Good. It will be best if our mate conceives soon."

"Hey, I'm right here," Ursula announced.

Gil's hand pressed against her belly. "Did you not wonder why you have not conceived since Crow was born? It is not because we do not fuck you."

"I know why," came the dry response. Ursula's voice hardened, "But as I told you before, I'm neither your broodmare nor your fuck toy. It would be nice to be consulted and to give my consent first."

Gil's hand slid down her abdomen and pressed between her thighs, the loose, flowing fabric of her skirt doing nothing to prevent her from feeling his intimate touch. Ursula's breath hitched. "Tonight we will proceed with the Rite of First Touch as a bound triad."

Ursula shivered as desire rippled through her body. She remembered her terror the night she'd escaped from the human embassy in a futile bid for freedom. She remembered encountering the hungry oryxis and the bloody, vicious battle in which Crow had engaged to defeat it and prevent it from eating her for supper. She remembered the suffocating feeling of Bran's mind overwhelming and opening her mind to them, forcing her to accept their claim, though their touch had not harmed her.

"Why is it necessary to go through the sequence of rites again?" she asked, the memory of dread making her reluctant to repeat the experience.

"To keep the balance," Bran answered. With a jut of his chin toward Zul, he added, "We must claim you as a triad, together, to secure the bond between mates and ensure your fertility."

Ursula's upper lip lifted and she reiterated, "I am not a fucking broodmare for the empire."

Gil's free hand stroked her hair. Zul's bleak gaze met hers, and he said, "If you do not wish to touch me or for me to touch you, I will not."

Ursula looked away, feeling ashamed. She took a deep breath then forced herself to meet his gaze once more. "It's not that I'm *not* attracted to you, Zul. It's… it's…" Her voice trailed off as she found herself unable to express the rationale for her reluctance.

"I am not Crow," Zul finished for her.

Her shoulders sagged and her head bowed. She sniffled. "No, you are not Crow."

"Zul is stronger than Crow, and there is no doubt as to his honor," Bran stated.

Gill added his proverbial two cents. "And he has given you and our son kindness. He has shown he can and will be gentle with you."

Ursula shook her head again and sighed, knowing she had no valid objection beyond not wanting her life arranged for her again. *I would have liked to have been given the privilege of choice.*

Bran's approval of Zul washed through her mind. *He gives you that privilege.*

Ursula's gaze flickered to Zul who continued to stare at her, his black eyes and closed expression revealing nothing. However, he could not conceal his dismay through the mental bond they shared through Bran. Through that bond which Bran held open for her, Zul could conceal nothing.

She saw his desire for her. He admired her beauty and delighted in her affectionate manner with her son. He felt both awe and puzzlement at her mates' trust in her to run her own business. She saw his curiosity at her love and skill for pottery. That her skill was creative rather than destructive satisfied something deep inside him and apparently proved her a feminine ideal to him.

Ursula sighed as her cheeks burned with shame. Zul was handsome and honorable, kind and surprisingly gentle. He would rather fall on his sword than harm her or Crow. He would protect her and her son with every lethal skill he commanded and be proud to die in doing so. He offered her all of himself and only hoped for her tolerance.

He will demand my obedience.

"We all demand your obedience," Bran said aloud. Gil stroked her hair again. Bran continued, "Our lenience and generosity allow you to forget where you are."

She snorted. "Oh, I *never* forget where I am, you big brute."

Gil's hand slid over her scalp again, soothing her. "No, *elska'adir*, you do not forget you live on Uribern now, but you do not yet truly understand our culture. Look at your First."

She obeyed.

"See his size. Compare it to yours." He tweaked a nipple. She gasped. "Urib females of every species are smaller than their males. Humans are smaller yet and so delicate." He tweaked the other nipple. "We allow you privileges so we can withdraw them to protect you."

Ursula squirmed on his lap, but the hand pressing between her thighs kept her anchored in place. "I don't think so." She took a stronger metaphorical grip on her thoughts and added, "Urib males believe females are less than them."

"You are smaller and much weaker," Bran pointed out. "You do not have the speed, strength, or skill to protect yourself."

She raised her chin. "But that doesn't mean I'm mentally deficient. It doesn't mean I'm incompetent, incapable of rational thought, or unable to make good decisions."

"Of course, not," Gil assured her. "Females are creators of beauty and wellsprings of pleasure. All that confers civilization upon us and makes us superior to wild beasts comes from females."

"We *cherish* our females," Bran concluded.

Unable to refute the reality of her experience as their mate, she lashed out one last time: "Your government has been trying to get you killed, so they can *place*" —she gestured with air quotes, a gesture her mates had learned conveyed irony or sarcasm— "me with another triad to breed more babies! And I would have no recourse!"

"Ah, *elska'adir*, I understand your distress," Bran said. "Why do you think I have searched these years for a new Third to complete our triad? Zul is not the only suitable male I have considered, but he is the only suitable male *you* would consider."

Ursula's jaw dropped. "I hadn't realized you'd been parading potential Thirds through the house."

"Not all of them," he clarified.

"But, yes, some of them," Gil added. He chuckled. "And it is strangely appropriate that you found our Third all by yourself."

Ursula felt herself flush as Gil's approval and amusement washed over her and he pulled the fabric of her skirt up her legs. She felt her body moisten in readiness. "Well, I didn't exactly *find* him."

"You know what Gil means," Bran gently reproached her.

"I do," she said on a gasp as Gil eased a thick finger inside her. She sharply inhaled again as the heavy muscles in his thighs bunched and released beneath her as he rose from the chair while holding her against his body. He allowed her to sink several inches, impaling her upon his thumb as his splayed fingers curved around her buttocks. "This isn't like last time."

Bran chuckled at her breathy words and fixed his gaze on her exposed thighs and the shallow lift and fall of her breasts beneath the light, loose fabric of her dress as she panted. "No, mate, this will be *better*."

Ursula's eyelids fluttered shut. She felt the press of Bran's thumb above her right eye and the slide of his hand beneath her bottom to support her weight because her feet dangled at least a foot above the floor. She heard rather than saw Zul's slow, careful approach and inhaled his clean scent when he drew near.

"Steady her," Gil said as he lifted his hand away from her abdomen and pressed the pad of his thumb above her left eye.

A hand, broad and calloused, pressed against her ribs, the placement of fingers carefully avoiding any unnecessary intimacy. A third thumb pressed against her forehead between the other two.

""I am the First of your mates, Brannal cen'Vyr, Prime of Fangrys Triad. Your honor and pleasure are mine and my love is yours. Receive me with joy," Bran intoned.

Gil spoke next. "I am Gilvane cen'Vyr, Second of the Fangrys Triad, and the Forever of your mates to accompany you for so long as you live. Your honor and pleasure are mine, and my love is yours. Receive me with joy."

Finally, Zul spoke, his voice filled with awe. "I am Zullar cen'Vyr, Third of the Fangrys Triad, and the Bridge who connects the First and the Forever. Your honor and pleasure are mine, and my love is yours. Receive me with joy."

Simultaneously, they lifted their thumbs from Ursula's brow, each leaving behind a shimmering imprint: gold for Bran, turquoise for Gil, and ruby for Zul. Ursula moaned as her mind opened to the warrior triad. Two of those minds were familiar, easing the blast of heat, desire, and excitement of the third.

"The psychic bond is established," Bran whispered. He pressed a kiss to her temple. "Tomorrow we will complete the Rite of First Taste."

Ursula exhaled a shuddering sigh as her channel tightened around Gil's thumb.

"Let him see you take your pleasure," Gil murmured. "Give him this gift."

Gil flexed his thumb to press and stroke against that magical spot within her body that never failed to stoke her passion. Another hand—she recognized Bran's touch—pinched her nipples. As though an electric line ran directly from her nipples to her G-spot, she cried out as her climax burst. The musky smell of her passion filled the air and mixed with her panted breaths.

Connected to her mind through the bond, Zul felt Ursula's pleasure swell and burst. His own cock swelled and demanded release.

"Soon, this, too, will be yours to share," Bran said to Zul as Gil's hands shifted to hold their mate's open thighs and support her weight. The golden Prime stepped between her spread legs and lifted his kilt to expose his turgid, pulsing cock.

Zul's jaw dropped as, fascinated, he watched Bran position his cock at the entrance of their mate's body and slowly push inside. Ursula's throaty moan sounded like sultry music to his ears. The base of his horns heated with fiery lust, and he clamped a hand around his own swollen cock.

"You need not stay if you do not wish it," Gil whispered to him.

However, Zul could not pull himself away. He could not summon that discipline or mastery of his own body, but stroked himself and watched as his new Prime fucked their mate. The wet, squelching sounds twined with Bran's soft grunts and the rapid movement of Zul's hand as he squeezed and stroked. He gurgled, swallowing a cry and tightening his grip as Bran hissed his release, sharing his pleasure through the mental bond with his triad.

After a long moment, Bran withdrew from Ursula's body, then he and Gil shifted her with practiced ease. His seed and the drops of her passion dribbled from her body and splattered on the floor. Gil transferred her to Bran's arms, and he supported her while Gil moved the fabric of her clothing out of the way and speared his cock into her from behind. Zul choked back a growl as Gil set a punishing rhythm, his hips slapping into their mate's buttocks. Soon, Gil, too, reached his climax as Ursula cried out and her body shuddered in an explosion of matching pleasure.

Zul, too, found his release, catching the spew of his seed in his hand. He grunted then sighed. Tomorrow he would taste her, and she would taste him. And then they would fuck.

CHAPTER 9

Zul stepped into the sheltered courtyard then paused in confusion. The youngling leaned his head against his forearm which was pressed against the base of a statue. He counted slowly, uttering a whispered bit of nonsense between each number: "four Mississippi ... five Mississippi ..." After reaching "ten Mississippi," the child raised his head, blinked against the bright sunshine from Uribern's two suns, and called out, "Ready or not, here I come!"

Standing in the doorway, Zul watched as the child looked about, obviously searching for something or someone. The boy decided upon a direction and began prowling, searching beneath shrubs and behind statuary and under benches. He watched as young Crow dashed here and there, occasionally calling in a sing-song voice, "Come out, come out, wherever you are!"

A flutter of pale green caught Zul's attention. He took a sniff and caught her scent. Hiding in the branches of a well-pruned tree was the boy's mother. He met her eyes, and she grinned at him. Although he was taken aback—not for the first time—by the friendly intent of her bared teeth, he felt no animosity or fear or anger in her, but rather an indulgent amusement.

What are you doing? he asked, initiating mind-to-mind conversation with her for the first time and hoping she would not repudiate him for it.

Playing hide-and-go-seek with Crow.

Is this an... an Earth game?

It is. Children love this game.

Is this game used to teach human children how to hunt? He felt her mental pause of surprise as she considered his question.

Her response came slowly. *No, we don't use it like that—at least my childhood friends and I never did. It was simply fun.*

The idea of play for its own sake puzzled him. Rather than risk the danger of disapproval, Zul decided to pursue his questioning to learn more about her alien customs. *What happens when he catches you?*

Her silent chuckle rippled across the mental connection and tickled his mind. *If he catches me, then I owe him a kiss, and it's his turn to hide while I seek. If I deliberately reveal myself to him, then I get to tickle him, and again it's his turn to hide.*

Zul decided he, too, would like to play this hunting game that wasn't training to hunt. He, too, would enjoy the stakes of capturing his quarry. *I would like to join you in this play.*

"Mama, where are you? I can't find you," Crow cried out and stomped a foot in frustration.

Leaves rustled as Ursula climbed down, showing an unseemly amount of leg. The sight made Zul exhale slowly in a self-reminder that they were in an enclosed courtyard which, although large, was private. Not even a single castratus was present, although he was certain they were monitoring the activity just in case either the Prima or the youngling managed to injure themselves.

"Here I am," Ursula called out as she landed on the ground.

"Mama!" Crow shouted and ran toward her, small, pointed teeth bared in a happy smile. He launched himself into her open arms. When she wrapped her arms around him and nuzzled his head, he whimpered, "I thought maybe you left me."

"Oh, my darling, I would *never* do such a thing to you," she assured him then pressed a kiss to his pate. "When you are old enough, we will take our game outside. Until then, we'll play in the courtyard where you can keep me safe."

Listening, Zul approved of her words and the way the young-ling puffed his chest at the thought of being considered strong and fierce enough to protect his beloved mama.

"Are you ready to pay the penalty?" she asked, rubbing her nose against her son's.

"Yes, Mama!"

Zul watched in astonishment as Ursula wriggled her fingers against the child's sides. As she counted to five with the same use of nonsense syllables between each number, the boy wiggled and laughed. Then she stopped and said, "Done!"

"Your turn!" Crow announced, still giggling.

"Zul would like to play. Will you let him join us, Crow?"

Crow's eyes brightened at the idea of another playmate. "Does he know how to play?"

Approaching them at a slow walk, Zul paused and suggested, "Why don't you teach me?"

"Okay," the child agreed, pleased to be the one teaching rather than the one being taught. Drawing himself up to his full, if diminutive, height, the child took hold of Zul's hand and led him to the statue. "You have to cover your eyes, so you can't see where she's hiding, and count to ten. You have to count slowly. Mama says saying 'Mississippi' after each number is proper."

"And then?" Zul asked.

"And then you have to find her. She says I only get three minutes 'cause the courtyard is small. If you find her, that means she's it."

"It?"

"Uh-huh. Then it's her turn to find me!"

"Shall we begin?"

"Cover your eyes, Master Zul. I'll cover mine, too, to make it fair."

Copying the boy's actions from earlier, Zul leaned against the statue and covered his eyes. He counted aloud as the boy instructed and listened to the light patter of Ursula's feet and the rustle of leaves.

When he reached ten, Crow took his hand again. He peered, squinting his golden eyes as though to pierce through the foliage and other items behind or under which Ursula could hide.

"Shall I show you a different method to hunt... er... *find* your mother?" Zul whispered.

Crow's eyes widened. "Yes!"

"Sniff the air," Zul instructed. Crow inhaled, more a snort than a sniff. "Try again." He demonstrated. Crow sniffed the air. "What do you smell?"

Taking another, deeper inhale, Crow's nostrils flared. He squinted again as he tried to discern the different scents. Slowly, he replied, "I smell the ponds. They smell cool and wet."

"Very good. What else?" Zul prompted.

"I smell the flowers, especially the sunfloss. It smells like candy." Crow's eyes opened wide. "I *love* candy, don't you?"

Zul gave him a close-mouthed smile of indulgence. "I do. What else do you smell?"

Crow took another breath then shook his head. "I don't know."

"All right," Zul said. "I will find your mother. When we find her, sniff her. Memorize her scent, and you will always be able to find her."

Crow nodded and watched in amazement as Zul took an ostentatious sniff, nostrils flaring. He again caught her scent and felt his groin tighten. Ruthlessly quelling his lust, he took the boy's hand and said, "Follow me."

Zul slowly followed the scent trail with unerring accuracy to the hidden bench where Ursula waited for them.

"You found me!" she cried out and opened her arms. Crow ran to her embrace.

"Now Zul has to kiss you," Crow said.

She tilted her head back, the finely scaled skin over her cheekbones flushing a darker pink. Her expression turned sultry and her voice thickened as she said, "Yes, now he must kiss me."

Zul chuckled, enjoying the fascinating play of color. "I caught you. I believe it is you who owes me a kiss."

Ursula smiled. "I do believe you're correct." She extended a hand. He captured it in his big paw to help her stand. "Bend down, Zul."

He bent down and stared into her eyes. She gave him a mischievous grin and darted to the side to give him a peck on the cheek.

It was less than he wanted and more than he hoped for—and the quickly delivered, light touch of her lips made him feel as though he were going to catch fire. After a long moment during which he took several deep breaths to calm his libido, he said, "Crow, take your mother's scent. Memorize it."

The child wrapped his arms around his mother's legs and buried his nose in her skirts. When he lifted his head, he asked, "Can we try again?"

"Yes," Zul said. "Your mama shall hide again, and this time *you* shall find her."

You're teaching him to hunt.

It's never too early for a Urib warrior breed to learn basic hunting skills.

Ursula gave him a small smile then said, "Yes, let's try again. This is how people on Earth train scent hounds to track."

"What's a scent hound?" Crow asked.

"It's a dog that finds things by their sense of smell," she explained.

What's a dog?

I'll tell you later. Aloud she said, "The three-minute rule is still in effect."

"Okay, Mama."

Crow retreated to the statue, pressed his forearm against the base and head head against his forearm, and began the laborious process of counting to ten. That time, Zul did not bother covering his eyes.

"Did you cover your eyes?" the boy asked.

"No."

"You *have* to cover your eyes," Crow insisted. "It's the rules. Now I have to count again."

"All right," Zul replied. He covered his eyes and Crow did the same, repeating the count to ten.

"Ready or not, here I come!" the child called out.

Before the child could take a step, Zul crouched beside him and laid his hand on his shoulder. "Do you remember your mother's scent?"

Crow nodded. "Uh-huh."

"Now sniff the air like I taught you."

His eyes closed and his face twisted in concentration, Crow took a slow sniff.

"Think about the smells in the air. Do you smell your mother?"

The boy took another long sniff, concentrated, exhaled, and inhaled again. His eyes popped wide open. "I got it!"

"Good. Now follow where the scent leads you."

The boy sniffed again while turning in a slow circle. Watching him, Zul saw the moment Crow locked on to his mother's scent.

"This way," Crow whispered loudly and began to tiptoe down the sandy path.

The child paused four times in his search, sniffing. He altered his direction twice. As the three-minute deadline drew close with only a few seconds to spare, he called out, "I found you, Mama! I found you!"

Ursula smiled and welcomed her son into her embrace. "Well done, Crow. Well done."

"You have to kiss me now, Mama."

She grinned at him. "Of course, I do." Then she bussed him on the nose. Before Crow could demand that she kiss Zul, too, she rose to her full height, dusted off her skirts, and said, "I think it's time to head back indoors. It's getting rather too hot out here for comfort."

Zul shot her a knowing look that made her feel even hotter.

CHAPTER 10

Ursula retreated to her studio to throw pottery. Zul joined Bran and Gil in the library. He sat in a comfortable chair and alternated gazing out the tall window, thinking, and reading. The freedom he experienced in his new home felt fragile and precious. His former prime had treated him more or less as a dangerous animal: to be both respected and restrained for his unpredictable savagery.

Effective ventilation systems kept the bright sunlight streaming through the windows from overheating the room. After collecting his thoughts, he said, "I want to know more about Ursula."

Bran looked up from the ledgers he was reviewing, and Gil set down the book he was reading. The triad's Second gave him a considering look and replied, "What would you like to know?"

Zul decided to start with the difficult questions first. "What are her expectations of us? Of me?"

Gil chuckled and slowly shook his head. "You must bear in mind at all times that our beloved mate is not from Uribern. In her country—"

"Country?" Zul echoed.

"Ah, first a quick lesson," Gil said. "Earth, the planet Ursula is from, is divided into many nations and peoples who are further divided by a multitude of languages and cultures. Even people within the same nation are divided by regional customs, religious beliefs, and political preferences."

Zul blinked at the complexity of Earth's human population. "How backward."

"Indeed," Gil agreed. "However, humanity has a plethora of females, and those females are—with some genetic conversion—biologically compatible with Urib males. As you are well aware, Uribern suffers a desperate paucity of females in general and breeding females in specific."

Zul nodded. That much he already knew.

Gil continued. "The culture in which our *elska'adir* lived guaranteed females many privileges and responsibilities that her people call rights. From my research, I have concluded this has created both many advantages and disadvantages for both the males and females in her culture. For instance, females are expected to carry and fulfill the same responsibilities as males, such as securing employment to earn wages to cover living expenses, and still bear their young and maintain their households. Many, if not most, males in her homeland expect and rely on the income earned by their females."

"Foolish," Zul muttered.

"Ursula came to Uribern for employment, although she did not realize she was being sent here from Earth." Bran frowned. "Humans are often duplicitous, especially their politicians."

"For *employment*?" Zul shook his head in disapproval, thinking that human politicians had much in common with politicians on any planet, including Uribern. Overall, they were loathsome, dishonest, self-serving, and utterly lacking in honor. The broad sweep of his horns narrowly missed knocking over a lamp.

Gil nodded and continued, "Females in Ursula's homeland may go about as they please. They may go anywhere and do whatever they wish without a male's protection."

"Is Earth so safe then that females need not worry about being attacked?"

Gil chuckled and shook his head. "Many of the males in Earth's cultures consider females their prey. I have made a brief study of this. Too few males act to protect them."

Zul was appalled. "Do the males of Earth have no honor?"

Gil shrugged. "The males of Earth are puny compared to us, but still larger, stronger, and faster than the females. Most are neither warriors themselves nor affluent enough to purchase protection for their females." He leaned forward, his expression twisting with disapproval. "I have read that, oftentimes, females carry weapons and learn to fight to protect themselves."

Zul blinked at this astonishing revelation. He shared Gil's disapproval.

"You're getting off-track," Bran murmured from where he sat at his desk.

"Right," Gil said. "In short, Ursula demands many of the same rights here that she had on Earth. It pleases us to indulge her as long as she does not act foolishly. Except for the attack by the rosvoi—for which she is not to be blamed—she has demonstrated good sense and has not betrayed our trust."

"And if it does not please you to indulge her?" Zul asked. "Do you simply forbid her what she wants, and does she accept it?"

Bran snorted.

Grinning, Gil said, "We often compromise. We do not wish to crush her spirit; that is a good part of why we love her. We will listen to her arguments and decide accordingly."

"She is not obedient then."

"She is often obedient because we do not abuse our authority," Bran commented. "We do not make unreasonable demands of her, and we always listen to her objections." He aimed a pointed look at Zul. "She is not a mindless animal or irrational child who needs to be controlled to prevent her from harming herself and others."

Gil nodded in agreement. "We were not best pleased to allow her to have her little shop in the village, but when we realized how proud she is of her work and how well she runs her small business, we understood how important it is to her. What is important to her is important to us."

"So," Zul voiced his questions again, "what will she expect of us? Of me?"

"Ursula will expect your respect as well as your affection," Gil replied.

"Respect?"

"Treat her as an equal, even though she is small and weak compared to any Urib female. She is smart and resourceful, and you would be wise to respect those qualities."

Zul snorted. "She has no claws and blunt teeth. She cannot harm me if I make her angry."

"But she can withhold access to her body," Bran said. The base of Zul's horns itched at the idea of being denied access to his mate's lovely, luscious body. "We do not and *will not* force intimacy upon her. We fuck her only if and when she is willing."

Zul nodded and replied, "To do otherwise is dishonorable."

Gil grinned again, his eyes shining with amusement. "Luckily, our *elska'adir* is nearly always willing and receives us with joy."

Zul cocked his head to one side, musing on that statement. "She does not know about our pheromones, does she?"

"We have not discussed it," Bran admitted. "But our mating pheromones facilitate intimacy, both physical and emotional, with her. If she were to believe she was being manipulated…" He shuddered. "Ursula has mostly settled into acceptance of Urib ways, and we wish to keep her happy, so we do that through compromise, as Gil said."

"What does Ursula like?" Zul asked, thinking of ways to not lose her favor and be denied access to her body.

"Anything sweet," Gil answered with a laugh.

"We import a viscous liquid from Earth called honey," Bran admitted with a sheepish grin. "She drizzles it over almost everything."

"She especially likes it on her breakfast foods," Gil added.

Bran nodded. "I tasted it once. It is *very* sweet."

"And then there's cake," Gil added.

"Cake?"

Gil explained, "A confection from Earth. It comes in different flavors and varies in texture. Ursula prefers one flavor called chocolate. She says it makes her happy."

Zul was skeptical. "Does it really?"

"She certainly enjoys it, so Gil ensures we import it," Bran said. "Such treats are small enough indulgences to help keep her content with her exile."

"Exile?" Zul echoed.

"Humans have barely ventured into space," Gil explained. "They are bound to their planet. Coming here, for her, was a terrible banishment from home that she did nothing to deserve. We wish to make her life here pleasant and preferable to returning to Earth."

"Even though she cannot return?"

"Even though she cannot return," Bran said. "An unhappy mate would make for a miserable existence."

Zul could understand the logic of that and wondered if Ursula understood the vast power she wielded over them.

Catching the unvoiced thought through their mental connection, Bran answered, "If she does, she does not abuse that power, just as we do not abuse our authority over her."

"That balance is crucial to her well-being and ours," Gil said.

"This is a good discussion," Bran said, laying his hands flat on the desk. "Gil and I must depart the day after tomorrow, so we will be leaving our mate in your care."

Gil ran a palm along the curl of one silvery horn. "We should refresh ourselves. It is nearly time for supper."

Zul took the hint and rose from the chair. He shut the book and returned it to the shelf, careful not to damage it with his claws or through rough handling. Musing on what he'd learned about their hybrid mate as he followed Bran and Gil from the room, he realized he had more in common with Ursula than he originally thought and vowed to allow her all the freedoms he had never been granted until his Prime and Second had perished in battle. Ursula, he understood, had gone from freedom to captivity—

luxurious and gentle captivity, but captivity nonetheless. Having been a captive, figuratively speaking, with few freedoms and little luxury, he had no desire to impose that burden upon his mate.

CHAPTER 11

They ate a light supper. None of them wished to go through the Rite of First Taste or the Rite of First Union logy from full bellies. Casting the occasional nervous glance at Zul, Ursula drank an extra glass of wine, thinking she'd need to be *very* relaxed to accommodate him.

They retreated to the central bedchamber in what Ursula thought of as the marital suite. From this central chamber with its enormous bed radiated an equally spacious bathing room and four more suites, one en suite bedchamber for each of them. After completing the Right of First Union which would finish the process of joining their souls, Zul would move from his guest quarters to occupy the space formerly occupied by Crow. She wondered if the castrati had cleaned it and cleared it of Crow's presence and felt guilty for not ensuring that task was already taken care of.

The chamber is prepared, Gil murmured reassurance in her mind as they walked toward the master suite. Young Crow had been dismissed to Suvesh's care in the nursery.

Ursula's heart clenched. It had been years since Crow's death, yet she still missed him terribly. A piece of her soul had died with him.

Zul will fill your heart and complete your soul, Gil promised. He reached out to stroke her hair.

Zul saw the comforting gesture and paused. The others stopped, too. Zul dared touch her shoulder with his fingertip, careful not to snag the fabric of her dress on his claw, and asked, "Are you reluctant?"

Perhaps it was the wine, but Ursula found her tongue loosen. She took a deep breath and said, "I do not fear you will harm me, Zul. But I miss Crow and do not wish to forget him. You cannot replace him."

Zul did not visibly flinch, but she felt the twinge of pain through their mental connection. "I know I cannot replace him."

After a pause, he turned away.

Appalled that she'd hurt him, Ursula reached out and touched his arm. He went still.

"I'm sorry, Zul. I mean no disrespect. It's just that... that... he..."

"You loved him and you do not love me," he stated plainly. He swallowed his disappointment. "We need not complete the ritual tonight."

"Ursula, you did not love us when we first claimed you," Bran reminded her, his reproof gentle. "Yet you did come to love us, did you not?"

She hung her head. "Yes."

"Then give Zul the chance to earn your love as we earned yours," he said, lifting her chin with his fingertip. "I have seen into his soul and he already bears you great affection."

"You will find him most devoted," Gil added.

Zul growled. "Stop. Cease attempting to persuade her to do what she is not ready to accept. If Ursula is ever ready to accept me as her Bridge, then I will be most honored. But I will not stand for coercion. I do not want a mate who does not want me."

Ursula winced. Waves of raw pain radiated through the bond. Her throat raw with unshed tears, she whispered, "I'm sorry. I'm so, so sorry."

Breaking beneath the weight of Zul's pain and Bran and Gil's disappointment, she fled.

"Aren't you going to go after her?" Zul rasped as she disappeared around a corner.

"No, I think you should," Bran said. Gil nodded in agreement.

"She does not want me."

Gil sighed. "She *does* want you, but she feels conflicted."

"She feels as though she betrays Crow and possibly us by accepting you as the Third in our triad," Bran explained.

"After you've known her for a good while, you'll realize that our mate is complicated. She is not as naturally submissive as an Ilmadrin female. She will need some time to consider this, but not so much time that she will convince herself accepting a new Bridge is betrayal."

"I do not wish to cause her distress."

"Your care for her speaks to your favor," Bran assured him. He patted Zul's shoulder. "Go to her. She's most likely retreated to the courtyard or to her studio."

"She won't harm you," Gil said, eyes gleaming with encouragement.

Zul would have objected. Ursula's reluctance to accept him as her Bridge made him feel as though she'd ripped out both his hearts with her dainty hands. Shoulders tense, he headed down the corridor and followed her scent to her studio, a room he had never entered because it was *her* space, private to her and solely for her use. It was a place he did not feel welcome.

He heard a slam when he entered the studio, easing the door open and sidling through. His horn nearly knocked the door when he turned his head to confront the violent noise only to see her peel the glob of pale pink clay off a flat stone surface, smash it between her hands, and throw it against the stone again. He waited a long moment, watching her as she slammed the clay against the countertop while tears trickled down her cheeks.

Zul knew nothing of pottery, but he thought she had abused the clay enough. Approaching her on silent feet, he settled his hand over both of hers. "Surely, you have punished it enough?"

She raised eyes shimmering with tears to meet his gaze. Her shoulders shook and she bowed over the countertop with a harsh sob. Zul lifted her hands from the clay and turned her toward him.

Feeling both daring and awkward, he drew her against him and wrapped his arms around her as he had seen her do with her son. Ursula yielded to his control, accepted his comfort, and wept.

Sniffling, she finally said, "I'm sorry, Zul. I'm so sorry."

He leaned down and pressed a kiss to the top of her head, again as he'd witnessed her do with Crow and as Gil and Bran often did to her. Through their bond, he felt the honesty of her words and the candid insight of Bran and Gil's words. Their little hybrid mate was indeed a complicated being. Unaccustomed to gentleness, Zul felt forgiveness swell within him. He wasn't sure he liked it, but he knew it was necessary.

"We do not have to complete the ritual now," he assured her. "I will wait until you are ready; and" —he swallowed a lump of painful disappointment— "if you are never ready, then I will respect that."

Ursula's sobs resumed.

"I will not harm you," he whispered, each word feeling like broken glass inside his throat.

His thoughts raced, conjuring and rejecting various options to persuade her to complete the ritual of her own free will. That was the sticking point: he wanted her to freely choose him without guilt, without regret, without sorrow. He knew he would neither force her nor manipulate her compliance. While any of the Triad could, they wouldn't. Not this time.

As she quieted, the sobs dwindling into watery sniffles, Zul looked around the studio. He saw shelves stocked with hefty blocks of pink clay, the finest Uribern had to offer. He saw jars of pigments waiting to be mixed into glazes. A potter's wheel was placed beneath a window which would capture the morning sunlight. Another wheel, the purpose of which he was not sure, stood nearby. Three more tables, one with what he guessed was a press, were placed around the room. Each had a cabinet he was sure was stocked with the implements necessary to achieve various decorative effects. He noted the four fat-bellied kilns near which were more shelves bearing various vessels and figurines, some drying and others awaiting their turn to be fired in the kiln. In the center of the room was an island with a large sink. Everything was tidy. The castrati maintained a high standard of cleanliness within the Fangrys household.

Feeling the need to make a connection with her that did not involve sinking his cock into her body and enhancing her feelings of betrayal, Zul hit upon an idea. "Will you show me? Teach me?"

"What do you mean?" she asked, pulling a handkerchief from an unseen pocket in her dress. Particularly after Crow's birth, she'd adopted the habit of always carrying a handkerchief. They came in handy. Ursula blew her nose, feeling further embarrassed by the loud noise.

Zul gestured. "Show me what you do."

Her eyes widened, then narrowed. "Do you truly want to know, or are you just trying to be nice?"

"I want to know. This is important to you; therefore, it must also be important to me."

Eyes watering again, she blinked away the tears and nodded. "All right." She turned away from him to face the countertop and picked up the lump of clay. "This is the Urib equivalent of porcelain clay on Earth. It's the finest clay and a bit tricky to work with. It has a smooth, fine texture and is known for its translucence after being fired."

She took his hand and set the lump into his palm. His fingers automatically closed around the moist, cool, malleable substance.

"Work it in your hands a bit and learn its feel."

Ursula gestured toward the shelves behind them as he worked the lump of clay. "There are blocks of stoneware clay over there, too. Stoneware clay works well for mugs, pitchers, and plates for everyday use. Porcelain clay works best for fine ceramics and delicate work. Most of the wares in my shop are made with stoneware clay."

"Why were you throwing it on the countertop?" Zul asked. He squeezed the lump of clay in his hand, folded it over, and squeezed it again.

"Do you know how magnetism works?" she asked. "Like how the ions in iron need to all be aligned in the same direction for the magnet to work?"

He nodded.

"Clay is like that. Slamming the clay aligns the particles, so they run in the same direction. It makes the clay stronger and more stable and easier to work with."

Zul began to suspect that pottery was a good bit more complicated than he anticipated. Just like her.

"We'll start with slab pottery first, a tall vase," she said and walked to the table with the press on it. Turning a wheel, she adjusted the space between the smooth steel roller and the flat surface of the table beneath it. "The goal here is to flatten and stretch the clay into a uniform shape and thickness."

With her direction, he patted the lump into a more or less oblong shape and fed it through the press. She handed the somewhat flattened piece to him and adjusted the roller. He fed the clay through again. After several runs through the press, the clay had flattened to the desired thinness and its surface was smooth and unbroken.

"Would you like to emboss the surface?" she asked.

He blinked. She opened a drawer and pulled out a length of heavy lace, a silicone sheet with a pattern stamped on it, and other items, including a rolling pin.

"Pick a pattern or two that appeal to you."

He touched a fingertip to the lace and to a length of chain with interesting links.

"Place the lace on the clay."

He did so and she adjusted it.

"What do you intend for the chain?"

"A border?"

She gave him a quick smile and laid the chain above one edge of the lace. "The patterns look nice together."

Her praise warmed his heart, but not as much as the way she'd begun to relax in his presence. He felt pride in having found an effective way to connect with her and set her mind at ease.

She led him through the process of pressing the patterns into the sheet of clay, just hard enough to emboss the surface. Unfortunately, he had to repeat the entire process of preparing the clay four times before he managed the lightness and delicacy of touch needed. She showed him how to cut the clay into a clean strip and wrap it around a form to create an evenly proportioned cylinder. She taught him how to score the clay and paint on a light wash of slurry to meld the edges and secure a watertight seal. She showed him how to cut the base and gently marry it to the cylinder. When they finished that night, a new vase had been placed on the shelf to dry beneath a clear dome which would prevent the clay from drying too quickly and, thus, cracking.

"The clay should be dry in a couple of days," she said as they washed their hands and tools. She draped the wet lace and the chain over a rod to dry. The scoring tool and small paintbrush were thoroughly rinsed and set in a jar to dry. She wiped down the countertop and table, anywhere and anything the clay had touched, to ensure its cleanliness when it would be used next. "Then we'll pick out glazes. I'll show you how to mix them."

"Thank you," Zul said.

She blinked at the simple gratitude in his voice. "You're welcome. I... I enjoyed it. I enjoyed teaching you."

At that moment, Zul realized that neither Bran nor Gil had given her the opportunity to teach them. They instructed her; she was always the student and never the master. Softly, he took her hand and said, "It was my pleasure to learn."

"Doesn't Urib culture forbid males from doing... er... creative things?"

The corners of his mouth lifted in a small smile. "Not forbid. Discourage, perhaps. Warriors are bred to fight, and we excel at it." He gestured toward the shelves. "But it's nice to know that fighting is not all we're good for."

She favored him with a melancholy smile and took her hand in his. Giving it a light squeeze, she thanked him then walked away.

He did not ask her what she thanked him for. He knew.

CHAPTER 12

Zul met Ursula in the studio again and joined her, Bran, and Gil at meals the next day, but the triad did not advance to the Rite of First Taste. Ursula agreed to proceed, but Zul noticed she was not altogether comfortable with doing so. Regardless of her words, she could not hide the trepidation and guilt she felt: the mental connection revealed those thoughts and feelings.

"You take a great risk," Gil warned him as he and Bran made ready to leave for their deployment the morning of their departure.

"We are a bonded triad now," Zul replied, keeping his voice quiet. "The Council Supreme knows and will end this latest deployment quickly, so we can get to the business of breeding more warriors for them."

Bran nodded, early morning sunlight glinting off his golden horns. "You are a wise choice for our triad and our mate."

Zul wanted to preen with pride at those words of praise. However, he had more self-control than that. He merely nodded and pressed his fist to the center of his chest in a gesture of solidarity and respect. "Glory and honor be yours."

The golden and turquoise warriors thumped their chests with their fists and bowed their heads, then they turned away, heading toward the transport that awaited them.

"I'll never get over how those bricks fly," Ursula commented as she watched them enter the vehicle.

Hearing her voice, Zul glanced behind him, surprised she had approached without him noticing. He chastised himself for such inattention and returned his focus to the departing warriors. When the door closed behind them, short, stubby wings fanned out, and the vehicle rose with a soft whine of unseen power. It hovered a moment, then shot upward into the cloudless sky and soon vanished from view. As the distance between them grew, the mental bond linking Ursula with Bran and Zul thinned and snapped.

Zul read Ursula's pensive expression and interpreted her thoughts and feelings without the bond. He murmured, "You are worried."

She sighed and nodded. "I always worry." They turned to head back indoors. As they walked, she continued, "When I was a kid, one of my best friends had a dad who was in the military. I forget which branch. Anyway, he was deployed overseas and returned a few months later in a casket. I remember how devastated my friend and her family were. They moved away soon after." She shook her head and sighed again. "I cannot imagine losing another mate or, God forbid, both of them."

"I do not think you need to worry about that this time," Zul said. "The Council Supreme knows about our triad. They cannot—"

"Cannot?" she interrupted, her tone sardonic.

"Will not," he corrected, "rescind the deployment orders, but they can and probably will redirect their service to a new assignment, one less likely to get one of them killed."

"You almost make them sound conscientious and considerate," she muttered. Scoffing, she added, "We know they are neither."

Zul shook his head and agreed with her. "No, they are not. They use the military for their own aggrandizement, something I hope will soon be rectified."

Ursula paused and looked at him, eyes narrowing. "You know something."

He gave her a small, close-lipped smile. "I know many things."

"Tell me," she demanded.

He cupped her cheek with one massive hand, sweeping his thumb over the fine, silky skin. "I do not endanger innocents."

Ursula stared at him, seeking a chink in his unyielding black gaze. Not finding what she sought, she took a step backward. He let his hand drop.

"You won't tell me what's going on, what Bran and Gil have planned."

"I will not," he confirmed. "I do not know the whole of it, only the intent."

"That should be sufficient to tell me."

"No."

"You would prefer me ignorant?"

"I would prefer you safe."

Ursula quelled the childish urge to stomp her foot. Straightening her spine and squaring her shoulders, she declared, "I'm going to town."

"I will accompany you."

His mild tone annoyed her precisely because he gave her nothing to fight against, no command or expectation of unthinking obedience. "There's no need."

He disagreed. "There is every need. I will ensure your protection."

"There have been no more reports of rosvoi in the area," she snapped.

"That does not mean there is no danger. Predators roam Uribern, predators that would see you as no more than a tasty morsel."

Ursula pressed her lips together in a thin line of anger. However, she knew when she was beaten. "I leave in thirty minutes. Don't be late."

Zul knew she wasn't joking: she *would* leave without him. He headed toward her studio to supervise the loading of wares into the hoverwagon to which two numpties had been hitched. The castrati had the task well in hand, having streamlined the process into an efficient science, ensuring porcelain and stoneware items made the journey intact and undamaged. Seeing the castrati needed neither his supervision nor assistance, he took some time to return to his quarters and arm himself.

Ursula met him at the hoverwagon a few minutes before the appointed time, Crow's hand clasped in hers. Her sour expression conveyed more clearly than words her annoyance that he had not been late. The castrati assisted her and her son in climbing into the hoverwagon. Another servant hopped up beside her and picked up the reins.

"Are you not riding?" she inquired, her tone haughty.

"I'll escort you on foot," he replied and took a step. The castratus driving the hoverwagon said nothing, but flicked the reins. Suvesh, still recuperating from his injuries, would remain at the manor while Hurvi took charge of the youngling. The numpties lurched forward and kept pace with him.

The journey ended without incident at the intended destination. Accompanied by her mate, Sifgul, Mistress Addilli emerged from their storefront and greeted her. Sifgul, the more lenient of her two mates, allowed Addilli to dash forward and take Ursula's hand in friendship.

"I see the warrior remains, so the rumors must be true," Addilli whispered, casting curious glances at Zul. "Gallik and Sifgul have kept watchful eyes on your shop. There has been no trouble."

Ursula gave her hand a light squeeze and smiled. "It's so lovely to see you again. I've been wanting to have a nice chat with another woman." She glanced at the berserker. "Men. Ugh. They're so overbearing."

Addilli giggled and darted a glance at Sifgul who nodded at her, giving her permission to continue to socialize with their Prima. "So, is the rumor true? Is he the new Third in the Fangrys Triad?"

"Yes, he is," Ursula replied and forced herself to give credit where credit was due. "He's a good male and a good match for us."

"You must tell me all about him over *ti'chal*. I have a fresh pot brewed."

The two females retreated to catch up on local gossip as the Prima's castrati finished unloading her wares. Ursula enjoyed hearing the local gossip even if she shared little of her own. Addilli fussed over Crow, plying him with snacks and praise while his mama allowed the indulgence. The female also cast furtive glances at the hulking red berserker who stationed himself within sight of them while still keeping a watchful eye over the shop. Nearly bursting with curiosity and questions, Addilli respected Ursula's reticence and contained the urge to pester her friend for details.

With a fond farewell and a promise to meet socially for *ti'chal* and cookies baked by the Prima herself—Addilli practically quivered with excitement at being invited to visit the Fangrys compound—Ursula set herself to the task of displaying her wares while keeping a watchful eye on her son.

As he was accustomed to doing, Crow occupied himself with the stash of toys his mother kept for him in the shop's back room while Hurvi hovered nearby, one eye on the shop and one eye on him.

Zul noticed the castratus' vigilance and approached him. "I will see to the Prima's safety. You need only concern yourself with the youngling."

"Yes, my lord." The castratus bowed and disappeared into the back room.

Heat warmed the base of his horns at the servant's words. He'd been called by his military rank, as "Third," and a host of other names—some less than complimentary—but never as "my lord." The privileges of being the Third of the Fangrys Triad made him feel guilty as though he'd stolen something valuable rather than having been gifted something priceless. Scanning the shop, he found a corner that wasn't packed with merchandise and which gave him an optimal view of the space. He stationed himself there and stood guard.

Ursula found herself relaxing under Zul's watchful presence. The anxiety she'd refused to acknowledge eased: the berserker—*her* berserker—would keep her safe from all manner of assault ranging from mere rudeness to outright violence. Even if he never said a word, his mere presence served as a deterrent.

She finished wiping down the newly unpacked wares, and they gleamed in the sunshine streaming through the storefront's large windows. She clustered the half dozen bowls and vases Zul had made under her tutelage, pleased with the way they'd turned out. They'd quickly learned that he preferred to work with the more forgiving stoneware clay, and his wares had a rugged, masculine appearance that her finer work did not. She thought they might appeal to the many bachelors in the village, and he had not objected to her suggestion that they be offered for sale in her shop. If his skin were not red, she thought she might have detected a bashful blush across his sharp cheekbones when she'd made that suggestion.

News spread quickly through the village that the Prima's shop had reopened for business. Before long, the first customers entered. Gazes flickering to the hulking berserker lurking in the corner, they bowed and greeted the Prima before looking over the merchandise. They bid her a polite farewell and departed.

"Does this happen often?" Zul inquired, joining her at the counter.

She blinked at him. "Does what happen often?"

"People come into your shop, gawk, and leave."

She shrugged. "Sometimes, yes. That's the reality of retail. Many customers are simply curious and just want to snoop. Some actually want to buy."

"Why do you not hire employees?"

She grinned at him, and he felt his cock twitch. "My shop barely makes rent; it certainly doesn't generate enough revenue to pay an employee. When I can't be here, I rely on one or two castrati from Fangrys to work here. Besides, I like interacting with people. It's why I became an event planner in the first place." She glanced through a window. "However, event centers really don't seem to be a thing here on Uribern, at least not that I've seen."

"Tell me about them."

Ursula's expression grew dreamy as she recounted the festivals, conventions, conferences, and parties she'd both attended and organized. "It's a lot of work demanding long hours, but the delight attendees experience makes it all worthwhile." Her expression turned sober, perhaps even melancholy. "However, free association doesn't seem to be a Urib thing."

"Explain."

"At a community festival or arts and craft show, for example, everyone is welcome. It doesn't matter who someone is or where someone comes from, each person who wants to attend is welcome to do so. A really good event will draw attendees from hundreds or even thousands of miles away. Such an event will have exhibitors and vendors, most participating in the hope of selling goods and services. It's a way to meet a lot of different people, build your clientele, and perhaps make a bit of money. They're generally a lot of fun, even if they're not profitable."

"Everyone is welcome?" he echoed, an idea forming in his mind. He didn't know what a mile was, but grasped the concept of people traveling long distances for entertainment. After all, they did so for war, and what was such an event as she described but a polite, mostly friendly battle for customers?

"Everyone," she said.

"You should do that here."

She blinked, jaw dropping in surprise. After a moment, she closed her mouth and considered his suggestion. Tilting her head, she said, "You know, that's an excellent idea." Her expression clouded. "But I don't know that Gil and Bran would permit it. They're rather overprotective."

Zul opened his mouth to reply, but the door opened and more customers entered. He returned to his corner to lurk, trying not to scare away her customers while the Prima exerted her charm to sell them her wares. When they left with their purchases, he rejoined her at the counter and resumed the conversation. "As long as one of us is with you at all times, I believe you would be permitted to plan such an event."

"Do you really think so?" Her eyes brightened. "But I'd have to get the mayor and the sheriff's permission—and they certainly don't approve of the freedoms Bran and Gil already allow me."

Zul bared his pointed teeth in a fierce smile. "I am now the Fangrys Third, am I not?"

Ursula's lips spread in an answering smile. "You certainly are."

"Then I outrank both the mayor and the sheriff."

Since Uribern's feudal society deeply respected its caste system, Ursula immediately understood where he was going with this. "Yes, you certainly do."

"Then you shall pick a day and plan a festival."

Ursula threw herself at Zul and wrapped her arms around him in an enthusiastic hug. His body responded to the press of hers against him, releasing pheromones to which her flesh responded with the heady aroma of feminine arousal. Only by fierce control did he refrain from pressing his advantage of greater strength and nearly overwhelming desire. She released him and stepped back, her cheeks flushed and her gaze averted.

"I… I'm sorry, Zul."

He pressed a fingertip under her chin and lifted her face to meet his gaze. "You never need to apologize for touching me."

"But… but…" She gestured vaguely at the tented front of his kilt.

"My cock is not my master," he assured her even though he desperately wanted to yield to its throbbing demand.

CHAPTER 13

A few days after Ursula pored over ideas for a festival, the sheriff and the mayor objected to her proposal with the usual protests of propriety and safety, particularly concerning any females whose permissive guardians would be so lax as to allow them to attend and participate. Ursula ground her molars in exasperation, wanting to add her voice to the argument and knowing that doing so would result in categorical denial. Finally, her patience ran out.

"Fine," she snapped. The sheriff and mayor gaped at the impertinence of her interruption. She looked at Zul. "We'll hold the festival at Fangrys."

"But—" the mayor blurted.

"You cannot," the sheriff blustered, taking a belligerent step toward the berserker. The mayor followed close behind him.

She leaned forward and glared at them. "Am I not the Prima of Fangrys?"

"Of course, you are," the mayor said, nodding his agreement in a futile effort to smooth her ruffled feathers. "And as such—"

"And is Fangrys public property?" she demanded, hands fisted on her hips. "Does it belong to the village?"

"Of course not," the sheriff replied, eyes narrowed in suspicion of the direction of her argument.

She smiled, knowing what baring her teeth at them meant and meaning it. "Then you have neither control nor say as to what I, the Fangrys Prima, do in *my own home.*"

"But your mates—"

She cut him off again, this time gesturing with a sharp cutting motion of her hand. "No. You do *not* speak for them."

The sheriff turned a fulminating look at Suvesh, who properly stood four paces behind his mistress. "You, castratus."

Suvesh nodded in acknowledgement, but did not glance at his Prima.

"Do the Lords cen'Vyr allow such insolence?"

Suvesh replied, his voice calm and sure, "My Lord Brannal cen'Vyr, Prime of Fangrys, commands us to serve his Prima as we would him and my Lord Gilvan cen'Vyr, Second of Fangrys, and Zullar cen'Vyr, Third of Fangrys."

"Third?" the mayor echoed, eyes widening.

Zul bared his teeth. "Do you gainsay *me*?"

The sheriff's stiff posture sagged. He shook his head. "No, my lord."

Zul turned his head toward his mate, the curling sweep of horns causing the other males to retreat to avoid being hit by them. "*Elska'adir*, what day do you wish to hold this festival?"

Ursula smiled, his use of the endearment melting her reservations toward completing the mating bond. She smiled at him, a different kind of smile that still included bared teeth. She named an upcoming holiday.

"What day is that?" the mayor asked.

She explained. "I reconciled the day with the calendar on Earth." The mayor and sheriff frowned. "The closest I could come up with is Halloween, a day my homeland uses to celebrate all things autumn."

"Autumn?" the sheriff repeated. "What is this *autumn*?"

"Autumn is a season that transitions from summer to winter in my homeland." She figured the mayor and sheriff would not be interested in a brief history of Halloween or its many customs both commercial and occult.

The village's two highest ranked officials shook their heads, still not understanding. However, Zul, who had traveled widely in his long life, explained the concept of seasons. "In many places throughout the universe, there are planets with only one sun that experience wide variations in temperature. Those variations create seasons. Summer is considered a season of heat, and winter is a season of cold."

"Ah," the mayor said, nodding his head and adopting a wise expression.

"What has this to do with Uribern?" the sheriff demanded. "We do not celebrate this day of *Halloween*."

Ursula, feeling a bit belligerent, leaned forward. "But *I* do." Silently, she added *you moron.* "It will be *fun*."

"Fun?" the sheriff parroted as though the concept were entirely alien. Perhaps it was.

"Fun," she repeated, her tone decisive. "We'll have music. Dancing. Lots of food. Games and competitions. Market stalls for anyone who wants to sell their handcrafted wares. Children—and even adults—may dress in costume. Children will go from stall to stall and receive treats given out by the vendors. Market stalls will be decorated and festive, too."

"It sounds chaotic," the mayor muttered and shook his head.

"Dangerous," the sheriff snarled. "No."

"You can't tell me what to do in my own home," Ursula reminded him with a saccharine smile. She placed a hand on Zul's muscled arm. "Only my mates have that authority."

Zul barely refrained from standing straighter and taller and puffing out his chest, but he did slide a hand around her slender waist and gently draw her close while concealing his amusement at her verbal acknowledgement of their authority over her—an authority she disavowed in private and sometimes flouted without conscience.

Ursula glanced up at him. *I'm not that bad.*

Oh, yes, you are. But I find you endearing nonetheless.

The mayor bowed his head in submission to the vagrant berserker who had somehow become the Third of the Fangrys

Triad. Bowing to any female, even the Fangrys Prima, would never happen. Raising his eyes to meet the berserker's he murmured, "Excuse us, my lord."

He tapped the sheriff on the back of his shoulder and gave him a speaking look. The sheriff huffed a sigh and followed the mayor's retreat several steps away.

"The Prima will have this festival," the mayor whispered. "If we allow it in the village, we will retain control and ensure it does not become something shameful."

"If we allow the festival, we will have submitted to her demand and unreasonable expectations," the sheriff countered.

The mayor pursed his lips and considered a compromise. "We will allow her to hold this festival in the village, but she must comply with a set of rules that we will draft."

The sheriff's eyes flashed with ire, but he sighed and agreed. The mayor was correct: the festival would happen regardless of their order. Neither wanted the berserker's rage unleashed upon them. Nor did they wish to attract the ire of the Fangrys Prime or his Second, who were also fierce warriors. The Fangrys Triad, the two males agreed yet again, allowed their mate far too much leeway.

"Our mate shall not attend," the sheriff stated.

The mayor shook his head. "No, it would not be seemly. Her absence will show other males the error of their thinking should they allow their mates to participate."

"I can hear you, you know," Ursula commented loudly. "What do you think will be more influential: what your Prima does or what the mate of two petty government functionaries does?"

The sheriff's eyes glittered with rage, and the mayor hissed in affront. "Petty government functionaries?" They turned to face her, glowering.

The hulking warrior beside her showed no expression, but pride and amusement radiated from his body.

"He will be lax as well," the mayor muttered in disappointment.

"The festival was my idea," the berserker commented, again showing that the mayor and sheriff had not retreated beyond earshot.

The sheriff growled in barely repressed fury.

"Have you lost all dignity?" the mayor gasped.

"There are more things in Heaven and Earth, Horatio, than are dreamt of in your philosophy," Ursula said.

The sheriff and mayor looked confused. The latter said, "I do not understand."

"It means that your understanding is limited," she replied succinctly.

"My mate wishes to host a community event of entertainment and commerce to the benefit and enjoyment of all Fangrys," Zul said. "There is no evil in this desire and much to be admired, for she invites all of Fangrys to participate, not just the ruling caste."

Although the Fangrys Third seemed willing to compromise, the sheriff was not fooled. "We will allow this festival, but it will be conducted in accordance with Urib law and customs."

"I hadn't planned on organizing a public orgy," Ursula replied, her sarcasm biting.

"Do not mock us," the mayor warned, shaking his finger at her. "This will be a dignified affair."

Ursula's lips split in a mocking smile. "Dignified? I don't think so. The goal is for people to have fun, to *enjoy* themselves. Music and dancing, remember? Costumes? Children?" She shook her head. "Don't be stuffy."

The sheriff opened his mouth to lecture her on proper decorum, but the Prima beat him to it.

"You know? Forget it. Forget about it being a *community* event. I'll host the party at Fangrys. Anyone who wishes to come will be welcome. *And you will have nothing to say about it.*"

The sheriff drew himself up to his full height and snarled, but Zul stared him down.

"Leave," Zul ordered, his quiet command dripping with menace.

With a huff, the sheriff and mayor departed, walking with stiff dignity, their tails lashing.

"Fireworks," Ursula said.

"What?"

She smiled, a vicious, devious expression. "I'm going to put on the party to end all parties—and that requires fireworks.

Everyone for miles around will be talking about this festival for *years.*"

Zul frowned. "What are fireworks?"

She grinned at him, pure delight in her eyes. "Wait until I show you. You're gonna love them!"

CHAPTER 14

Zul had his doubts about the fireworks, but the pictures Ursula showed persuaded him to allow such incendiary frivolity.

"Now, we just need to acquire them and figure out how to launch them without blowing the place up," she muttered under her breath.

Having already given his permission, Zul was reluctant to rescind it, so he set himself and two of the castrati to researching fireworks. What he learned made him wonder if she'd hoodwinked him into doing something terribly foolish. Taking her aside one evening after supper, he cautioned her as to the danger of such entertainment.

"Well, of course, they're dangerous," she agreed with a chuckle. "That's why we need experts, people who understand how to handle gunpowder and explosives."

"I cannot risk you or Crow getting hurt."

Ursula's hands closed into fists which she propped on her hips. She glared at him. "Are you reneging?"

Zul's hearts constricted. His lungs seized with dread and he nearly gulped in fear, not fear of any physical retaliation she might bestow with her small stature, flat teeth, and blunt claws. She could not hurt him in that way. But she could withdraw her affection for him, which had been slowly building as her comfort in his presence grew. He extended a hand toward her. "No! No, I am not reneging. I will keep my word."

She nodded, a curt gesture. "Good." She threw a hard glare at him. "If I can't trust your word, then there's no future for us. Trust is *everything*."

He nodded. "I will see it done."

Ursula granted him a beatific smile and settled a hand on his arm, and all was right with his world once again. "Thank you, Zul. I know this is difficult for you, but I'm not inclined to run headlong into my own demise. Humans have been using fireworks for centuries. Yes, some have been injured or even killed, but the vast majority of fireworks result in no harm. Besides, we'll be well out of range of the explosives during the show."

Zul heaved a relieved breath and squinted his eyes. "You will take care of the rest of the arrangements?"

"I'm already on it," she replied with a grin. "Addilli's being a great help."

Zul blinked at her and waited for further explanation. She did not disappoint.

"Gallik and Sifgul have given their permission for Addilli to help me."

"They are not ignorant of the prestige of allying with the Fangrys Triad," Zul said.

Ursula nodded. "No, they're not. And I have assured them of Addilli's safety and well-being when she visits here."

"As if I would allow harm to come to any female!" Zul snarled, offended by the other two males' apparent distrust.

Ursula laughed, a sound he found simultaneously charming and offensive, for he thought she laughed at him. "No, Zul, they have no fear she shall come to any *physical* harm when we meet here. What they *do* fear is that I will contaminate her with my ideas of women's liberty and female agency."

"Explain."

Ursula pointed to herself. "Am I stupid?"

He reared back, sensing a trap. "No, of course not."

"Am I incompetent?"

"No, of course not."

"Am I foolish and incapable of making smart decisions?"

He paused, thinking of her determination to have fireworks at her festival, then rapidly said as her expression began to sour, "No, of course not!"

"Then, if I am a functioning, intelligent adult, why should I have to seek and obtain permission to do what I want?"

Trying to choose his words carefully so as not to insult his mate and earn her enmity, he slowly replied, "Because the world is a harsh and dangerous place, and females do not have the *physical* strength to prevail."

Ursula snorted and reached up to touch his cheek. "Just because I don't have a man's brute strength doesn't mean I can't figure out other ways to get things done."

He leaned over her, looming in a manner that would have been threatening if she didn't already know he would chew off his own arm before harming her. "I am stronger than you, faster than you, and much, much more dangerous than you, pretty mate." He bared his pointed teeth at her, and she retracted her hand. "*That* is why you must ask and obtain permission; otherwise, I cannot guarantee your safety and well-being."

Ursula sighed. "I hate to break it to you" —her tone indicated she did not actually regret her words— "but no one can *guarantee* my safety and well-being."

He nodded, because what she said was true. There was no guarantee. "Bran, Gil, and I make harming you and Crow much more difficult."

"That's true," she admitted, recalling how she and Zul had met. She said nothing about how, throughout history, women on Earth had needed protection from the very men who were supposed to protect and cherish them. She'd met several mated females in her years on Uribern, both full-blooded Uribs and hybrids, and all appeared to be doted upon by their mates. She clapped her hands together. "Well, I'd best get to work."

Before she could dash off, Zul said, "*Elska'adir*, you do know that I would protect you with my life?"

Although frustrated by her mates' inclination to, figuratively, wrap her in cotton wool and bubble wrap to keep her safe, Ursula realized she had some repairing to do. She'd hurt Zul's feelings. She wrapped her arms around the hulking berserker and laid her cheek against him. "I do, Zul. And do not think for one moment that I am ungrateful—"

"I do not want your *gratitude*," he growled.

She tilted her head back. "You have it nonetheless. And you have my love, too."

Both of Zul's hearts stuttered. "Your love?"

She pressed a kiss to his chest, for her lips could reach no higher, then smiled. "Yes, Zul, my love. You have earned my trust and affection. You *fit* with Bran and Gil. And I find it terribly difficult to resist you."

He sighed and ran a hand down the silky length of her hair. "We are mates. You should not resist me."

She patted him. "Until Bran and Gil return, I must."

Zul sighed again, knowing she spoke truly. He took her small hand in his big paw and lifted it. He turned it over and pressed his mouth to her palm. After kissing her palm, he said, "And I am a male of honor. But once we have performed the Rites of First Taste and First Union together, I will take great pleasure in fucking you" —his words made her shiver— "and you will receive great pleasure when I fuck you."

The musk of her arousal floated up to his nose. Zul put his arms around her and held her against his body, hoping Bran and Gil would return home soon before his fraying control snapped.

CHAPTER 15

The mayor and sheriff relented, and Ursula agreed to hold her festival within the village, much to the unvoiced relief of the Fangrys castrati. She soon discovered that organizing a community event was different from organizing a dedicated conference or party for a single organization. There were additional considerations to handle, including coordinating with other merchants on the streets that would be closed for the festival. Those entrepreneurs were, of course, busy running their businesses, and many were disinclined to speak directly to the Fangrys Prima, demanding instead to deal directly with the new Third of the Fangrys Triad.

That annoyed Ursula to no end. After wasting time and energy complaining, she changed strategy and sought and received introductions to the matriarchs of those business owners' families. She spoke with the wives of mated merchants and the mothers of unmated merchants. Most of the females were intrigued by her proposition to assist in the organization of the festival and delighted by the honor and prestige of helping the Prima of Fangrys.

The village ladies threw themselves into the project with an infectious enthusiasm that spread throughout the region and into neighboring provinces, including Omari. Ursula's former coworker and the Omari Prima called her.

"Carmen, it's wonderful to hear from you! How are you?" Ursula greeted her friend, another human-Urib hybrid bride.

"*Hola, chica*! I heard about your festival and wanted to let you know that the boys and I will be coming," Carmen replied.

"I assume 'the boys' includes your triad as well as the kids?"

"Of course!" Carmen laughed. "You know I never go anywhere without those big lugs." She paused, then asked, "How are you getting along?"

"It's been… weird."

"Weird how?"

"Well…" Ursula chewed on her bottom lip for a moment before launching into the story of meeting Zul and him being accepted as the new Third in her mated triad.

"Well, you know my men will just have to meet him!" Carmen giggled. "And I'd like to take a gander at him, too."

"Carmen!"

The other woman's delighted laugh chimed like bells. "I'm married, not dead!"

Ursula chuckled, glad of her friend's mirth. "Oh, and let me tell you what else I've been doing."

"Stirring up trouble?"

Ursula gasped with fake offense then laughed. "Of course. You know I can't resist causing trouble."

"That's my girl! Strike one for women's liberation!"

Ursula snorted. "The Women's Lib movement isn't coming to Uribern anytime soon. You know that just as well as I do."

"Bah. I can always dream." Carmen sighed. "You know, it's up to us, the human hybrids, to make it happen. We're the only ones with the fire and determination to lead the way for women's rights."

"But how far are we willing to go? How far are *you* willing to go?"

"Therein lies the rub," Carmen admitted. "It's really hard to justify rebellion when we're so richly cosseted. It's not like our husbands are drinking their income and coming home drunk to beat us because we didn't buy meat for supper."

"We'll have to find another angle," Ursula said. "Perhaps forced marriages?"

Carmen threw another roadblock in her way: "Have you met an unhappy Urib mate?"

"No, I have not," Ursula was forced to admit. "But it's not like I've met many."

"So, tell me what you're doing to cause the males of Fangrys to clutch their pearls."

Ursula snickered at the mixed metaphor and related her dealings with the village ladies.

"Oh, that is precious, just precious!" Carmen crowed. "I'll have to take a page from your book and duplicate your work here in Omari."

Ursula laughed again. "Can you *imagine* what would happen if we got all the human hybrid brides to hop on the bandwagon?" She shook her head in incredulity. "Talk about a grassroots uprising."

"I'd say it's worth a try."

"You're connected with the other brides, right?"

"Ah, my little networking party planner, I still have some connections in the embassy. It seems a few of those folks stationed at the embassy were not pleased when Ambassador Hamilton handed me over like so much chattel. Office administration has yet to recover from the loss of my superb efficiency. Anyway, they'll dig up the contact information for those women, and we'll get this grass roots revolution started."

They chatted a while longer, Ursula talking about her son, Crow, and his antics as well as her business and Carmen relating the typical family drama of being mated to a warrior triad and a mother of two children. She confessed to wanting a third child and her hope that maybe, just maybe, she might be blessed with a daughter.

"I'm drowning in testosterone," Carmen complained.

Ursula commiserated, "Tell me about it."

They ended the call, Ursula sighing with pleasure in knowing she had one good friend who understood her. She carried that happy feeling into her studio where she threw three more pots and glazed four.

We're back, elska'adir, Bran's voice rang through her thoughts.

I'm in my studio, she replied as she scrubbed her arms. *Just finishing up.*

Zul had an interesting tale to tell us.

Ursula sighed, dreading a decree to cease and desist with planning the festival.

We will not undermine Zul by canceling your festival, but this is something you should have discussed with all three of us first.

Ursula attempted to reason with him. *I'm a competent, intelligent adult who built a career organizing events. This is what I did for years before coming to Uribern. It's not like I'm attempting something dangerous that I've never done before.*

Gil interjected himself into the mental conversation. *You are intelligent, competent, and precious to us. However, this endeavor is a not-so-subtle attempt to assert your independence… and we cannot have that. You are our mate and the Prima of Fangrys.*

It is not just an attempt to "assert my independence" as you accuse me of doing, she objected. *The festival will draw additional business to the village, foster community spirit, and help people get to know one another better. It will be fun.*

I think we need to remind you who's in charge of you, Bran commented, his tone practically a purr. Ursula squeezed her thighs together as her body responded with heat and moisture. *Wear your hair down, elska'adir, so that we may entwine our hands in those silky strands.*

I will wrap your hair around my fist while I fuck you from behind, Gil added with a mental growl.

Ursula whimpered as lust sizzled through her flesh. She glanced at the time and quickly calculated how long it would take her mates to divest themselves of their gear, bathe, and dress in their at-home clothes. Of course, they'd want to spend time with Crow, too. Their son would have missed them as much as they missed him. It had been too long since she and her mates had sated their physical needs. *After supper?*

After supper, Gil and Bran promised.

Ursula shivered as her re-energized libido sent another surge of heat through her. She knew that evening Zul would join them and she would receive him with joy.

CHAPTER 16

She sat on Zul's lap at supper, this time knowing what to expect. On either side of her, Bran and Gil covered her right and left hands with their hands, gently pressing her palms to the table. One of Zul's arms wrapped around her waist to keep her securely pressed against the turgid length of his cock, and his tail slid beneath the fabric of her skirt and stroked her legs, lingering on her inner thighs and stoking her desire. Ursula's males sat closely enough that their horns occasionally tapped.

All three of them took turns feeding her the choicest morsels on the table. Someone—not Ursula—had informed the kitchen that the Rites of First Taste and First Union would be performed that night, so the kitchen had cooked accordingly. Every dish presented was already cut into bite-sized morsels or served as finger food. Every dish was considered a Urib aphrodisiac.

When Ursula declared her gustatory hunger satisfied, her mates carefully cleaned her fingers and wiped her lips before attending to their own hands and mouths. As one, they rose from the table. Ursula's legs dangled a split second before Zul's brawny arm scooped up the lower half of her body to carry her to their suite. They headed straight for the central bedchamber. Bran carried a large tyg fashioned of ruby glass and filled with the potent, pale green wine of ceremony.

Candles set at auspicious points in the large room cast a warm glow and released a heady, musky scent, adding to the romance. Folded blankets had been set aside, leaving the enormous mattress open and bare but for an arachnasilk covering stretched tightly over its expanse. Pillows were piled at one end. Pitchers of water and tumblers were lined atop a bureau. The castrati of Fangrys knew thirsty activity would last the long night. This time Gil did not silently question the absence of a mating rack; he knew they did not need it. Ursula preferred their warm hands to a cold metal contraption.

Zul carefully lowered Ursula until her bare feet settled on the floor. Surrounded by the three hulking males, she watched while Bran extended a claw and pierced his thumb. He dribbled four drops of his blood into the tyg. Gil and Zul followed suit. Bran set the tyg on the bureau. Then the three males turned toward her.

Zul said, "Hold on to me."

She gripped his arms, rock steady beneath her hands.

As one, Gil and Bran slid their hands beneath the neckline of her filmy dress and pulled, tearing the delicate layers of fabric in one long, savage rip. They flung the rags behind them. Zul's eyes bugged, seeing her body revealed to him for the first time. His tongue flicked out to moisten suddenly dry lips.

"Set her on the bed," Bran ordered.

Zul did as commanded, handling his dainty mate with careful delicacy as he settled her in the center of the huge mattress. Ursula spread out her arms and her legs fell open enough for him to see moisture glistening between her thighs. He took a deep breath, inhaling the delicious aroma of her desire.

Her mates quickly divested themselves of the minimal clothing they wore, then each kneeled on a different side of the bed, Zul enjoying the center position that allowed him to gaze directly upon the treasure he would soon plunder. Bran began to hum, setting the tone and pace of the ancient hymn demanded by the Rite of First Taste. As had happened once before, Gil soon picked up the melody. A moment later, Zul's deep voice joined in harmony, anchoring the triad's mating song with a baritone beat. Harmonized, the three males began to sing the words and language of the ancient hymn older than written history.

Only pleasure, Ursula reminded herself, her memory flashing back to the first time she'd gone through the Rite of First Taste.

Only pleasure, Bran and Gil repeated in her mind as their a capella song died away. Zul had no words, vocal or mental, as he struggled to control himself.

"Gently," Bran cautioned him.

"She is fragile," Gil reminded him.

Zul acknowledged their words with a curt nod as he slid his hands up her legs and down again, enjoying the soft, smooth texture of her skin as well as the way her little, clawless toes curled in delight. Ursula hummed in pleasure and smiled at the sight of the thick roll and bulge of Zul's heavy muscles beneath his skin as his arms moved his big hands up and down her legs. He locked his black eyes with her golden ones and edged forward, gently lifting her legs and resting each within the thick curve of a horn. As he moved closer to her, her legs widened exposing her fully to his greedy gaze and flared nostrils.

With a slow, light touch, he probed the delicate flesh between her thighs, shining with viscous evidence of her arousal. Ursula moaned again and would have squirmed, but Bran and Gil anchored her to the bed with the gentle press of their hands on her abdomen even as they leaned over her, each cupping a breast that felt heavy and swollen in their other hands. Together, Bran and Gil caressed her breasts, rolling and pinching the tightly furled points and kneading the sensitive mounds of flesh. Ursula moaned again, the sound drawing Zul's thick finger into deeper exploration, sliding through her slippery folds and easing into her weeping channel.

Zul growled as hot, wet silk clamped around his finger. His cock throbbed with urgent demand. The soft sounds of pleasure his mate made encouraged him to press more deeply into her body even as he stroked the passion-smeared skin of her inner thighs and puffy labia. With excruciating care, he eased his finger out until only the tip of it remained, careful to keep his claws retracted so as not to damage the delicate tissue and harm his lovely, fragile mate. He pushed his finger back in and soon established a sensuous rhythm that complemented the other two males who kissed, licked, and suckled her willing, pliant flesh.

When Zul felt her channel begin to ripple around his finger, he pulled it out and surged up the bed to replace it with his tongue. He groaned at her sweet succulence as he licked and slurped, drinking in the liquid of her passion. He edged in a fingertip to flick the tiny bundle of nerves that seemed especially sensitive. After a few gentle flicks combined with the worship of his lips and tongue, Ursula cried out as an orgasm erupted within her and her body gushed its heady juices into Zul's mouth even as a deep, rumbling purr emanated from his chest.

When Ursula's full body tremors subsided and Zul finished drinking her passion, he crawled further up her body and pressed his mouth to hers. She opened her lips willingly and met his tongue with hers. He tasted her mouth, twined his tongue with hers, shared the taste of her passion, then drew back before he lost all sense and drove his cock into her body.

Settling back on his heels and using his tail for balance, Zul reached over to the bureau and lifted the tyg. Bran and Gil propped Ursula into a sitting position as he brought the cup to her mouth. She grabbed onto two of the handles while he steadied it with a firm grip on the third and drank the blood-altered wine. When she drank her fill, he returned the tyg to the bureau. She eagerly accepted another claiming kiss from him.

Zul switched places with Gil. As he had many times before, Gil's long, elegant figures explored her body and touched her with erotic precision while Zul and Bran kissed and caressed her everywhere else. In moments, he had her quivering and crying out for release which he denied. He eased back and drove her near the precipice again, soon adding the torment of his mouth, lips, and tongue and enjoying the sexual torture that would lead to an explosive climax which would leave her feeling boneless with pleasure. When Ursula once more crested and splintered with a scream, Gil drank in her passion then shared the spicy-sweet taste of it with her as their tongues tangled.

As Zul had done, Gil offered her the cup of blood-altered wine. She accepted it and drank. After she handed the cup back to Gil and he returned it to the bureau, Bran took Gil's place. Ursula shivered, knowing from the hot gleam in his golden eyes that her Prime was prepared to deliver the orgasm of all orgasms.

Her legs draped over the wide sweep of his elegant horns, she lay beneath the sensual assault of her other two mates while Bran ruthlessly toyed with her oversensitive flesh. She panted, whimpered, gasped, moaned, and begged to no avail as he extracted every last drop of passion from her and still did not allow her to climax. Finally, hoarse and desperate, she wept with gratitude when his skilled touch drew her to the precipice and flung her over in a burst of heat and light that stole her sight and voice as her body convulsed and quivered in helpless reaction. After gently bringing her shattered consciousness back to her body, he shared her taste on his tongue and steadied the ceremonial cup of wine while she drank from it.

The three males let her relax a moment to catch her breath before Zul kneeled beside the bed and offered her the turgid length of his fat cock. His natural lubrication oozed down its length. She felt Gil's skilled fingers slide along her jaw to encourage her to open and relax her throat.

"Taste," Zul commanded, his voice a low, rumbling growl as he rubbed the bulbous tip of his cock over her lips and lubricated them. At her sigh of acceptance, he pressed into her mouth. His breath caught as her tongue fluttered against the underside of his cock where the thick veins pulsed. His essence dribbled into her mouth and her tongue pressed more firmly against his cock as she attempted to swallow. He cleared his throat and, his voice guttural, rasped, "I am Zullar cen'Vyr, Third of the Fangrys Triad, and the Bridge who connects the First and Forever. Your honor and pleasure are mine, and my love is yours. Receive me with joy."

Zul eased his hips forward, gently pushing his pulsing cock deeper into her mouth and gasping when he hit the back of her throat.

"She can take you deeper," Gil murmured, stroking his fingers along her jawline and neck to encourage her to open more and accept his full length.

Zul drew back and Ursula swallowed and gasped for air. His black eyes met hers, and she nodded, opening her mouth wide and relaxing her throat. Thus encouraged, he carefully pressed into the hot, wet cavern again and groaned at the sublime pleasure. He continued to slide deeper and deeper until his cock was lodged down the constriction of her throat and against the fluttering of her tongue, her nose buried against his pubis. He jolted when her delicate hand took hold of his heavy testicles and began to massage them, a fingertip sliding further back toward the underside of his tail and his taint. The unexpected caress broke the last threads of his control, and his hips bucked. Zul cried out as his seed spewed forth in hot spurts.

Panting for breath, he withdrew from his mate's slack mouth. His eyes bulged once again as she lazily licked her lips, catching the drops that leaked from her mouth. With a groan, he sank further down and pressed his mouth to hers to taste his pleasure on her tongue.

A light tap on Zul's shoulder reminded him that there were two other males who needed release. Bowing his head, he moved to let Gil take his place and watched in utter fascination while the ceremony repeated with the turquoise warrior finally achieving his climax within their mates' mouth and uttering the sacred words of bonding. When Gil finished, Bran took his place and repeated the process and spoke the ritual vow.

The four of them paused and availed themselves of the cool water to refresh themselves and rehydrate. They arranged themselves on the massive bed, cocks temporarily limp and quiescent. Their tails stroked her in languid motion, keeping Ursula's skin sensitized and stoking her desire. When the rapid, shallow pulse of her heart had slowed and she began to squirm in readiness again, the three of them proceeded to the Rite of First Union.

The base of Zul's horns burned. The heat spread through his body. "I burn."

"You burn for our mate," Bran said, stroking his cock which had once again risen to the occasion.

Ursula wriggled and spread her legs. She stretched out an arm beckoning her mates. "Please."

Bran took the lead. "First we touch."

He stroked her legs, and Gil and Zul followed suit, their hands wandering over her arms, shoulders, neck, breasts, and belly.

"Now we taste," Bran said and bent down to lick her weeping sex.

Again, Gil and Zul copied his actions. Stimulated beyond endurance, Ursula climaxed.

Bran focused his attention on Zul and said, "Because our bond with Ursula has long been established and sealed, you shall be the first tonight to complete the Rite of First Union."

Zul bowed his head in silent gratitude for the honor being given to him, knowing his former prime would not have been so generous. Taking a deep breath of air already heavy with the scent of spent passion, he positioned himself between Ursula's thighs. He stroked them, willing her to relax sufficiently to accommodate his girth and length without discomfort. He bent over her and pressed a gentle kiss to her lips and whispered, "My hearts are yours."

Ursula gave him a slow, soft smile and raised her hand to cup his cheek. She then said, "I receive you with joy, Zul."

He notched the tumescent eagerness of his sex at the shiny entrance of her body and hissed as he slowly pressed inside, "I am the Third of your mates and of the Fangrys Triad, Zullar cen'Vyr, the Bridge who connects the First and Forever. Your honor and pleasure are mine and my love is yours. Receive me with joy."

By the time he'd finished speaking, he'd sunk as deeply as he could into his mate's delectable, gorgeous body. He retreated, relishing the drag of his cock inside her hot, wet channel. Pleasure burst within him and sizzled through his veins, spurring irresistible instinct to thrust until his balls tightened and drew close to his body and the base of his spine began to burn. His gaze focused on the bouncing of his mate's breasts and his ears on the wet slap and suction of fucking. Instinct had him watch her for the slightest of signals of pain and pleasure until the pitch of her mewls and cries changed and her breathing hitched and she erupted around him in glorious ecstasy. Her sublime pleasure ignited his. Zul threw back his head and roared as he strained against her body and filled her womb with his seed.

He gasped for breath and bowed his head. His arms trembled, which surprised him. After a moment during which tremors of pleasure rippled sporadically through his cock and body, he managed to lean down without collapsing on top of his mate to press another gentle kiss to her lips. Rising from the kiss, he took a deep breath and reveled in the strength of the bond he felt, a bond he'd never before experienced and would weep inconsolably if he ever lost it.

After a long moment, Zul's cock softened sufficiently to withdraw from her body. He slid down and savored her soft cries of pleasure as he lapped at her core and cleaned her for Bran.

Zul watched with glittering eyes as Bran and Gil, the First and the Forever of their triad, took their turns, giving her their vows as they reveled in the hoarse cries of her pleasure. By the time they finished, Ursula lay as though boneless in her exhaustion. With a soft sigh, she said, "There is more."

"Ah, you remember," Bran said with a small smile as he held her steady in one arm and a cup of water to her lips in his free hand. She drank as she watched Gil retrieve a plug and lubricate it. Her bleary eyes blinked. Her ass clenched in anticipation. Bran continued as Gil handed him the plug, "You have mated us singly, and you will next mate us in union."

Ursula swallowed and nodded, her eyelids drooping. "So tired."

"We shall rest," he said, much to Zul's disappointment, though he, too, could have been forced to admit that he felt deliciously logy. Bran gently rolled her over and slid the lubricated plug into her ass, then said, "And when we wake, we shall eat and bathe and complete the Rite of First Union."

Ursula responded with a smile and let her eyes shut.

Uncertain as to what to do, Zul watched as Gil retreated to the en suite bathroom and returned a moment later with a warm wet cloth. After wiping their mate clean, he tossed the washcloth into the bathroom and fetched the blankets. Gil gestured toward their mate and murmured, "Climb in. We sleep with her tonight."

Zul climbed in, drawing his exhausted mate into the shelter of his body and thinking he had known no greater satisfaction in his entire life. Bran slid in on Ursula's other side. Gil unfolded the blanket over them and crawled in at the foot of the bed, so Ursula was surrounded by her mates.

CHAPTER 17

The next morning found Ursula nestled between Gil's legs in the humongous bathtub—a shallow pool, really—as he washed her clean of the previous night's sticky residue. Both her mates watched, occasionally pointing out a spot he'd missed or simply leaning over to press a kiss to her head or shoulder or offering her a sip of *ti'chal*, Uribern's favorite morning beverage. Zul and Bran had already bathed, and Gil would wash himself after the three of them deemed her properly clean—and that would only happen after Gil's clever fingers made sure she orgasmed at least twice.

Of course, watching Gil finger her to orgasm incited Bran and Zul to pull out their big cocks and stroke themselves to completion, making sure to spray her with their seed so that Gil needed to wash her again.

"Why do we not fuck her this morning and complete the Rite of First Union?" Zul asked as he lowered his kilt over his now flaccid cock.

"Our mate retains many of her human qualities," Bran answered, understanding the berserker's eagerness. "She is, as you see, small and delicate. Fragile. Her body needs to recover before she can take us again without pain or damage."

Zul nodded in understanding. He would have greatly preferred to continue the previous night's fucking, but did not wish to harm the small female who had already captured his soul. "No, our mate must not be harmed."

Bran's approval washed over him. The tension in Zul's shoulders eased, a tension he had not realized he carried until his Prime's approval melted it. Having long since become accustomed to solitude after the deaths of his original Prime and Second, Zul had not realized how much he still craved the triad connection and a prime's approval.

Filled with daring, Zul said, "I wish to be the one who bathes her next."

Gil tilted his head back and grinned at him. "Bathing our mate is most gratifying, especially when she is impaled on a cock."

The base of Zul's horns heated as he imagined sitting in the tub with their pretty female speared upon his cock as he washed her. His kilt tented.

"He likes that idea," Gil said with a chuckle.

"He's not the only one," Bran agreed, his lips curling at the flush that spread across Ursula's face, neck, and upper chest.

Gil finished rinsing Ursula's long white hair and squeezed out the excess water. He shifted so that she moved off his lap. Rising to his knees so his erection cleared the water, he tapped her on the shoulder and said, "I need your mouth, *elska'adir.*"

Ursula gave him a soft smile then braced her hands on his narrow hips and opened her mouth wide. Careful not to scrape him with her teeth, she lowered her mouth over his cock. Delicately, slowly, she began to lick and nip and suck. Steadying herself, she brought her hands into play, stroking and gently squeezing where her mouth could not reach. Gil's mouth slackened as pleasure coursed through him, but he refrained from directing her movement or forcing her to take the whole of him down her still-raw throat.

He grunted when she brought him to completion and swallowed his release. At that point, he cupped her face and murmured words of love and praise. He brushed a wet thumb over the corner of her mouth where a drop of semen remained, and wiped it away. Bran snapped open a large towel and lifted Ursula to her feet, wrapping the towel around her. He patted her dry, examining her with critical eyes for any bruising or abrasions. When she was dry, Bran handed her over to Zul to whom Gil had already handed a comb.

"I hope you know how to braid," Gil said. "Our *elska'adir* likes to have her hair braided."

Zul nodded and silently vowed to learn every variation on braiding hair. He guided his towel-wrapped mate to the vanity in her chamber and paused, trying to decide whether to sit her on the stool or to sit on the stool himself and position her on his lap. The second option won.

With a patience and care he'd not known he possessed, Zul carefully untangled her long tresses and combed them. Ursula, to his relief, did not complain of his ineptness and remained still throughout the procedure.

"I can braid it," she offered when he laid the comb on the vanity. "If you'd hand me a ribbon, please?"

Grateful to have been released from braiding duty until he'd mastered the skill, Zul opened a drawer and pulled out a pink ribbon. He gave her a hopeful look.

She smiled at him and said, "That will do." At his hesitance, she added, "Just set it on the vanity, please."

He dropped the ribbon on the vanity and watched as she deftly separated her hair into three long locks and began to weave them together. One hand holding the end of the long braid, she grabbed the ribbon and wound it around the end before tying it into a tight bow. Seeing how the color of the ribbon complemented her coloring, Zul gently set his mate on her feet and stood. He crossed the room, opened her wardrobe, and began searching her garments until he found one that closely matched the ribbon's rosy hue. He laid that gown on the bed, already refreshed and tidied by the Fangrys Triad's efficient servants, before rummaging in the large casket set on a low table near the vanity. Soon, he found what he searched for.

"Come," he said, extending his hand. Ursula placed her palm in his, and he drew her to him. "Allow me."

She smiled at him and did not protest as he dressed her in the rosy gown and adorned her hair, neck, wrists, and ankles with jewelry.

"Is this a berserker thing?" she asked.

"What?"

"This penchant for dressing your mate and bedecking her with jewelry."

He frowned. "Why do you ask?"

The smile she gave him was soft and melancholy. "Because Crow enjoyed doing that, too."

Zul felt a tug of sadness, grief for a fierce warrior he'd never truly known, and knew it for the echo of loss whispering across the bond linking mates. He made another silent, private vow to add to her collection of jewelry. After all, he had more than sufficient funds which were yet to be mingled with the Fangrys accounts: a bonded triad shared *everything*. He pressed a kiss to her head and replied, "Then Crow had exquisite taste."

Thus accoutred, Ursula again took the hand Zul extended to her, obligingly following along as he rejoined his triad in the corridor. In formation, they headed toward the dining room. Bran, being Prime, spearheaded the way. Gil walked beside their mate. Zul took the rear. None of them expected to be attacked in their own home, but the habits of protection were both instinctual and trained.

Ursula ate heartily, sending her compliments to the cook on the excellence of the eggs which were unlike any eggs found on Earth.

"Eggs," Gil said between bites, "was something I cooked for our mate when she first came to us."

Ursula snorted. "*First came.* You mean *first captured*."

Bran shrugged. "It was either *capture* you or leave you to be eaten by an oryxis or immolated by our suns."

Ursula visibly shuddered at the memory of the quick and brutal fight against the huge lizard that had stalked her as its prey the night she'd escaped from the embassy. She pointed her two-tined fork at Bran and said, "You'd already put in a bid for me, hadn't you?"

He nodded and replied, "Of course. We knew you were ours the moment we saw you."

"And being claimed by us has not ended so ill, has it?" Gil inquired, his expression worried.

Ursula sighed and let go of her lingering resentment. "No. No, I love you, all three of you." She sighed again. "It's that my own government was trafficking women that still makes me angry. We didn't agree to be sent to a distant planet. We didn't agree to be married off to strangers." She took another deep breath to compose herself. "There's a lot to be said for *consent*, you know."

"I have heard that Ahn'hudin discovered some human skulduggery in the trade for brides," Zul said.

"Oh?" Ursula shot a speaking look at her other two mates. "I don't get much news about Earth here."

Gil had the grace to look guilty. Bran met her glare with inscrutable calm.

"What happened?" she asked.

"The human females were being sterilized before being mated," Zul answered. He glanced at Bran and Gil. "Did you not hear of this?"

"We had," Bran admitted. "The Ahn'hudi are rectifying Earth's duplicity."

"Sterilizing?" Ursula echoed, her voice squeaking.

Bran met her gaze again and said, "Officials on Earth directed officials at their embassy on Ahn'hudin to render human brides incapable of breeding. The brides themselves discovered this treachery and brought it to the attention of their mates. The emperor of Ahn'hudin was rightfully outraged. Sanctions have been imposed upon Earth by all planets of the Triune Alliance, and the treaties are being renegotiated."

Ursula looked at her plate, not seeing the remains of her breakfast as she pondered what she heard. Lifting her head, she asked, "And what about the brides?"

"The ones who were sterilized?"

She nodded.

"Those females are mated. They will not be cast aside," Bran answered. "No honorable male would allow that."

"Earth will continue to send brides to allied planets, more brides than before," Gil added.

"And are they being trafficked?"

Gil shook his head. "Do not fret so, *elska'adir*. The new brides will be fully informed and must consent to being transported to Uribern, Ahn'hudin, or Kaan."

Ursula nodded and said nothing about the human government's propensity to engage in underhanded, dirty dealings. If there was a way to muck this up, the government would find it and capitalize on it to the detriment of those caught in its web of deceit.

Zul caught the tenor of her thoughts through the bond linking them all and commented, "You do not trust the government of your homeland?"

Ursula snorted. "Nobody with any sense trusts the government."

Gil reached across the table to pat her hand. "You are safe from their machinations now."

Bran blinked slowly at her and gave her a small grin. "In fact, we need to discuss your own machinations. The mayor and sheriff are in an uproar."

"Fusty old curmudgeons," she muttered under her breath. "Male chauvinist pigs, all of 'em."

"Yes, Ursula, I would hear more of this festival you are organizing," Gil said.

Ursula grinned. "Those misogynists in the village will soon realize that we women aren't incompetent idiots. We *can* do things that take organization and planning."

"Of course, you can," Bran said. "Art and music require great skill and perception. This is why they are the purview of females." He took a drink of *ti'chal*. "Were males left to our own devices, Urib culture would have no beauty or refinement."

"If I recall correctly, you sing beautifully," Gil added. His expression turned sad. "I have not heard you sing since Crow died."

"You sing?" Zul echoed. His expression turned hopeful. "Would you, some day perhaps, consent to sing for me? It has been long since I heard singing—any singing."

Ursula pursed her lips, thinking. She said slowly, "I hadn't realized it had been so long since I sang anything more than lullabies." She paused to think again. "There will be a stage set up for performances during the festival. I'll schedule myself into the program to sing a song or two."

"No," Bran said, his tone flat with disapproval.

She leaned toward him, eyes narrowed in instant fury. "*Yes*, I will."

"It is not seemly."

"Seemly-schmeemly," she dismissed his concern. "I'm not a toy to be set on the shelf when you're not playing with me. We've discussed this before."

"She will not be in any danger," Gil interjected, his tone calm and exuding reasonableness.

Disturbed by their mate's instantly negative reaction and fearing she would refuse to complete the Rite of First Union, Zul said, "No, she will not be in any danger. I will protect her."

"As will I," Gil added.

Expression sour, Bran bowed to the others' willingness to allow their mate to have her way. He nodded and said, "And, as will I." He gave her a hard, reproving look. "But you will go *nowhere* without escort from at least one of us."

Ursula knew better than to gloat. She gave Bran a soft smile of gratitude and reached across the table to lay her hand on his forearm. "Of course not, my love. I know better than to court danger."

Gil's soft snort did not go unnoticed, but it did go unmentioned.

Zul sighed with relief at her compliance. "I will be grateful to hear you sing, *elska'adir.*"

"By the way," Ursula said. "The Omari Triad and Carmen will be visiting for the festival. Apparently, word has spread far and wide about it."

"They are welcome to stay here," Bran said.

Ursula grinned. "And Carmen's going to dance the flamenco."

CHAPTER 18

Bran and Gil were deployed again before they could complete the Rite of First Union. Zul suspected that unnecessary deployment resulted from the Council Supreme's ire at having been thwarted in their aim to get them killed so they could give Ursula to another triad. Despite the Council's machinations, the two warriors returned home after another ten days of nearly constant skirmishing. Apparently, the Sivuul were taking advantage of the Ogranox retreat.

The day following Bran and Gil's return home with only minor injuries (which no doubt annoyed the Council Supreme), Ursula did not work at her shop. Instead she spent the day enjoying being pampered by her mates. Cognizant of her soreness following the night of their return, none of her mates permitted her feet to touch the ground. They carried her everywhere she wished to go, whether that was to her studio to work on her pottery, to the library to read, or to the courtyard to bask in the bright sunshine of Uribern's high desert climate. She spent hardly a minute apart from them, singly, in pairs, or all together. With at least one of her mates always nearby, she hardly saw any of the castrati and supposed they, too, were enjoying the relief from "Prima watching" duty. The thought made her chuckle.

"What's so funny?" Gil inquired, looking from the book he was reading to the woman nestled in his lap.

Ursula snuggled in closer, adjusting her position against his lean, muscular body. "I was just thinking about the castrati."

"Oh?"

She stroked his arm and chuckled again. "Yes. I was thinking that they were probably celebrating your return because it means they get a break from supervising me."

"Watching over you is not a chore."

She giggled at his serious tone. "You, Bran, and Zul might not think so, but I'm sure they do." She twisted around to look him in the chin. "I'm not very obedient, you know."

He then saw the humor and chuckled. Gil set aside the book and pulled up her skirt to bare the smooth, finely scaled skin. He ran his hand along her leg while bending his head down to nuzzle the top of her head. "You're *very* obedient in certain circumstances."

Ursula sighed as he stroked her delicate skin. Her nipples beaded even as her breasts swelled. Heat pooled low in her belly, and her core moistened. "I'd be silly not to."

Gil's nostrils flared as the perfume of her arousal rose in the warm air. His cock, ever eager, surged full and hard beneath his kilt. Across the triad bond, he broadcast, *She is ready.*

With a small grunt, he rose from the chair, keeping his mate cradled against him. His prehensile tail snatched the book from her slack grip and set it aside. When he arrived in the central bedchamber, both Bran and Zul awaited them, already naked and erect. Gil transferred her to Zul's arms while he divested himself of his clothing and Bran shredded her gown, somehow leaving all her jewelry undisturbed. Gil yanked the covers off the bed, and Zul lay her down.

Bran climbed onto the bed and lay down, his cock rising like a tower and leaking his own natural lubricant. Gil lifted her and settled her over Bran, holding her as she shuddered while sliding down his turgid length.

"Lean forward, *elska'adir,*" Bran whispered.

She leaned forward, quivering in anticipation as Gil climbed up behind her. She moaned softly as he first wriggled then withdrew the large plug from her ass. Zul had been assigned the task of ensuring her readiness there, and he'd taken great delight in fulfilling that charge regardless of how desperately he wished to fuck her again. She sighed when he smoothed the opening with additional lubricant.

"Relax," Gil commanded as he set the tip of his penis against her loosened sphincter.

Ursula took a deep breath and deliberately relaxed. She whimpered as he pressed forward, then moaned as he slid deep inside. "So full!"

"Open for Zul, *elska'adir*," Gil murmured.

The mattress dipped beneath the weight of the berserker who climbed on the bed and kneeled above their Prime. He stroked her jaw and let his fingertips slide down the elegant column of her slender neck. Obedient to Zul's unvoiced command, her jaw opened wide and her throat relaxed. He leaned down to press a kiss to her head before feeding her his cock. She clutched at the bulging muscles of his thighs to steady herself.

Zul growled as Ursula moaned around him when Bran and Gil began to move. They kept their synchronized thrusts shallow and slow. Their movement forced Ursula to duplicate the same rhythm as she slobbered around Zul's cock.

Stuffed by three cocks all moving within her body concentrated the pleasure zinging throughout her body, and Ursula's muffled cries of orgasm generated vibrations that quickly had Zul spurting down her throat. Bran and Gil soon followed in their release as her flesh clamped down and rippled along their cocks. All three males lay their hands upon her as she and they climaxed: Bran gently squeezed her breasts, Gil rubbed her butt, and Zul stroked her back.

When their cocks were spent and had softened, Zul carefully withdrew from Ursula's mouth first before Gil withdrew from her anus. Ursula panted as Bran gently lifted her off his spent cock. Gil retreated to the en suite bathroom to cleanse his cock. Ursula gave into the lassitude to recuperate during Gil's brief absence. When he returned, she was ready for the next round.

The males switched places: Gil beneath her, Bran at her mouth, and Zul at her ass. The scenario repeated, though somewhat less carefully as her body had softened and loosened to accommodate their use of her. Climax came swiftly, and Zul's eyes crossed as he felt the deafening pressure of her orgasm through her ass and against Gil's throbbing, pulsing release through the thin membrane that separated their cocks.

Zul, the mighty berserker, wondered if he might simply pass out from the pleasure of this triad mating of their beloved female who took them so sweetly into her soft, wondrous body. However, he found the strength and stamina to thrust into her pussy and catapult her into yet another explosive orgasm before he, Bran, and Gil also found their third shared release and the mating bond was sealed.

Exhausted by their passion, Gil and Zul curled up around their mate while Bran cleaned his cock then drew the covers over them all. They settled in for a restorative nap before waking, bathing, eating, and doing it all again and again.

When Ursula awoke after their third round, she was alone. A long, slow inhale took in the heavy odors of vigorous sex lingering in the air. She moaned as she left the bed, every muscle deliciously sore, and murmured a word of gratitude that somehow the architecture of the manor allowed for her central bedroom to have a large window that could be opened to admit fresh, clean air. She leaned out the opening, enjoying the play of the refreshing breeze across her still heated skin.

"Ursula!"

Startled, she yelped and turned away from the window. Zul rushed forth and wrapped a blanket around her naked body.

"You should not display yourself," he admonished.

"Nobody's out there," she protested.

He glanced out the window, his fierce gaze picking out what she had not seen. "On the contrary, there are three gardeners out there."

Ursula felt the flush of embarrassment burn. She turned her face into his body and muttered, "I'm sorry. I did not see them."

Zul's ire melted at her contrition. "You truly did not see them?"

She shook her head. "No. I just liked the feel of the breeze."

"Ah." He scooped her up into his arms. "Come, let me bathe you."

Ursula sighed and did not protest, for she'd long since learned that any of her mates intent upon caring for her would not be deterred. Zul carried her to the bathroom and bade her sit while he ran the water. As it poured from the faucet, he removed her jewelry which had somehow made it undisturbed through their hours of marathon sex. Freed of the jewelry and having long since lost any semblance of privacy among her three mates, Ursula emptied her bladder while Zul stripped. Her mate picked up jars and read their labels, sprinkling in those herbs that promised to soothe aching flesh and revitalize flagging energy. He climbed into the tub.

"Come here," he said.

She obeyed. Not willing to risk her slipping and falling on the slick surface, Zul picked her up and lifted her into the tub as he would a child. However, he did not treat her as a child when he settled her on his cock as they both sank into the seasoned, fragrant water. She gasped then sighed then relaxed against him, her back to his abdomen. First he merely stroked her, spreading the herb-infused water over her skin and resisting the urge to pump his hips. Then he reached for a washcloth and soap and began to clean her body of the sticky residue of vigorous sex.

"Mmm," she hummed as he washed her. Zul imagined he could feel the gentle vibration of her hum in his cock which flexed and pulsed with need inside her.

He tweaked a nipple and she squealed. "You will not again display yourself like that."

She moaned. He tweaked the other nipple, and she whimpered.

"Answer me, *elska'adir*."

She squirmed while impaled on his cock. "No, no, I won't do that again."

He rolled both nipples between his thumbs and forefingers and reveled in the way her channel rippled around his cock. "That's my sweet mate." He rolled his hips and she moaned. "Lean forward."

She leaned forward, but the water was too deep for what he had in mind. So, he rose to his feet, holding her impaled on him, and lifted her with his body. Knees bending so his petite mate could stand on the bottom of the tub, Zul said, "Brace yourself."

Ursula's hands shot forward and gripped the edge of the tub as Zul wrapped an arm around her abdomen and leaned over her.

"Are you steady?"

She nodded. With a low grunt of approval, he began to thrust, hard, deep, deliberate pumps of his hips that hit her G-spot every time even as his heavy balls slapped her clit. Her mind went blank and her arms and legs trembled as pleasure suffused her body. She cried out as an orgasm swept through her and he continued to thrust through it, prolonging the mindshattering pleasure. Without ceasing rhythm he soon drove her up and over the precipice again. By the fourth time, she was blubbering and shuddering, unable to hold herself up. The fifth time, he finally emptied himself into her.

His own arms and legs trembling from the strength of his climax, Zul carefully lowered them both back into the water. He allowed his spent cock to slip from her body before gently cleaning her reddened, puffy labia and watching his seed leak from her body and swirl in the bathwater. After a moment's rest, he turned his attention to washing and rinsing her hair.

Zul set her outside the tub before he got out. He ignored the chill of water drying on his own skin so he could tend to her first. When they were both dry, he carried her into the bedchamber and seated her on the stool in front of the vanity. First, he rummaged through her wardrobe for a dress and chose one of vibrant blue to match the Urib sky. Then he poked through her jewelry chest to find coordinating jewelry. She sat, compliant to his care, as he combed out the tangles from her hair and braided it.

"You learned to braid," she commented with a long, slow blink.

"A simple braid," he clarified. "I will master more complicated braids for you."

She grinned. "Do you intend to continue dressing me?"

"Always."

When he finished dressing and adorning her hair and body, he donned his own clothes. Extending his hand to her, he said, "Come. You must eat."

She laid her palm upon his. Looking up at him, Ursula said, "Please allow me to walk."

Zul frowned at her polite request. His tail slowly lashed like a cat's, an nonverbal display of indecision. He would have preferred to carry her, nestling her sweet-smelling, soft body against his chest. However, he realized no harm would come of allowing her this small independence. Indeed, she might very well look more favorably upon him and grant him continued use of her body and the sharing of such immense pleasure if he acceded to her small request. Deciding in favor of delayed gratification, he closed his hand around hers and nodded.

"I will escort you."

CHAPTER 19

Several days later during supper, Gil announced, "Some of the village council are in an uproar."

"No one has said anything to me," Ursula replied before taking a bite of food.

The three males had begrudgingly agreed to allow her the independence of feeding herself, although such feminine autonomy irked them.

"No, they wouldn't," Bran replied in a mild tone. He sighed, then took a drink. "They're complaining to us."

Ursula set her fork down. "So, what is it now?"

"You've involved the village's females in your project," Zul explained, "rather than relying upon the castrati to carry out your orders."

Ursula had to admit to herself that she'd seen this confrontation coming. Indeed, she had invited it. Carefully enunciating every syllable, she replied, "I'm organizing a *community* festival. Shouldn't members of the community be involved?" Before any of her mates could respond, she narrowed her eyes and said, "Or do the *females* not count as members of the community?"

Zul glanced at Bran, unwilling to wade into that minefield. Gently, Gil responded, "The males are members of the community, too, *elska'adir*, are they not?"

"Do they feel left out?" she asked.

The three males sensed a trap and did not answer.

Ursula didn't mind; she answered for them. "Did they tell you that I invited their input? Did they tell you that they refused to work with me because I'm a woman?"

"Did you expect otherwise?" Bran retorted, his tone still mild.

She huffed. "No, I did not expect otherwise, you idiot."

Zul nearly choked on his food to hear her speak so disrespectfully to their Prime. Gil cast him an amused glance. Bran held his silence, knowing it would work better on their mate than any remonstration or lecture.

After a long moment, Ursula sighed. "The committee of women I'm working with are really enthusiastic and thrilled to be involved. They've got wonderful ideas and have been so very helpful. Why is it such a terrible thing to have their help?"

"That is not a female's role in Urib culture," Gil replied.

Ursula shook her head. "I still don't get it. Why are women restricted to arts and crafts? Why can't we be involved in more important things?"

Zul felt compelled to reply. "Females embody creation. Creation is their very purpose, so the gods have given them the blessing of creativity. Without females, we would not have great art or music."

"Or architecture," Gil added.

"Architecture?" Ursula echoed with a small frown.

"Without the creative nature inherent to females, our buildings would have no beauty, no grace," Gil explained. He gave her a small smile. "You persist in thinking Urib females are uneducated and unskilled. Nothing could be further from the truth. Our females must be well-educated and highly skilled to manifest the very creations that make our culture superior to any other."

"Consider your friend, Addilli," Bran added.

"Addilli?" Ursula blinked. She hadn't thought that Bran knew of her friendship with the other female whose mates owned a restaurant a few doors down from her shop. Her own mates were more cognizant of what she knew and with whom she associated than she'd realized. Apparently, there was no hiding anything from them—not that she was deliberately concealing her friendship from them. Of course not.

Bran explained, "It is her creative insight and skill that enables her mates to produce such wonderful food. She created their recipes and designed their menu. But they are properly protective of her and wary that such a skilled and desirable female would be coveted by other unmated males, so they minimize her exposure to predation."

Gil added, "And, no, *elska'adir*, we would not forbid you her company just because she is lower caste. We know you cherish your friendships and need them."

Ursula felt the heat of embarrassment flood her cheeks. She lowered her gaze to her plate. "I'm sorry. I guess…"

Zul patted her hand. "We do not wish you to be lonely."

"Thank you," she murmured, knowing fully well that Zul understood what it was to be lonely. She chewed on her lip for a moment before looking up at her three mates. "Is the village truly against the festival?"

Bran gave her a small smile. "The *villagers* are somewhat conflicted. They are dubious about the reason for the event as they do not understand this Halloween of yours, but they do understand and appreciate the idea of a harvest festival."

"I'd say more are looking forward to it than not," Gil commented.

Ursula breathed a sigh of relief at this mild encouragement and gave him a grateful smile.

"And I doubt many males will forbid their mates from attending because they do not want their mates to be unhappy. More likely, they will attend in company with their mates just to please them and keep them safe."

"Oh, good."

Zul patted her hand again, still not quite believing he had the great good fortune to casually touch and comfort any female, much less his mate.

"Tread lightly, *elska'adir*, while finalizing these arrangements," Bran cautioned. "Try to reassure rather than antagonize."

Again, Ursula felt the burn of embarrassment.

"I look forward to the fireworks," Gil said to distract their mate from that embarrassment. "I watched some videos. Crow will enjoy them."

"Most boys do," Ursula said, flashing him a grateful smile. "I remember going to Independence Day shows with friends and their families. The boys would always be so excited and not at all bothered by the noise."

"Noise?" Zul repeated with a frown.

"Gunpowder," Ursula explained. "It's explosive and loud when it goes off."

He frowned at her.

"You can't have fireworks without big booms."

He shook his head.

Did he suffer from PTSD? She frowned. "Are you okay, Zul? *Will* you be okay?"

He gave her a reassuring smile and patted her hand again. "I will endure."

Gil sent Bran a speaking glance. *We will help him endure.*

"What are your favorite fireworks, Ursula?" Bran asked to distract her from worry. Zul sent a whisper of gratitude across their bond. He did not wish to appear weak in front of their mate. Bran responded directly to him, mind to mind. *Soon you will understand she does not always need you to be strong. She will appreciate your vulnerability. You can trust her to protect you.*

Protect me? How could such a delicate female protect me?

Bran did not answer. Zul would learn soon enough.

"I've always liked the ones with the willow effect," Ursula answered the question. She took a sip and said nothing about knowing he was distracting her. Instead, she let it slide, appreciating his care for both her feelings and Zul's.

"What are the 'willow' ones?" Gil asked.

She answered, "The willow fireworks create big stars with the arms falling gracefully like a willow tree's branches." At their blank expressions, she added, "You'll have to look it up. I'm not exactly sure how to explain a willow tree to you guys."

"This is a type of tree found on Earth?" Zul murmured.

Ursula nodded. "Fireworks have been around on Earth for over a thousand years in a country called China. Humans haven't had any communication with alien civilizations until recently, so names for things refer to what's either on Earth or what we can see from Earth's surface."

"Makes sense," Zul said with a nod.

CHAPTER 20

Ursula met with her committee of Urib brides. Of the dozen females, only one was actually Urib. The others including herself were imports from biologically compatible species. Of the biologically compatible species, all had been altered at the genetic level the same as Ursula. The very paucity of female Urib presence only underscored the planet's dire need for fertile brides.

The other females, who eschewed the term "women" as a human-centric word, discussed final arrangements and updates with polite enthusiasm. Each of them was cognizant that their continued participation depended greatly upon their seemly behavior and their mates' permission. Thus far, none of the males mated to the women had protested or objected to such an extent that they'd withdrawn permission. Cynically, Ursula figured they prized the privileged association with the Fangrys Prima and Triad over any semblance of impropriety. She did what she could to discreetly reward such self-serving toler-ance in the hope that her beneficence would encourage more allowances for the females. In this quietly subversive manner, she stoked her conspirators' desire for greater autonomy in their lives and undermined their mates' control.

While she worked on the Halloween festival, she noticed the frequent arrival and departure of visitors to whom Bran,

Gil, and Zul did not introduce her. When she asked about them, they reassured her that all was well and not to worry. To be fair, those visitors often stayed for a short time, less than the length of a morning or afternoon. However, her mates—the one not hovering in attendance as her escort on any given day—closeted themselves in the library for those weighty discussions to which she was not privy.

Ursula didn't think she'd mind that they did not involve her in those meetings or even condescend to discuss what they talked about, except that they did question her about her meetings with her festival committee and required that she divulge all details to them.

It all seemed a bit lopsided and unfair to her.

"Why won't you tell me what's going on?" she asked Gil as they lay on his bed, pleasantly exhausted from a vigorous bout of one-on-one lovemaking, thinking he might be the weak link in the united wall of silence her mates presented.

"It has nothing to do with you, *elka'adir*," he reassured her and stroked her hair. "Do not worry—"

"If you tell me not to worry my pretty little head over it, I'll throttle you," she warned, her voice growling.

He chuckled because her threat had no teeth. "My fierce little bride."

"So, tell me, Gil. What would my puny female mind not understand?"

He refrained from wincing at her sarcastic tone. "It is Urib politics, my sweet."

Ursula grimaced. "Politics? Ugh."

He chuckled again. "Exactly."

Her eyes narrowed, because that was just too easy. She traced invisible patterns on his muscled chest with a solitary fingertip. His pectoral muscle contracted beneath her touch. "I'm getting an interesting education in local politics with my festival."

Gil lay still, knowing that his beloved mate was homing in for the kill shot. However, he kept his voice relaxed and conversational: "I have noticed. You're doing well dealing with the mayor, the sheriff, and the village council, much better than when you first started this project."

"Thank you." Although his praise warmed her heart, Ursula did not let it deter her. "Anyway, what I'm learning at the local level makes me curious as to how things are done at the national level."

He rolled over to his side to face her and cupped one of her breasts. He used his thumb to rub gentle circles around her nipple which beaded into a tight point. "It will be many, many years—likely centuries, if ever—before the Urib government accepts female counselors. We cannot risk our brides in such a manner."

She frowned. "Oh, yes, I'd forgotten: we're useful as breeding stock, but not for much else."

It was Gil's turn to frown. "Now you know that isn't true. You are beloved by us. We see you as much more than merely a fertile womb."

"*You* do, but the government doesn't."

He couldn't refute that and refused to lie to her, so he redirected the conversation. "What is it you wish to accomplish?"

"I want to know what you, Bran, and Zul are doing that involves national politics."

He frowned again and his hand stilled. "What makes you think that?"

"That you're discussing national politics?"

"Yes."

Ursula slid her hand down his body to stroke his once-again erect cock with a teasing, feather-light touch. "If you were discussing local politics, I would have heard about it by now."

Gil's gut clenched. She was too perceptive. Ursula gave him a sultry grin and pushed at him with her other hand. He obliged and rolled to his back. She crawled over him, centered her core, and sank down. He groaned as her sex enveloped his and indescribable pleasure zinged through his veins. She began to roll her hips, and he groaned again and slid his tail into her anus.

She moaned at the delicious intrusion, then said, "I'll get my answers, Gil."

He grasped her hips to control her movement and rolled them over. Grinning at her, he thrust into her body and made her gasp. "Not from me."

With the stamina of his kind, he tortured his bride for attempting to manipulate him with sex. He drove her to the precipice of orgasm only to stop her from taking the leap to climax until she sobbed and pleaded to be allowed fulfillment. When he finally did have mercy, she screamed loudly and long as her body shook helplessly beneath overwhelming waves of pleasure. Only when she lay quiescent and lax beneath him did Gil drive himself to his own completion.

As usual, he recovered first and carried her into the adjoining bathroom where he washed her and brought her to yet another climax.

The next morning when alone with Zul, she asked him. That time, however, she did not attempt to manipulate him through sex as she was certain Gil would have informed the other two of his warrior triad what she'd attempted to do. She knew they shared mental conversations like that, conversations to which she was not privy. Ursula was rather tired of not being included in conversations.

She lay languorous beside Zul in his bed for the same reason she'd lain beside Gil the previous afternoon. "Zul?"

His tail prodded her swollen folds and stroked through their seed-slicked wetness. "You wish to speak of the visitors to Fangrys."

She sighed. "Yes. Why won't any of you tell me what's going on?"

He rolled over her, propping himself up on his arms and wedging his hips between her legs. "Because it doesn't affect you."

"There are a lot of things that don't affect me directly, yet I know about them," she pointed out and gasped as he drove forward, drilling his revived cock into her body even as his tail moved to penetrate her ass. She squealed as he set a punishing rhythm that had her breasts bouncing and her thoughts melting.

Zul concentrated on driving his mate to orgasm then found his release while her walls contracted around his cock. After his cock deflated sufficiently to withdraw from her body without causing her to further contract around him, he indulged himself and her in the usual after-care of a bath during which he brought her to yet two more climaxes. Zul enjoyed that almost as much as finding his own release. Caring for her satisfied something deep and needy within his soul, a gentle, nurturing aspect of being mated that puzzled, delighted, and calmed his berserker nature.

Ursula spent that afternoon in her studio adding to the inventory for her shop. She did not see the arrival of yet another mysterious visitor, but she noticed the scurry of castrati which indicated a disruption in their normal routines and deduced what was going on. As the clay rose and fell beneath her skilled hands and gradually took the sensuous shape she envisioned, she considered whether it might be worth the risk to eavesdrop on the conversation.

Don't even consider it, came Bran's mental admonition. *The castrati will be instructed to prevent you from eavesdropping.*

Ursula sighed. She wished she could read her mates' thoughts as they read hers, but the bond didn't work that way. The clay bent under her hand, the vase ruined. With a muttered curse, she pulled the wet clay from the wheel and set it aside. Her concentration as ruined as her project, she washed her hands and cleaned the workstation.

To distract herself from growing ire and resentment, she headed for the courtyard to join Crow in a bout of joyful, childish play.

Ursula spent the next day at her shop. Gil lurked in a corner, ensuring no one—customer or fellow merchant—dared offer her insult. Business that day was brisk, so she managed to ignore him while putting on a smile and offering compliments to her customers' good taste. She continued to ignore Gil during lunch which she ate in the back room with Addilli who happily chattered about her offspring and the upcoming festival.

"Gallik and Sifgul are actually excited about the festival," Addilli confided with a twinkle in her eye. "Though they won't admit it, you know. They're far too preoccupied with the prospect of losing face by admitting your idea is wonderful."

Ursula grinned and finished her sandwich. She wiped her fingers on a cloth napkin and said, "I think the children will enjoy the trick-or-treating most. I know I always did when I was a kid."

Addilli tilted her head to one side. "Tell me about this trick-or-treating custom. It sounds terribly dangerous."

Ursula laughed, then sighed at the memory. "I grew up in a middle class suburb. I know that doesn't mean anything to you. Anyway, we knew our neighbors and socialized with them. It was exciting to dress in costumes and trek from house to house to collect candy. Because we knew our neighbors, we weren't afraid. Everyone's mom, dad, or grandparent kept their collective eye on us to make sure no one got lost or ran into any trouble."

"Were you not escorted by your fathers?"

"There were a few adults escorting kids, but for the most part, we kids roamed at will and stuck to our familiar neighborhoods." At Addilli's shocked expression, Ursula felt the need to explain. "Families are different where I come from, Addilli. Some households had both a mother and a father. Many had only mothers, and a few just fathers. I even knew a couple of kids who were being raised by their grandparents because their dad wasn't in the picture and their mother had abandoned them to pursue her own dreams."

Addilli frowned. "That sounds very selfish."

With a sigh, Ursula nodded. "It was. It *is*. When my parents were young, divorce was still somewhat scandalous. When I was young, it was common. Even having and raising children without being married was common and accepted. The social stigma had disappeared."

"That does not sound good for the stability of human society."

She shook her head. "No, it's not. By the time I was sent to Uribern, my homeland was starting to finally figure that out. It took unprovoked riots and the murder of a good man to force us to examine our culture's moral decay."

Addilli patted her knee. "Then I am doubly glad you have come to Uribern where you can live protected in a stable society."

Ursula glanced through the open doorway where Gil lurked just beyond. "I'm safer, yes, but stifled."

The other female gave her a sharp glance. "Are you truly *stifled*, Prima? Or do you tell yourself that to justify stoking your anger and resentment?"

Addilli's insight made Ursula pause to think. She didn't have an answer because she suspected that the other female might very well be correct. Her freedoms of life, liberty, and the pursuit of happiness had driven her to answer a vague employment advertisement out of desperation. She'd had no real safety net, no one looking out for her welfare—and now she had an abundance of such tender loving care directed at her. She wondered what freedoms she had truly lost, since she had to be honest with herself in admitting she hadn't taken advantage of many of the freedoms available to her when she lived on Earth. She'd only tried to fulfill the obligations of a responsible adult living on her own. *Perhaps I should have at least voted in the presidential election.*

"You're very perceptive," she murmured.

Addilli gave her a typically Urib close-mouthed smile then said, "As you like to say, I'm not just another pretty face."

CHAPTER 21

The morning before the festival and her body still thrumming from thorough ravishment by her three mates, Ursula greeted her former colleague and good friend, Carmen, with a cry of joy and a hug. Her three mates lingered a few steps behind with Crow bouncing on his toes. Carmen's own triad waited a few steps behind her with their two sons who eager to play with Crow. The warrior males exchanged murmurs of formal greeting and glances of indulgent amusement at their mates' antics.

"You boys do whatever it is you plan on doing," Ursula said with a wave of dismissal at their mates. She ignored Zul's snort and continued, "Crow, you and Carmen's boys mind Suvesh. Auntie Carmen and I are going to catch up."

The two women walked off, arm in arm, toward the drawing room Ursula preferred to use when meeting with friends and acquaintances. It was furnished with comfortable seating and decorated in soothing pastels. Small tables bore smaller trays of sweetmeats and other tiny confections ladies could neatly pop into their mouths. Tall windows let in plenty of natural light despite that day's unusual drizzle.

"I love that you call me auntie. It makes me feel like I have family here." Carmen took off her damp wrap and handed it to a waiting castratus. "The desert will really bloom after this."

Two more castrati stationed themselves in the room, ready to serve their mistress and her most honored guest.

"I know. It'll be gorgeous! Would you like lemonade or *ti'chal*?"

Carmen eyed the small, sugar-coated balls that reminded her of almond puffs. "Lemonade, please. Were you able to procure lemon trees for your greenhouse?"

"I was!"

One of the two castrati poured Carmen a glass of lemonade and handed it to her. The other castratus, seeing the direction of her gaze, began filling a small plate with her favorite treats.

"*Ti'chal*, please."

The castratus poured Ursula a cup of the fragrant hot beverage. She smiled and glanced out the nearest window. "I love how everything just bursts into bloom after a rain. The world will smell like nutmeg when the firethorn blooms—heavenly!"

Carmen seated herself, and the castratus set her plate on the small table beside her. "And it's just in time for your festival."

"It is." Ursula seated herself opposite her friend. "So, which of your men is going to be your partner dancing the flamenco?"

Carmen grinned. "Pako's going to play the guitar, can you imagine it?"

Ursula snickered, trying and unable to imagine the hulking male strumming guitar strings without snapping them with his claws. "And?"

"Yiis will be my *cantante*, my singer. You'll be surprised, but he has a really wonderful voice."

"It's a shame Urib culture discourages artistic pursuits among males," Ursula commented.

"It is. I had to *cry* to get them to agree to accompany me."

"You little manipulator," Ursula wheezed through her giggles.

Carmen's rich laughter filled the room. "Oh, they knew *exactly* what I was doing, but the big bad warriors' inability to endure a few crocodile tears gave them the excuse they needed to indulge me."

Ursula leaned forward. "And did that indulgence…"

"Oh, you know it did," Carmen crowed while the light caramel color of her cheeks turned rosy. She leaned forward, too. "And I'm pregnant again."

"That's wonderful. Are you still able to dance?"

"I'm *able*. The question was whether I'm *allowed*," Carmen admitted. She leaned back and took a sip of lemonade. "But as I'm not yet showing *and* because I've delivered two children without any issues before, my triad agreed to let me fulfill my commitment to you." She grinned. "I had to remind them that exercise is good for pregnant women."

Ursula pressed her hand against her own abdomen and wondered when she might next conceive. Since the Rite of First Union, all three of her mates had been most assiduous in their attentions, singly and together. She was healthy and still young. Surely, she'd conceive soon. "So, how is Mosk at dancing?"

"Adequate." Carmen's eyes twinkled and she grinned. "He likes the stomping parts."

"Well, he *is* your berserker."

"Indeed he is." Carmen popped a pastry into her mouth and chewed. "We were hoping to avail ourselves of your Suvesh to watch our sons during our performance."

"Of course, although Zul volunteered for babysitting duty," Ursula said. "You know, I offered Suvesh the day off, but he absolutely refused to accept it. I've got to admit, Crow minds no one else as well as he does Suvesh, and Suvesh really is good with him. So is Zul."

"Zul is that hunk-a-licious berserker who's your new Third?" Carmen grinned.

"He is a beautiful brute of a male, isn't he?" Ursula held out her hands to display the heavy, bejeweled bracelets encircling her wrists. "And generous, too. Yesterday's gifts, just because. He has a crazy need to drape me in jewelry."

"But you're not complaining."

"No, I'm not. He has exquisite taste. And, of course, Gil and Bran feel compelled to match his generosity. My jewelry chest is overflowing. If I ever have a daughter, her mates will never need to buy her anything sparkly. I'll just give her half my stuff."

"So, tell me the schedule," Carmen said, switching the subject while she ran her fingertips over the heavy, intricate links of the bejeweled necklace draped across her own collarbones. The sparkling clip in her thick black hair matched. Her own triad enjoyed bedecking her in arachnasilk and gemstones, too. She subtly wriggled in her seat, feeling the movement of the gold plug buried within her ass. Luckily, the guest quarters were located a good distance from her hostess' suite, and the walls and doors of the manse were thick and insulating, so she wouldn't have to fret over her hostess and her mates overhearing the loud sounds of vigorous and enthusiastic fornication.

Ursula let her friend steer the conversation to the festival being held the day after next. After several minutes of detailed discussion, she asked, "Will your triad be helping with setup?"

Carmen shook her head. "No, I do believe they'll be sequestered with *your* triad in finalizing whatever sneaky plans they've been discussing on the sly."

Ursula's eyes narrowed. "So, the Omari Triad is in cahoots with the Fangrys Triad?"

Carmen nodded. "You bet."

"Do you know what it's about?"

Carmen shook her head. "Not a clue. I can usually tease out what I want to know from my men, but not this time, not about this topic—whatever that topic is."

"Same here. It's frustrating."

"I know. I don't like it when they keep secrets from me."

"Especially when I'm not allowed to keep secrets from them."

"Fucking double standards," Carmen muttered under her breath.

The two women munched on confections and tiny pastries and sipped at their beverages in companionable quiet for a moment before restarting their conversation.

Meanwhile, comfortably gathered in the manse's conference room, the Fangrys and Omari Triads met via virtual video and audio connections with their co-conspirators to discuss treason.

Their seditious conversation was not recorded; Bran made sure of that. Soon, they promised themselves, *soon* a new government—a new Council Supreme elected by the very people they governed—would represent the will of the Urib people and serve their best interests. All that was left was to ensure the right people were in place, the right weapons were in place, and the right date and time were set.

Bran and Gil looked forward to the day when broken triads were not deployed away from their mates in not-so-covert attempts to kill them off—and the high caste survivors of broken dyads were not assassinated—so their brides could be reassigned to new mates to produce more offspring. They also wanted to open access to imported brides for the lower castes as well, for those folk were just as crucial to the well-ordered operation of Urib society and commerce as were the high castes.

"Ursula would be astonished to hear of our egalitarian ambitions," Bran commented when the brief meeting concluded.

"Egalitarian does not preclude authoritarian," Pako pointed out. "Our ambitions do not include giving our females the freedoms they used to have on Earth."

"True," Zul said. "Our females must remain protected."

The other five males in the room nodded their agreement.

"Are you prepared to serve as the Council Supreme's new chairman?" Gil asked the Omari Prime.

The male nodded and replied, "Only with the Fangrys Triad and Mosk and Yiis as my advisors."

"The Ulscanti Triad will arrive tomorrow," Gil confirmed. "The official reason is to accompany their mate to the Halloween festival, but they will be bringing important communiques."

"And the others?" Yiis prompted.

Bran answered, "They are ready to support us."

"As long as we do not divulge their names," Zul added, tasting the sour note in his voice.

Yiis shrugged. "When we succeed, they need not fear retribution. Until then, they are wise to be leery of discovery."

"But are we certain of their loyalty?" Pako looked worried.

"Yes," said Zul.

Bran smiled, revealing pointed teeth. "Yes. I made sure of it."

Yiis blinked. "You didn't?"

"I did."

"You could establish yourself as a warlord with that kind of psychic strength."

"I could, but I don't want to," Bran replied. He glanced at Gil and Zul. "It is sufficient to lead my triad."

Gil and Zul nodded, the latter commenting, "He is a wise leader."

Mosk's eyes narrowed as he looked at Zul, then opened wide. "You were the Third of the Uk'khadir Triad. Borsulvar cen'Gyrah was your Prime."

Zul nodded. "He was. You knew him?"

"I did. We were younglings together." Mosk, with his customary blunt candor, then said, "You were well rid of him when he was killed in battle."

Zul's jaw clenched against the urge to snarl, and he maintained a stoic silence.

"Borsulvar was a bully," Mosk stated.

Zul could not deny that and didn't try.

CHAPTER 22

Each accompanied by two of their three mates, Ursula and Carmen went to the village of Fangrys to set up for the following day's events. Armed with printed diagrams and lists and pens and a coterie of female volunteers accompanied by their mates, brothers, or fathers, Ursula set everyone to work. She gave diagrams and signs to those who would be marking assigned spaces around the village's central square. She assigned several males to build a temporary stage at the far end of a side street, which the sheriff agreed to barricade against vehicular traffic. Other village streets were also barricaded. She checked in with each vendor to ensure they found their assigned spaces and received any assistance as needed. Bran and Zul shook their heads at the barely controlled chaos of event organization.

"There's a lot more that goes into planning a party than I guessed," Carmen quipped after she finished helping a local vendor set up his market stall, much to that male's nearly gibbering horror. The Omari Prime chuckled while keeping a close watch over his mate and offering the merchant a word of reassurance that human hybrids were less docile than other hybrid females.

"It's not just a party," Ursula explained. "It's a market combined with a roster of performances. There are a *lot* of moving parts to align so everything goes off smoothly." A crash resounded, and she winced. "And it never goes smoothly."

With a quick smile, she headed off to see what had happened and to rectify the problem. Zul rushed after her, ready to lend a muscular arm, a skilled hand, or a stern glare. Bran looked at Pako and shrugged.

"The things we do to keep our mates happy."

Pako grinned and glanced at Carmen who was already haggling with a vendor to buy something at a discount. That vendor sent a pleading glance at the Omari Prime for help. "I'd better rescue that poor male, or he'll find my mate has robbed him of everything valuable."

"And your finances much depleted anyway," Bran murmured.

Pako laughed and headed off to save the flustered merchant.

"My Lord cen'Vyr," someone hailed.

The Fangrys Prime turned to face the mayor. "What is it?"

The male paused in his approach, then found his courage and continued walking toward the Fangrys Prime until he stopped at a respectable three large steps from the lord of the region. He took a deep breath and said, "I have received complaints from several males."

"About what?" Bran inquired, his tail slowly swishing.

The mayor's own tail curled. "The females are giving them orders!"

"Would those males know what to do if the females in charge of the festival did not tell them?" Bran asked, keeping his tone reasonable.

"It is unseemly for a female to tell a male what to do!"

"Ah, it seems they would not," Bran concluded. He took a step toward the mayor, and the mayor scrambled backward to remain the respectful distance just beyond the reach of Bran's heavily muscled arm and sharp claws.

"No good will come of this violation of the natural order," the mayor threatened.

Bran glanced at the busy people surrounding them, listening to chatter and laughter and even some off-key singing. He saw a handful of children running about on errands or just chasing each other for fun. "I see nothing untoward."

"You give your mate too much lenience. You are too permissive with her."

Bran's eyes narrowed and he leaned forward, angling his long, sharply pointed horns toward the mayor. "My mate is none of your concern."

The mayor huffed. "It will be when she disgraces you with her loose behavior."

"Loose?" Bran echoed in astonishment. Then he laughed. "If there is anything—anything at all—of which I am certain, it is my mate's fidelity."

"No male can be certain of that."

"Do you not share your mind with your mate?"

The mayor was appalled. "And weaken my intellect by sharing a female's imbecility?" He stiffened his spine and puffed his chest. "This explains your woeful permissiveness with the Prima."

Bran drew himself to his full height. The bright sunshine gleaming against his golden hide made him appear regal and intimidating, reminding all who saw him as to why *he* was a warrior triad's *prime*. "Mayor, present yourself, your mate, and your dyad bond to me the day following the festival."

Thinking he had impressed the Fangrys Prime, the mayor bowed and took his leave, although he had not gotten the immediate concession of the Fangrys Triad controlling their wayward, insolent mate as he had hoped. Perhaps arrangements had gone too far to disrupt them right then, and the Fangrys Prime would take his mate in hand following the festival, as was proper.

Bran, surmising the mayor's conjecture, said nothing to correct him. Doing so in public would shame that male who, perhaps, did not quite deserve such harsh treatment. He planned to set his lovely mate to speaking with the mayor's mate to discern whether that female was being mistreated. If so, public humiliation would be the least of the mayor's worries.

He turned around to join Ursula and Zul, but they were already headed back toward him. He met them halfway and asked, "What else is there to be done?"

"I've got to stick around for a while longer," Ursula said. "Some vendors are coming in from out of town to set up, and I should be here when they arrive."

"She has established a deadline for setup today," Zul explained, resting a hand lightly on Ursula's shoulder. "I will stay to protect her if you wish to return home."

Bran gave him a small smile, mouth closed so as not to reveal any pointed teeth. "No, Zul, I think it sends a necessary message if we are both here."

"Lending my little festival your royal consequence?" Ursula remarked.

"Something like that," Bran replied. "If you thought the mayor was disappointed that you were actually allowed to organize something more complicated than a dinner, then you would not believe how outraged he is to see that you have actually been allowed a position of authority."

"Allowed?" she parroted, eyebrows rising.

"His word, not mine."

Ursula snorted. "No, I think that's your word. Regardless, this is what I do, and I'm damned good at it."

Zul nodded. "Yes, she is."

"I know. Her competence impressed me at the embassy gala where we met."

Ursula chuckled. "I thought it was my singing."

"That, too." Bran traced the back of a knuckle down her cheek. "And your beauty and your fierce defense of your friend."

"I was the whole package, huh?"

Zul looked confused.

"Everything and more," Bran said. "I have not regretted claiming you, and I never will."

"No matter how much blame you catch for *allowing* me too much freedom?"

"Everything Gil, Zul, and I do is in the best interests of you and Crow. We want nothing more than your happiness."

Ursula smiled and threw herself at her mate. Bran rocked when she collided with him, but did not move. She wrapped her arms around his brawny body and hugged him tightly. Bran closed his arms around her, careful not to squeeze her too snugly.

Zul set a ruddy hand on her hip and gave her a light squeeze. "You are precious to each of us. We would die before allowing any harm to come to you."

Face pressed against Bran's chest, she said, "I was beginning to worry that I was in trouble. That the mayor had convinced you I'd brought shame upon you."

Bran stroked a hand down her long white hair. "You caught my emotion, *elska'adir*? Fear not. I am never angry with you."

He met Zul's eyes over her head.

She was worried, Zul said, mind to mind.

Bran cast him a knowing look. *As much as our lovely mate wishes to be independent, she needs us. She needs our support and approval.*

It must be difficult for her to reconcile both her need for independence and her need for us, Zul replied.

She struggles with it, Bran acknowledged. *We try to ease that struggle. Part of that means reminding her of her importance to us: she is more than a breeder for the next generation.*

She is precious to us, necessary for our very souls.

Indeed.

CHAPTER 23

Suffering from a last-minute attack of anxiety, Ursula whispered before mounting the stage, "I don't see a microphone. How are they going to hear me?"

Gil turned her around to face him and straightened the tiara which had been knocked slightly askew. The headdress radiated spokes fanned from an intricately designed base like filigreed rays of a bejeweled sun. "The amplifiers will work. They will carry your voice to every corner of the village."

"I don't see any amplifiers."

"I installed them myself, *elska'adir.*"

Ursula's eyes widened. She hadn't realized the Second of the Fangrys Triad was so handy. *You've been keeping secrets, you silver-horned devil.*

He grinned at her and whispered, "We all have our little secrets. Now—how do you say it—go pull their socks down."

"*Knock* their socks *off,*" she corrected with a smile before taking a deep breath to calm her nerves. "Do I look all right?"

"You are beautiful," Gil reassured her. "The most beautiful female I have ever seen."

Ursula took another deep breath, closed her eyes, then summoned her courage and opened them. She climbed the three steps and walked onto the stage, the thin soles of her slippers shuffling softly against the smooth, hard floor. *Carmen's dancing shoes will sound wonderful against this material.* She found the center of the stage, took another deep breath, straightened her spine, threw her shoulders back, and turned to face the crowd. She raised an arm, the sleeve falling back to reveal the sparkling bracelets encircling her wrist and the jeweled rings on four of her fingers. Faceted stone and gleaming metal caught and reflected the morning sunshine as though she were surrounded in a brilliant nimbus of sparkling light.

"Good morning, Fangrys Village!" Ursula spoke in her very best imitation of Robin William's iconic greeting in *Good Morning, Vietnam.* She knew nobody except Carmen would understand the pop culture reference, but she enjoyed using it anyway. Carmen's delighted smile and thumbs-up gesture showed that the other woman appreciated it. She took a breath and looked at the crowd of expectant attendees all garbed in their finest.

Turning her head to look at the crowd, the morning sunlight made the spokes of her jeweled tiara sparkle. "I am delighted you could attend what I hope will be the first of an annual festival here. As many of you know, I'm one of the brides sent from the planet Earth. Back in my homeland, we celebrate an autumn or harvesttime festival called Halloween. Halloween benefits from a mixture of Earth cultures and customs, some of which I have integrated into this event, as well as other events I am sure all of you—and especially our children—will enjoy and appreciate."

Ursula paused and again let her gaze roam across the gathered crowd. No one smiled. No one clapped. They gave her their solemn attention. She wondered briefly if that was merely because of her high caste status as the Fangrys Prima. Forcing a broad, welcoming smile that she in no way intended as threatening despite the baring of her teeth, she clapped her hands together and said, "So, without further ado, let's get this shindig started!" She gestured to her left. "We have many wonderful vendors offering an amazing variety of handcrafted items." She gestured to her right. "And we have a plethora of food vendors to tempt everyone's tastebuds."

She raised both arms. "And here on stage, we have a full program of performances. First up is Omari Prima Carmen Sanchez and her warrior triad performing a Spanish flamenco!"

After Ursula exited stage left, Pako mounted the stage first, carrying an instrument that didn't quite look like a guitar. Ursula assumed it was the Urib version of the stringed instrument. He pulled over a stool and carefully positioned it before taking a seat, balancing the not-guitar on one knee. Yiis walked on stage next, carrying a drum. He, too, pulled over a stool, carefully positioned it, and sat with the tall drum placed between his knees. He rested his palms on the drum's taut leather top. Mosk and Carmen climbed the stairs next, her hand in his. Mosk positioned himself center forward and struck a pose, looking both supercilious and sexy in a costume Carmen had adapted to the Urib male's physique. Dressed in a skin-tight, red dress with a skirt of cascading, flame-colored ruffles, Carmen posed beside him, raising one arm and extending the other, castanets in each hand. Her large chandelier earrings matched the flame colors of her skirt.

Pako began the performance, his claws strumming the not-guitar with flawless precision. Yiis' hands struck a rhythm on the drum in perfect counterpoint. After a moment, he began to sing, his resonant tenor starting low and increasing in volume as he verbalized deep emotions of love, loss, joy, and grief, his voice rising and descending with the not-guitar's music. As he sang, Carmen and Mosk began to dance, drawing gasps of astonishment from the crowd who had gathered to watch this spectacle of Earth culture. When the performance ended with Carmen gracefully draped backward over Mosk's brawny arm and the clacking castanets finally silent, Ursula joined them onstage and applauded with obvious enthusiasm. The Urib crowd quickly followed suit and clapped, emulating their Prima's expression of appreciation. The Omari Triad and their Prima bowed.

"Wasn't that *absolutely magnificent?*" she called out. She glanced at her program as the Omari Triad and their Prima left the stage. "Next up we have an acrobatic performance by our very own warrior recruits!"

She clapped again and exited the stage as a group of six young males, not a berserker among them, dragged mats onto the stage and placed them to form a softer landing than the hard surface below. The adolescent males had choreographed martial arts kicks, hits, parries, and tumbles, some with empty hands and some with blunt wooden weapons. When they finished, the crowd remembered the appropriate response—appropriate according to their Prima—and applauded. The young males took a cue from the first act and bowed, chests heaving as they panted from their athletic exertions.

As the young males dragged their mats off the stage, Ursula once again addressed the crowd. "We have one more performance before a break in the program. Please use that break to visit our festival market. Parents, please take your little ones to the children's activity area where they can have their faces painted and try out a variety of crafts. And, everyone, don't forget to sample the food. It's *amazing*!"

The crowd lingered, politely waiting for the third performance before they felt free to explore. However, that time, Ursula didn't leave the stage. Instead, she announced, "The last performance of this morning is me."

Folks gasped, although some murmured among themselves that the Fangrys Prima was known for being odd and overly bold—and her mates altogether too permissive.

"I'm going to sing three songs," she said. "The first is 'Think of Me' from *The Phantom of the Opera*. This is the song that first caught my mates' notice." She glanced at them hovering nearby and smiled. "My second song is 'I Will Always Love You' by Dolly Parton, a personal favorite, and my final song will be 'Let It Go,' the theme song from the Walt Disney movie *Frozen*." She looked at Gil and said, "Hit it."

Recorded music swelled and filled the entire village. Ursula saw no speakers, but trusted in his assurance that instrumentals of each recorded song would play without static or other sounds distracting from her performance. On cue, she lifted her voice, the aria soaring toward the sky as she worked to reach and sustain those high notes. When she finished, the crowd of Urib males and mixed assembly of pure and hybrid females gaped before remembering their newly learned response of clapping. After a pause, she launched into the next song. When the third song concluded, Ursula curtsied and bowed her head. Upon rising, she thanked them for listening and again urged them to enjoy themselves before the afternoon's performances began.

"You… were… *awesome*," Carmen enthused, wrapping her friend in a hug. She pulled back, grinned, and said, "Come. Yiis doesn't like manning your booth, and Bran has a picnic waiting for you there."

Ursula blinked. "*Yiis* is staffing my booth?"

Carmen giggled. "He caught some young thug attempting to make off with one of your vases and decided to keep watch. Then a customer approached and he found himself obligated to serve as your salesman." She giggled again. "He's a *terrible* salesman."

"I'll bet," Ursula replied in an arid tone as Zul moved behind the two women and placed a big hand lightly on his mate's shoulder to indicate his readiness to escort them to her market stall. Pako moved into place beside Carmen and took her hand in his. "I'd better get over there before he scares away all my customers."

Carmen shook her head and chuckled. Eyes twinkling, she offered, "Do you want me to set my men to rounding up customers for you?"

Ursula laughed. "No, thanks anyway. I'll have lunch with my triad, then shoo them away so I can serve my customers until it's time for the afternoon's first performance."

"I'll staff the booth for you then. Yiis won't mind *too* much." She grinned. "I can be *very* persuasive."

Ursula laughed. "With moves like I saw in your dance, you'll seduce every male in the village into buying something. Do you want a job?"

Carmen laughed and shook her head. "Nah. I'm happy being a housewife these days."

CHAPTER 24

Zul made sure Ursula was occupied in her parlor when the mayor, the sheriff, and their mate arrived at the Fangrys triad's manse in obedience to the Fangrys Prime's command. The visitors looked about in awe, not quite gaping, at the majestic edifice in which the warrior triad lived as a supercilious castratus led them to Bran's office. Bran remained seated when they entered, surmising that standing and looming over them would be unnecessarily intimidating.

"We are here as you ordered, my lord," the mayor said with a shallow bow of perfunctory respect.

Standing between her mates, the thin female sank into a deep curtsey, keeping her eyes downcast and her head properly covered. Bran noted her lack of adornment, the plain fabrics in dull colors she wore. Beside her, the sheriff bowed and said nothing.

"Mistress Soraia," Bran addressed the female, who visibly flinched, "the castratus will take you to visit with the Prima."

"Our mate goes nowhere without escort by either me or my bond," the sheriff growled.

Bran leveled a cool look at him. "Do you imply your mate is in danger here?"

"Of course not, my lord."

"Then why should she not visit with the Prima? The Prima's friendship does your mate honor."

"The Prima may unwittingly give offense," the sheriff said, squaring his shoulders.

Bran tilted his head to one side—just a little. "Offense? Why don't you elaborate? Explain how the Prima could possibly offend."

"She does not know her place," the mayor said."

Bran leaned back in his chair. "So, you believe that a little time in my mate's company will irrevocably corrupt your mate? Is your mate so weak of will, so impressionable that she cannot withstand association with the Prima?"

The female's eyes widened even as she kept her gaze fixed on the floor. She seemed to shrink, to shrivel within herself.

"Hurvi, escort Mistress Soraia to the Prima's parlor where she may relax and enjoy some refreshments."

The female glanced at her mates whose small nods of permission released her from the oppressive weight of the Fangry's Prime's disapproval, though she did not sense he disapproved of her. She shivered with dread, for their humiliation at the Prime's hand would undoubtedly land upon her.

"Oh, hello," the Prima looked up in surprise. She smiled, which made the other female hesitate and hastily consider leaving the pretty room to which the castratus had led her. The Prima shot a speaking glance at the hulking berserker lurking in a corner and returned her attention to her unexpected visitor. She bared her teeth again and extended her hand toward the other female who looked at it in confusion. The Prima lowered her hand and sighed. "I do apologize."

The female's eyes widened at the Prima apologizing to her.

"I forget that you folks don't smile or shake hands," the Prima said with a small chuckle. "You'll have to forgive me for being gauche."

The female gulped at the concept of forgiving the Prima of any wrongdoing.

The Prima gestured. "Please, have a seat. Would you care for a refreshment?"

The female scurried to the chair and gingerly perched on the edge of the cushion. A castratus dashed forward at an unseen signal from his mistress and filled a small plate with small morsels of delectable treats. The female accepted the plate and wondered what to do next.

Seeing her guest's discomfiture, the Prima sought to put her at ease. "I'll have some, too."

The castratus filled a plate and handed it to her when she reseated herself. The Prima popped a small, bite-sized pastry into her mouth, chewed, and swallowed. "I do love those."

She leaned forward, balancing the plate on her knee. She smiled again, keeping her lips closed and her teeth covered. The other female responded with a hesitant flicker of an answering smile.

"So, I'm Ursula. What's your name?"

Fixing her eyes on her lap, the female answered in a soft whisper, "Soraia, my lady."

Ursula glanced again at Zul. *You knew she was coming.*

I knew. Bran asked me to make sure you were available to greet her.

Ursula sighed. *He could have just asked me.*

She felt his amusement. *It's more fun this way.*

Hah. Very funny. This poor woman is terrified. She refocused her attention on Soraia. "Please do try the chocolate truffles. I had to work with the chef here for months to get them just right."

Soraia looked at the confections on her plate in confusion.

"The dark brown ones."

Soraia carefully picked upon one of the chocolate puffs and bit into it. She chewed, eyes widening again as the flavor filled her mouth.

"Good, aren't they?" Ursula asked, popping another into her mouth. "The flavor pairs well with *ti'chal.*"

A castratus dashed forward at the mention of *ti'chal* to pour a dainty cupful and hand it to the Prima's guest.

Soraia nodded and popped the rest of the morsel into her mouth. Her eyes widened at the rich, decadent flavor. "What is this?"

"Chocolate truffle. It's a treat from Earth."

"Earth?"

"The planet where I come from," Ursula explained.

"Is all Earth food this wondrous?" Soraia picked up another truffle and chewed slowly to savor it.

Ursula chuckled. "Hardly. But I'd never feed a guest brussels sprouts or kale. That would be cruel."

The two women lapsed into a less brittle quiet as they ate a few more snacks.

"So, what brings you to Fangrys?" Ursula examined the shy woman sitting opposite her. It was difficult to discern age among the Urib, but she sensed the female was older.

"The Prime summoned my mates," the female answered.

"Ah," Ursula replied with a shallow nod. She raised an eyebrow. "And they couldn't leave you unsupervised?"

"I was summoned, too," Soraiaya admitted. "I do not know why."

"Who are your mates? Perhaps I know them."

"The mayor and sheriff of Fangrys Village."

Ursula bit back a guffaw and the disparaging comment that might have followed. *Those two morons did something to offend Bran, didn't they?*

They insulted you, came Zul's reply.

Well, it wouldn't have been the first time.

Zul had no answer to that because it was true.

Ursula sighed. *What does Bran expect me to do with this poor woman?*

Engage her in conversation.

That's not helpful.

He shrugged.

Ursula smiled, again making sure not to show her teeth. Reaching for an appropriately innocuous topic of conversation, she glanced out a window. "The firethorn is beautiful, is it not? I love seeing the desert bloom after a rain."

Soraia's shoulders relaxed at the safe topic and allowed her hostess to engage her in conversation. Ursula paid no attention to the passage of time and concealed her relief when the door opened. Soraia shot to her feet.

"The sheriff and mayor are ready to depart," Hurvi announced.

Soraia drew her mantilla back over her hair, having let it fall away during her pleasant conversation with the Prima. Her shoulders tensed and her gaze focused on the floor. Ursula's eyes narrowed. She recognized fear when she saw it. Approaching the other woman, she settled a hand lightly on Soraia's arm. Soraia flinched as though struck.

"If you need help, I will help you," Ursula said in a low voice.

Still looking at the floor, Soraia shook her head and said nothing.

"Abuse is wrong, Soraia."

Soraia said nothing.

Ursula sighed and patted her arm. "We won't force anything on you, but please do visit again. You are always welcome here."

Soraia whispered a thank-you, but did not look up.

"Hurvi, I'll walk with Soraia back to the front door."

The castratus nodded and led the way. Ursula linked her arm with the other woman's and walked beside her. Zul fell into step behind them, keeping a watchful eye on his mate as always.

When she met Bran and Gil at the door where they stood facing the sheriff and mayor, the latter two wore closed, wooden expressions on their faces. Soraia disengaged herself from her hostess' light grasp and scuttled to take her place between her mates.

"Remember what I said," Bran said as Hurvi and another castratus opened the tall doors leading outside.

The sheriff and mayor bowed their heads, a gesture of both acknowledgement and subservience as they submitted to the Prime's crushing dominance. Without further ado, they turned, ushering their mate ahead of them, and departed.

When the doors closed behind them, Ursula said, "What the hell was that about?"

Gil answered, "The sheriff and mayor gave offense."

"They have seen the error of their ways," Bran added, propping his hands on his waist. His tone oozed satisfaction.

Ursula snorted. "I doubt that."

Gil grinned, showing his teeth. "Oh, Bran's locked in to them now. Any misstep on their part, and we get to tear them to pieces."

Ursula's eyes widened. The bloodthirsty tone of Gil's voice indicated that he meant what he said—and looked forward to the violence. She took a breath. "Soraia's terrified of them, you know."

"She no longer needs to fear them, but she will need your friendship to build her courage," Bran said with confidence.

"She has it," Ursula vowed. If anyone needed a friend and advocate, it was the sheriff and mayor's mate.

CHAPTER 25

"Be nice to Zul," Gil said as he and Bran bade their mate and their son goodbye two days after the festival. Zul stood behind their mate, his hand resting possessively on her shoulder. Crow huddled against his mother's leg, his hand tightly clutching her vivid blue skirt. He'd bade goodbye to his fathers all too often already in his young life.

"When are you coming back?" Ursula asked again because they hadn't answered the question the first six times she asked. Perhaps the seventh time was the charm.

"We don't know, *elska'adir*," Bran replied. Honesty compelled him to finally admit, "We might not be able to return."

Ursula paled, her usual pink complexion going ashen. "Are we at war again?"

"Still," Bran corrected her, his voice gentle if somber. "But, no, we have not been deployed. We are…"

His voice died away as he searched for the right words.

Gil rescued him. "We're headed to the capital for political reasons."

Liberté, égalité, fraternité, she thought and whispered, "Who's playing Napoleon?"

"Napoleon?" the two males echoed in confusion.

"Nevermind," she said with a wave of her hand. "I'm not stupid. I know all those secret discussions I'm not supposed to be aware of have had something to do with politics. I know you—and I—have been unhappy with the Council Supreme's machinations to reassign fertile brides to unbroken triad and dyad bonds."

Gil, Zul, and Bran exchanged glances over her head.

"You're very... perceptive," Zul murmured, his hand tightening on their mate's shoulder.

"Like I said: I'm not stupid."

All three males winced at her acerbic tone.

She explained how she came to her insight: "If you're engaging in political activity that may result in you being unable to return home, then it means you're engaging in *illegal* activity, possibly sedition or even treason."

"As he said, you're perceptive," Bran acknowledged with grim pride. "You must say *nothing* to anyone."

She nodded. "I can keep a secret." She paused and frowned before asking, "Would the authorities even think of questioning me, a lowly and stupid female?"

"They might not, but Zul will not take that chance," Bran said. "If everything goes wrong and we do not effect the change we desire—"

"And what change is that, exactly?" she interrupted.

Bran hesitated. Gil's lips remained pressed in a thin line. So, Zul answered her with blunt candor: "A new Council Supreme."

Ursula nodded with surprising equanimity. "Treason then."

"I expected more of a reaction," Gil finally commented.

Ursula shrugged. "The country I'm from basically came into being as a sovereign nation due to treason. The USA rebelled against England over the issue of taxation without representation." She glared at the two males standing before her. "And I'll be extremely disappointed in you both if you succeed in your aims and don't work to grant women some God-given rights."

The three males again exchanged speaking glances.

"If we fail," Bran said, his tone measured, "then you and Crow will go with Zul. He will protect you."

Ursula nodded, understanding that if they failed they would face execution for their crimes.

"You're brave," Zul complimented her after Bran and Gil hugged and kissed her and Crow.

"Not really," Ursula said as she watched them climb into the brick-shaped conveyance that defied all laws of physics and would fly them to the Urib version of a subway which would then propel the conveyance to the capital at high speed. "But I know they're doing what they think is right and just, so I *must* support them. The Council Supreme is corrupt and needs to be replaced—preferably on a regular basis."

Zul stared at her. What strange philosophy was this?

Turning toward him as the vehicle lifted from the ground and rose with ponderous grace into the sky, Ursula correctly interpreted his expression and said, "In my homeland, citizens vote for our political leaders. It's a civic duty, although no one is compelled to exercise that duty. I feel obligated because a lot of women suffered and even died to earn me that legal right to vote. I hope to see women acquire such political suffrage in my lifetime here on Uribern."

Zul blinked in astonishment. "Women—females... did what? Protested? Rebelled against the natural order?"

His mate sighed and decided a short history lesson was in order. "A century before I was born, women had few, if any, rights. Only under certain specific circumstances could women own property: they were, in essence, chattel themselves. Women even ceased to exist as legal entities upon marriage and only became legal entities again when widowed." She paused at Zul's puzzled expression and forebore to give him a much-abridged summary history of Western civilization and political philosophy. "Regardless, women comprised half the population and had no say in the laws affecting them. Thousands of women protested and lobbied until they were finally granted the right to vote. That was just the first step."

"First step?" Zul echoed in awe of the ferocity of human females. "There's more?"

Ursula gave him a grim smile. "Oh, yeah, there's more. A lot more."

He shook his head. "No wonder you are so fierce."

She smiled at him. "And I hope you appreciate it."

He nodded, fearing her reaction if he expressed disapproval. Truly, he thought, I need to read more about my mate's people and their history.

"Let's go in, Mama," Crow whined, pressing his face against her leg.

Ursula dropped into a squat and wrapped her arms around her son, knowing he was sad, knowing he did not understand why his fathers were leaving again. "Shall we play in the courtyard, sweetie?"

The boy sighed, sniffled, and shook his head. "Don't wanna."

"All right," she said, rubbing his back. "How about we go to the library? I'll read you your favorite stories, and we'll get Suvesh to bring us some hot cocoa?"

Crow perked up. "With marshmallows?"

She smiled tenderly at him. "Is there any other way?"

He shook his head. "Nope."

"Marshmallows?" Zul parroted, wondering what they were talking about.

Rising to her full height which was much shorter than Zul's, Ursula took his hand in hers and said, "Let me introduce you to one of the seven wonders of the universe: hot cocoa."

"And marshmallows!" Crow added as he grasped his mother's other hand. As they began walking back toward the manor, he asked, "And can we have cookies?"

"Tonight, we're throwing out the rules," Ursula said with a soft smile at her son. "Do you remember what that means?"

"No vegetables!"

"That's right. We'll eat what we want and go to bed when we feel like it. But the rules start again tomorrow morning, remember?"

He nodded. Days without rules helped ameliorate the melancholy of his fathers' departure.

"Do you do this often, *elska'adir*?"

"Only on the days when Bran and Gil both leave—and not always then. You weren't with us when we last decided on a no-rules day."

Zul nodded, assuming he'd been in the library or wandering about the grounds when that had happened. He hadn't noticed at the time any raucousness or evidence of festivities. Indeed, his mate and her son apparently kept their no-rules days quiet, focusing on comfort rather than entertainment. He could not deny them that solution to their solemn worry, so he decided he would join them. "What are cookies?"

Crow's eyes widened. "Cookies are… are… the best things ever!"

Ursula grinned and explained, "Cookies are baked goods, treats where I come from. Gil makes sure we always have a supply of chocolate chips on hand, so you'll get to experience chocolate chip cookies today."

He gave her a suspicious look.

"I spoke to Suvesh this morning. He'll have long since notified the cook."

"These cookies do not take long to make?"

"Not really. And, given the enormous ovens our kitchen has, the cook can make several dozen at a time." Ursula redirected her attention to Crow. "Do you want milk to drink with your cookies? I think milk's the best with cookies."

The boy nodded. "Yes, milk! Earth milk!"

"Milk?" Zul repeated, now fretting that his mate was unknowingly feeding her son foreign substances that his Urib body could not digest and would make him ill. "What is this Earth milk?"

"Milk usually comes from cows or goats, although some cultures drink the milk of camels, sheep, and horses. I prefer to drink cow's milk; it's much less… pungent. Gil gets fresh milk shipped in from Earth. It's outrageously expensive, but that jerkwad, Argosie, owes me, and he knows it. Anyway, since Gil goes to the effort of getting milk sent to Uribern, I make sure that he specifies the good stuff."

"What's the good stuff?" Zul asked, now genuinely curious.

"Jersey milk." She gave him an impish smile. "There ain't nothing else like it." She looked at her son and said, "We'll do milk and cookies now and have hot cocoa with marshmallows after supper. How does that sound?"

Crow nodded and smiled.

Zul figuratively girded his loins for the worst as they climbed the stairs to the manor's imposing front entrance. "I will have to try this milk and cookies."

"I think you'll be pleasantly surprised."

A castratus opened the door and stood aside while his mistress, her Bridge, and her son entered. Ursula thanked the castratus, relying on the good manners taught to her in childhood to show appreciation rather than taking his service for granted. A sweet, rich, alluring aroma wafted through the large building. Zul inhaled and his mouth watered. "Is that—?"

"It is." Ursula inhaled deeply and sighed with pleasure as they turned down the corridor that led to the manor's vast kitchen. "Chocolate chip cookies for everyone."

Zul was not surprised that his mate would share these delectable-smelling treats with the castrati. "These treats will not upset Crow's digestion?"

"A couple of cookies won't hurt," she said. "That's all he's permitted to eat at a time."

"Ah, so no-rules day does have some rules after all."

She nodded. "No rules in moderation, of course."

CHAPTER 26

Ursula noticed almost immediately that the servants disallowed her any news. Printed news releases were burned before she could get her hands on them. Video releases failed to display on any device. They offered no disrespect, but would not accede to her demands for updates. Frustrated, she aimed her accusatory glare at Zul who met her ire with bland equanimity.

He lowered his cup of *ti'chal* and asked in a mild tone, "Something disturbs you, *elska'adir*?"

Trying not to grind her molars into powder, Ursula set her cup down with a decisive click on the saucer and said, "Yes, *darling*, something disturbs me."

He blinked and maintained his silence, waiting.

"I hate when you do that," she muttered under her breath. Then, before he could say anything in response, she said, "What's going on in the capital?"

"Nothing for you to worry about," he replied.

Ursula's eyes narrowed. "My mates are engaged in dangerous activity. Do *not* tell me *not* to worry."

He nodded. "Then I will not tell you."

Her fists clenched. She took a deep breath to calm herself, counting silently to ten. Then she took another breath because the first failed its purpose. When she could finally speak without shrieking, she said, "Please tell me what's going on. Not knowing is driving me crazy."

"Your ignorance keeps you and Crow safe," he replied and took another sip as though there were nothing to worry about and she were being unreasonable. He met her gaze, his own implacable. "What you do not know you cannot divulge."

With icy fury, Ursula rose from the chair, every movement controlled and precise. She slid the chair under the table and turned toward him. "You know being treated like this infuriates me."

Zul nodded. "I know."

"And you do not care."

His expression did not change, but something glinted in his eyes. Perhaps it was regret. Or maybe it was just annoyance. "I do care."

"But you will not relent."

"No."

Her voice throbbing with the force of her emotion, she still managed to avoid yelling and said in a low tone, "Then go… to… hell."

She turned on her heel and left the room. The door closed quietly behind her, a servant scrambling to ensure it did not slam. The castratus' attention to that detail was not necessary.

Fists clenched, Zul leaned back in the chair and tilted his head so his face was parallel to the vaulted ceiling far above. He exhaled and relaxed his fists, pressing his palms flat on the table. The castratus in the room gazed at him, eyes wide with wariness and ready to flee. An enraged berserker was dangerous. Meeting the servant's wide-eyed fright, he exhaled again and murmured, "She's both scary and impressive when she's furious, isn't she?"

The castratus squeaked and fled.

Zul exhaled an expletive. The profane word felt cathartic and helped him master his own emotions. He knew his berserker nature intimately: emotions were difficult to control, and control was critical to avoid hurting innocents. He had to admit to himself that no one had ever roused his emotions like his gorgeous mate.

He didn't know whether he wanted to throttle her or fuck her, but he refused to yield to the impulse of the first and knew she would not welcome the impulse of the second. She had vowed to receive him in joy, not anger.

He heard the jingle and rattle of harness through the window and looked outside. With another muttered curse, he stood and rushed to join his mate and her son before they left without him. Ignoring his arrival, she grabbed the lines from the servant sitting next to her and snapped them against the numpties' broad backs and set them into lumbering motion. Zul fell into step beside the hoverwagon.

"Good morning, Papa Zul," Crow greeted him with a bright smile.

"Good morning, Crow," Zul replied as he easily kept pace.

The child glanced at his mother then leaned down toward the berserker and whispered, "Mama's *mad*."

Zul nodded. "Yes, I know."

"Do you know why?"

Zul refused to lie to the youngling. "I do."

"Is she mad at you?"

Zul accepted the blame. "Yes."

"Then why don't you fix it?"

Zul shook his head. "I am keeping you and your mama safe."

The child frowned, trying to understand why efforts to keep him and his mother safe would anger her. Drawing himself up to his less than intimidating height even seated on the hoverwagon, he demanded, "Explain."

Zul chuckled, seeing the commanding nature of a golden warrior breed in the youngling. Bran would have to work hard to keep the boy from becoming a bully, as none understood the nature of a high caste warrior breed better than another, just as none understood the challenges of a berserker better than another.

"You're a bit young to impose your will upon *me*, Crow," he chided gently.

The youngling frowned at being thwarted and ducked his head. He pursed his lips, then looked at the third of his patriarchal triad. "Some day you will obey me."

Zul shrugged. "By the time you are strong enough to control one such as I, you will be ready to form your own warrior triad."

So, that's what it is: Bran controls you, so you feel it necessary to control me.

The icy blast of her words in his mind surprised him. However, he mustered calm and replied, *Do you think me so petty?*

She responded with frosty silence which he interpreted as yes, she did think him so petty. Her poor opinion made his gut clench and the natural sway of his tail as he walked turned into a tight wringing motion, the only outward sign of his unsettled emotion.

Nervous clicking sounds came from the castratus sitting in the back of the hoverwagon with the new inventory.

When they reached Ursula's shop, Zul helped the castrati unload what little cargo there was, carefully setting down the crates so his mate could place each new piece where she thought it would be best displayed. He'd quickly learned to allow her this menial labor, as it gave her satisfaction and did no harm.

After each crate was emptied and removed from the floor back to the hoverwagon by the castrati, Zul took his usual position in a corner where he had visual command over all the storefront and a good bit into the back room. No sooner had he seated himself when Addilli entered, accompanied by Master Gallik and two castrati.

"Good morning, Master Crow," the male greeted the youngling with a bow of respect.

Crow smiled and bowed. "Good morning, Master Gallik. Have you come to see Mama?" Guileless, the child took a step forward, leaned closer to the familiar male, and whispered, "Mama's *mad*."

Ursula rolled her eyes as Addilli giggled.

"Prima," the male began, his stiff voice exhibiting discomfort in addressing another female, "we are hoping our order is ready."

"Of course," Ursula replied with a tight smile.

Addilli correctly interpreted the other female's expression and attempted to ameliorate Ursula's visible ire. "Sifgul is eager to receive the new plates and bowls. He says the beauty of your wares makes our food taste even better."

Ursula blinked in surprise, her ill humor evaporating. "Really? He said that?"

Addilli tilted her head and smiled. "Have I ever lied to you?"

Ursula sighed and wiped away a sudden tear that sprang to her eye. "Oh, Addilli, you are a treasure. That compliment was just what I needed."

Addilli patted her arm and looked at her mate. Gallik gave her a nod of approval.

Ursula gestured toward the back room and said, "There are four boxes marked with your name, Mr. Gallik. Everything you ordered is in there, but please be sure to reconcile your records with the content to make sure."

The restaurateur bowed and replied, "I am certain you are correct, Prima. It is an honor to do business with you."

With a flick of his fingers, he signaled his castrati to fetch the boxes.

Addilli's eyes flickered toward Zul who sat silent and watchful. Alluding to the berserker's consistent presence when Ursula's males generally rotated their guarding, she asked, "Have Prime Bran and Second Gil been deployed again?"

Ursula's lips pressed together in a thin line as she took a second to ponder her answer. After that brief hesitation, she replied, "Yes."

And that, elska'adir, *is why I keep you ignorant. You are a less than convincing liar.*

Lying isn't honorable, she flung back at him.

But sometimes it is prudent.

Addilli, who had no interest in politics, blinked and sighed, understanding that the distracted look in her friend's eyes meant mental communication was going on. Again she patted Ursula's arm and she murmured, "They protect you."

"That's what he claims," Ursula muttered in a bitter tone.

"Then you must believe him. Your mates cannot lie to you."

"Do you truly believe that?" Ursula's tone made her doubt clear.

Addilli nodded. "The connection we have with our mates is intimate and allows for no falsehood. They would rather keep you ignorant than risk breaking your trust and their honor."

Ursula gave her a rueful smile. "I hope you're right. Because if you're not, I'm going to kick some ass."

Addilli's eyes widened in astonishment at the other female's violent words. Then she chuckled. "And if I'm wrong, I am sure they will let you... er... kick their asses." She grinned. "I *like* that expression. Do you mind if I use it?"

Ursula gave her a conspiratorial grin. "Be my guest."

Zul did not wince, but he wanted to. Gallik looked horrified but dared not mention in the berserker's hearing that the Prima was a bad influence on his sweet-natured, submissive mate.

CHAPTER 27

Even if the capital's populace did not particularly care that broken triads and dyads were frequently sent into danger to kill them off so the Supreme Council could reassign their mates, the native males of Uribern absolutely did *not* appreciate revelations that the Council Supreme played favorites with the distribution of brides. More revelations, accompanied by recorded evidence, of the council members' accepting bribes, enriching themselves at their people's expense, and consolidating political and financial power among themselves made simmering resentments based on suspicion boil over into outright rebellion and heated demands for political change.

Mated males fortunate enough to have secured human brides and pained by their mates' resentment of Uribern's cultural restrictions imposed upon females joined the rebellion, if only to secure their mates' affections rather than from any dedication to or support for what the human-Urib hybrids called "women's suffrage" or "women's liberation." Many hybrid females from other planets, much to the surprise of their mates, also joined the protests and demanded that they be treated as citizens equal under the law, too.

The members of the Council Supreme were not amused by the societal unrest and rampant calls for abdication of their exalted positions. They charged Bran and Gil with treason and sent a company of the council guard to arrest the golden Prime.

Bran exchanged glances with Pako and the Ulscanti Triad prime, a celebrated war hero who had traveled extensively and had joined their cause. Gathered behind them to confront the unlucky warrior dispatched to arrest them were Gil, Yiis, and a horde of other Urib breeds spanning the diverse strata of Urib society. Over the length of the season, Gil and Yiis had organized the groups to ensure each order had its duly approved representatives. They agreed that a representative form of government was more equitable than a council consisting of an elite class of males who had never gone to war or served at the pleasure of other masters.

(Mosk, like Zul, remained behind in Omari to ensure their mate's and their son's safety.)

"Brannal cen'Vyr, you are ordered to submit for reckoning," the leader of the Council Supreme's guard called out.

Bran had expected the confrontation. Open-handed and unarmed, he emerged from the modest building in which he and Gil had been staying and stood, his posture erect and proud. The harsh sunshine glinted off his golden horns and his golden scales, turning him into a brightly light statue of inspiration. He replied loudly, "I will meet with the Council Supreme, but I will not submit."

The guards raised their weapons.

Doors from every building in the neighborhood opened and armed Urib males emerged, all leveling their weapons at the guards. More than one guard looked at the unexpected response from the citizenry and silently murmured petitions to their gods.

"*We* will no longer submit to the tyranny and corruption of the Council Supreme," Bran proclaimed.

Standing a step behind his prime and slightly to the right, Gil leveled his sword. Sunshine gleamed off the long length of razor sharp metal. He called out, "Your aggression will be met with death."

Pako stepped beside Bran, another horned figure of gleaming gold to strike inspiration and confidence among the rebels.

He looked down his nose at the guards and said, "Tell the Council Supreme we will meet with them tomorrow at dawn at the High Temple of the Suns."

Yiis stepped forward. "They will have the opportunity to resign with dignity."

"The Council Supreme has no honor!" someone from the crowd shouted.

The guards looked about to determine who had spoken, but faced only a sea of obdurate animosity. The commanding officer of the guards lowered his weapon and took a step forward. He met Bran's gaze without flinching.

"We will inform them, but you must accompany us."

"Do you guarantee upon your honor that Brannal cen'Vyr will not be harmed?" Gil demanded.

"We will not harm him," the commanding officer promised.

"Not good enough," Yiis stated. "Guarantee Brannal cen'Vyr will not be harmed."

"I cannot do that," the officer said. "I do not command the entirety of the Guard Supreme."

"I will go," Bran said in a low voice so as not to be heard by anyone other than Pako or Gil.

"They're likely to order your immediate execution," Gil pointed out.

"Then you will avenge my death and lead the rebellion," Bran said. *I fully expect treachery by the council. They have no honor.*

"I know the Guard Supreme's commander," the Omari Prime murmured. "I'll contact him."

"What leverage do you have over him?" Gil asked, sotto voce.

"He owes me a favor."

Gil nodded. The details were not important.

"I will go with you," Bran called out. A hush fell over the crowd. "As everyone sees, I go peacefully!"

"Aggression will be met with death!" Yiis yelled.

Pako then shouted, "Brannal cen'Vyr will join us tomorrow at dawn at the High Temple of the Suns—unharmed—accompanied by the Council Supreme, or there will be blood!"

The crowd erupted in cheers and shouts as Bran descended the steps to join the guards in the street. He met the commanding officer with a curt nod and did not challenge the guards who surrounded him. The officer ordered the guards to march forward, and the crowd parted to allow them to pass.

Gil looked at Pako, his expression worried. "This won't go well."

"Probably not," Pako agreed, his own expression grim. "At the very least, they'll torture him."

They turned to walk back inside the building.

"As long as they do not kill him, they will claim to have not harmed him," Gil said.

"They'd better take more care than not killing him," Pako said. "Amputation, castration—anything that permanently alters him will be considered harm, and I will ensure every member of the Council Supreme dies for it."

Yiis nodded. "What they should understand is that Bran's death will definitely mean outright revolt and sanction their own executions."

Gil sighed. "Let's hope they're not that stupid."

Pako snorted, expressing his doubt. "I have to contact the Guard Supreme's commander and remind him of his debt of honor to me. Gil, you and Yiis deal with the rest of our council-to-be. There's not a warrior among them, and they'll need reassurance."

Gil nodded. "They are not warriors, but several of them are wickedly smart. We'd do ourselves a disservice to underestimate them."

"Intelligence combined with cowardice does not impress me," Pako muttered before turning down the hallway toward the room he shared with Yiis.

Gil and Yiis stopped walking to turn around and extend their arms to prevent their co-conspirators from following him. "Leaders, let us meet and discuss our next steps."

The group of sixteen males, eight dyads representing the diverse castes of Urib society except for the warrior caste, followed Yiis and Gil to a large conference room where they began to hammer out a list of demands to present to the currently reigning Council Supreme and a list of concessions they were willing to make for the sake of compromise and progress.

Although everyone hoped for a peaceful regime change, only the two warrior triads did not fear the outburst of violent rebellion.

Revolution was due.

And blood would flow.

CHAPTER 28

As the days passed, Ursula maintained her frosty, resentful silence, only speaking to Zul whenever necessary. She'd realized the futility of trying to badger information from the castrati and the berserker.

Outwardly, Zul's stoic demeanor did not waver, but he felt like raging. He sensed her enduring anger through their bond, and she remained cold to any romantic overtures. Touching her when she obviously resented his touch made his hearts and gut clench, and he dared not attempt to tease or persuade her. In short, he found himself at an impasse.

Having only recently known the joy and fulfillment of being mated, the denial of her affection left him feeling frozen and, dared he admit it, angry as well. What right did she have to deny him? However, she never once told him no or demanded he not touch her. Instead, she ignored his touch even as she pretended to ignore his words. True, he could have forced her to submit, but, if he gave into that impulse, Zul knew such forced intimacy would turn whatever affection she had for him to fear and hatred—and that he could not endure.

The reality and delicacy of daily life with a female shattered his previously uninformed ideal of an always willing and available mate who'd make no demands upon him beyond welcoming bedsport. The layered complexity of this female drew his grudging respect even as she denied him physical intimacy. Before being mated, he'd never considered a female capable of thoughts and wishes and dreams that did not reflect her mates' desires.

His emotions raw, Zul scrutinized the daily reports he received from the capital and took small comfort in knowing that as long as the reports came, he needed not to worry for Ursula and Crow's welfare. Daily he tested the triad bond with Bran and Gil, fearing to lose that connection as he had apparently lost the connection with their mate. Bran did not acknowledge the wordless inquiries, but Gil did: *Hold fast.*

Time passed. The season turned. Zul maintained the fiction that Bran and Gil had been deployed for an indefinite length of time. And Ursula continued giving him the silent treatment.

Retreat! The sharp, urgent command came late one night, accompanied by a sharp burst of pain. Zul bolted upright in his lonely bed, every mental alarm ringing and every muscle tensed and ready for battle. He sent an unspoken question along the triad bond, but found the connection blocked. At once, he understood that Bran had cut himself and Gil off to protect him, Ursula, and Crow. Plans they had crafted much earlier now came into play. He remembered Gil's prediction of torture and surmised the cause of Bran's pain, an agony so severe he could not prevent it from traveling across the triad bond.

He left his room and entered the suite where his mate slept. He tiptoed through the room and opened the door. The castratus stationed in the central bedchamber who had been assigned nighttime guard duty—an assignment made without informing the Prima—glanced at him. Zul shut the door behind him and whispered, "Alert Suvesh."

The castratus nodded and raced away to wake Suvesh. Zul entered the bedchamber and squatted beside his mate's bed. Gently placing his hand over her mouth, he whispered, "Wake up, *elska'adir.*"

Ursula's eyelids flipped open. Seeing a dark figure looming over her, she screamed, but the hand pressed over her mouth stifled the sound. Terrified, she began to struggle.

"Hush, Ursula," Zul ordered both aloud and through the emotional bond that still connected them. Panting through her nose, her body grew still. His voice low and thrumming with urgency, he said, "We must leave."

"Crow?" she asked, her lips rubbing against his palm.

"Suvesh has him."

Ursula misunderstood, and her eyes flashed with hot fury. "He belongs with *me*."

Zul wasted no time on apologies. "They will meet us in the stableyard."

Ursula closed her eyes in relief: Zul did not intend to separate her from her son. When he removed his hand from her face, she hissed, "What's going on?"

He ignored her question. "Get dressed in your most practical clothes and pack enough for a few days. Pack only the essentials. *Quickly*. We must leave."

Zul retreated to his suite where he dressed for battle. Their transportation would soon arrive.

Ursula glared at the bedchamber door and pressed her lips together to stem the questions that clogged her throat and crowded her mouth. Obedient to the urgency she felt through their bond, she rose naked from her bed and headed for the en suite bathing room where she emptied her bladder before digging out her most practical clothes—which weren't very—and getting dressed.

As her skirts swished around her legs, she wished for a much more practical pair of blue jeans. However, she had to make do with the garb Urb culture deemed appropriate for females. At least the fine fabric was made of some type of dark wool rather than the filmy, floaty, pastel-colored cloth her mates preferred she wear. She pulled on stockings and quickly fastened the buckles on her boots.

Dressed, she pulled out the bag she used when visiting Omari for two or three days. She understood "packing lightly" meant no jewelry. With a lingering glance at the chest containing her jewelry, she sighed, then got to the business of pragmatism, determined no one would have reason to accuse her of being frivolous. She drew on a shawl, then buckled the bag closed and slung the strap over her shoulder.

Emerging from her suite, she raised her gaze to Zul's, noticing that he carried two large satchels and wore his battle kilt and boots, and asked, "What's going on?"

Again, he did not answer her. "Come."

Clenching her jaw, she followed him. Carrying two bags, Zul moved swiftly and silently through the manor, a stealthy progress which Ursula decided shouldn't have been possible considering his size. Following him, she caught the dull glint of dark metal and realized Zul wore more than his battle kilt: he was garbed in full battle regalia. A tube of sharp spikes was affixed to the end of his tail. Spiked spaulders protected his shoulders and greaves his shins. Gauntlets covered the backs of his hands, but left his talons bare. Short, sharp fins protruded from the vambraces on his forearms. Lethal spurs were strapped to his legs and protruded at wicked angles from behind his ankles. A gorget protected his throat and clavicles. Beneath the gorget, he wore a heavy shirt like a hauberk, but it wasn't made of metal. A spiked plate of metal covered the span of his skull between his horns.

Ursula wondered if she'd need armor, too. Would Crow? Would Suvesh?

Her footsteps stuttered to a stop when she saw long, sinuous necks, the dull gleam of scales beneath the dim illumination of the moon, and the malevolent glint of reptilian eyes. She did not notice Zul dropping the two satchels to the ground.

"What the *hell* are those?" she hissed.

Long, heavy reins dropped from thick rings at the beasts' auditory openings. Castrati held on to those reins with grim determination, each also holding a goad. A wet gurgle sounded from one of the beasts.

"Our transportation to safety," Zul said.

"They look like they'd rather eat us than not," she objected. "Crow is not getting near one of those evil things."

Zul fixed her gaze with his. "We have no time for debate. Crow will ride with Suvesh, and you will ride with me."

"Not on that thing."

"Yes, on that thing." He did not try to tell her it was perfectly safe because, as she'd reminded him more than once, she wasn't stupid. One of the beasts yawned, displaying fearsome teeth.

Reluctant to take one step nearer the beasts or to let Crow near it, she objected again, "Won't whatever we're fleeing from be able to track those things?"

"No."

"Mama, what's going on?" Crow whined as he and Suvesh joined them, the castratus lugging two satchels slung over one shoulder. He held onto the youngling's hand with his free hand. Crow rubbed his eyes. Suvesh dropped the satchels to the ground.

Zul crouched down to look at the youngling eye to eye and did not attempt to dissemble. "We are in danger and must flee."

Crow jutted out his chin. "I will fight."

Zul nodded. "You may have to. It is your duty to defend your mama at all costs."

"No!" Ursula protested. "I'm his *mother*. It's my duty to protect *him*."

Zul ignored her and handed the child a small knife in its leather sheath. "You are a golden warrior breed. You will not shame your lineage."

The child clutched the sheathed knife and nodded. "I will uphold the honor of my ancestors."

Zul nodded then rose to his full height as Suvesh gently took the knife from the child and attached it to Crow's belt. More castrati darted forward to pick up the satchels and attach them to the beasts' harnesses, positioning the bags so they lay smoothly against each animal's hide and did not protrude too far or hinder movement.

"If you're giving a *child* a weapon, you'd better give me one, too," Ursula hissed.

"No." He reached back to grasp Ursula's hand and glanced at Suvesh. "Mount up."

She gasped as one of the restive beasts snapped out a leathery wing. She squeaked, "That's a fucking dragon!"

Terrified and desperate to grab her son and flee, Ursula tugged her hand, but she could neither break Zul's grip nor slip from it. She shrieked when he tossed her up into the saddle and huffed when he settled an instant later behind her. She glanced at the other beast to note that Suvesh had mounted the beast with Crow seated in front of him, sheltered by the castratus' body as she was sheltered by Zul's.

"Hold on to the pommel," Zul ordered.

Ursula's hands shot out to clench the padded ridge in front of her. Her knuckles whitened with the tightness of her grasp. Zul and Suvesh picked up the reins, and the servants handed each of them a goad.

"Have they fed recently?" Zul asked the nearest servant.

"At dusk," the servant replied.

Zul nodded and gave the rein a sharp tug. The beast snarled. Suvesh did the same, and the beast he and Crow rode turned its head to deliver a baleful glare. Ursula looked over to her son who clutched the pommel and stared at the dragon with wide-eyed awe.

"You know where we're going?" Zul asked.

"No!" Ursula snapped.

"I know our first stop," Suvesh replied, indicating that he understood wherever they landed would not be where they stayed.

"If we are separated, you know what to do," Zul said.

"Yes, my lord," Suvesh replied. "My honor is yours."

Ursula opened her mouth to object once more, or perhaps demand just what the hell was going on, but her words raced back down her throat in a shrill gasp of terror as the dragon roared and darted forward. Her eyes squeezed shut as the great beast ran several steps. She whimpered when she heard the snap of leathery wings and whimpered again when the beast leaped into the air with a grunt.

Bowing her head against the rushing air, she wheezed, "Please, where are you taking us?"

Zul's grim answer did not reassure her: "To safety."

Ursula shrank against him and lowered her head even more. She ducked to look beneath Zul's outstretched arm and felt her gorge rise. She gagged and swallowed, managing not to vomit as she peered past the huge flapping wings to see the other dragon flying behind them. She could not see her son cuddled against Suvesh's body, but she did catch a glimpse of the castratus who appeared to be handling the dragon with skill and confidence.

Her wordless surprise reverberated across the mate bond. Zul addressed it with a calm reply, *Suvesh's family raises and trains wyverns.*

Wyverns? What the hell is a wyvern? Thoroughly discombobulated, Ursula forgot her resentful anger. *And won't they be tracked?*

It's highly unlikely.

Please tell me what's happened. Are Bran and Gil …

They're alive. That's all I know. Zul did not lie; he knew they were alive because Bran kept the triad bond blocked. If they were dead, that connection would have disappeared and Gil would have taken charge of it.

Ursula shuddered with relief. *I assume something went very, very wrong with Bran and Gil's revolution.*

Yes.

Do you know what?

Not yet.

When you do, will you tell me?

When it's safe to do so.

She sighed. *I hate you sometimes.*

I know.

CHAPTER 29

Ursula fell asleep cuddled against Zul's broad body as the wyverns carried them through the night. When they arrived at their first destination, the beasts were weary and subdued and disinclined to hunt. Zul knew they would rest before hunger and thirst drove them to hunt for meat and water.

He hoped the beasts would head for home, but doubted Suvesh's family would be so lucky. The Fangrys Triad would have to reimburse them for the loss of such valuable beasts. Regardless, he, Suvesh, Crow, and Ursula needed to move beyond the wyverns' notice or become prey themselves.

"Can you carry the boy?" Zul asked, his voice a hoarse whisper.

Suvesh nodded as he slung the straps of the two satchels over his shoulders. Crow, exhausted, slept curled at Suvesh's booted feet. "Do you know where we are going, my lord?"

Zul nodded. "It's a place I've visited many times over the years."

He shrugged the straps of the other satchels over his shoulders and scooped Ursula into his arms, cradling her against his chest.

Without further discussion, Zul started walking. The small, wiry castratus—still taller than the hybrid female—picked up the exhausted youngling and followed in his footsteps. He wondered why Suvesh had pursued a life in domestic service and submitted to castration, but did not voice his curiosity. Of greater importance was the castratus' strength, stamina, and loyalty.

They walked for hours, the first hour at speed to put as much distance between them and the wyverns as possible before the beasts roused themselves to hunt. He'd landed them near a water hole where wildlife gathered to drink for that very reason: the wyverns would prefer easily found prey. He just hoped there were no other wyverns in the area. Perhaps there would be an oryxis. The wyverns would enjoy the vicious fight after which they could gorge upon its flesh. Engorged wyverns tended to be sluggish, which would also work in their favor.

Zul varied their speed as they hiked across the high desert, alternating the speed of a battle march with the less strenuous pace of a parade march. As the horizon brightened, Zul adjusted his direction. It was easier navigating at dawn than in the darkness of night.

Ursula stirred. "Wha… who?" She blinked against the early morning sunshine aiming for her eyes. She began to squirm, and the arms confining her tightened.

"Settle," Zul ordered.

Her eyes flew open, and she remembered what was happening. "Where are we? Where is Crow?"

"Suvesh is right behind us carrying Crow," Zul replied. "We've another two leagues to go before we can stop."

Ursula tried to remember how long a league was, then gave up. A Urib league was measured differently than an imperial league which was three miles. She squirmed again. "I can walk."

"I can walk faster," Zul replied, not lying but also not telling her that he'd rather enjoyed carrying his mate and relished the press of her body against his.

"I have to pee."

"Mama? Mama!"

"My lord?"

Zul stopped and reluctantly set his mate down, ensuring she was steady on her feet before relinquishing his hold. Crow ran to his mother who crouched down and opened her arms to embrace him. He watched in silence as mother and son held each other.

"Relieve yourselves, then we'll proceed."

"But Crow—" Ursula automatically began to protest.

"Crow is a golden warrior breed. He will not suffer for walking," Zul said.

Ursula looked at Suvesh who nodded and ventured to offer his opinion, "He is bred for strength, endurance, and speed."

"But he's just a little boy," she objected.

"He will grow to be an elite Urib warrior. Trust in Lord Zul's judgment."

Ursula cast a sour look at the berserker then a worried look at Crow. "Crow, you will tell me if and when you get tired."

The boy nodded. "Yes, Mama."

She took his hand and looked around for a suitable spot to relieve themselves. "We'll be just beyond that clump of shrubbery."

Zul nodded in approval and dug out a canteen from one of the satchels. Suvesh did the same.

"You are well-prepared, Suvesh."

The castratus accepted the compliment with a small, closed-mouth smile. "Breeding and training wyverns demands resourcefulness and acceptance of hardship. I've spent more than one night in the wilderness, my lord."

Zul nodded. "Bran chose well when he hired you to care for the youngling."

Suvesh favored him with another small smile after he took a drink and wiped his mouth. "Actually, it was Lord Gil who hired me."

Zul nodded. "I stand corrected."

Ursula and Crow rejoined them. Zul offered her his canteen, and Suvesh offered his to Crow, murmuring, "Just a small sip, no more."

"But I'm thirsty!" the boy protested as his mother looked on, holding the canteen in her hands. He turned a pleading look at Ursula.

"We must not squander our resources," Suvesh said.

"Just drink a little as Suvesh says," Ursula said. "We can have more later."

Crow sighed and nodded and raised the canteen to his lips. After he swallowed his mouthful of water and handed the canteen back to Suvesh, Ursula took a drink, restricting herself to a small sip as she'd advised her son. Zul's gaze heated as she licked her lips to catch every last drop of moisture. She handed the canteen back to him and smoothed the loose strands of hair away from her face.

"Ready?" Zul asked.

Ursula nodded and stooped to pick up one of the satchels, determined to share the workload.

"No."

She looked up at him. "I can help."

"These are heavy, and you will need your strength to keep up," he said and gently took the strap from her hand.

Ursula huffed, but did not bother to argue. A moment later, she held Crow's hand as they walked behind Zul and Suvesh followed them.

Crow endured better than his mother expected, and she endured less well than she expected of herself. After she stumbled a second time, Zul turned on his heel and scooped her into his arms.

"Hey!"

"Settle," he ordered.

She squirmed. "I can walk."

"You are weary already."

Ursula huffed in disgust with her own lack of strength and stamina. "I ought to be in better shape."

"You are female."

"That has nothing to do with it. Besides, I'm too heavy to carry."

Zul snorted. She hardly weighed more than two of the packs he carried.

"I'm going to have to start exercising after we get back home," she muttered. After a pause, she asked, "We will go back home, won't we?"

"I hope so," he replied, not sure there would be a home to go back to. If the Council Supreme succeeded in squelching the rebellion, they'd raze the manor to the ground, have both Gil and Bran executed, and confiscate their wealth. If that happened, he would be responsible for ensuring his mate and her son had sufficient food, clothing, and shelter. Perhaps he could find work as a mercenary or a guard on some other planet, because exile from Uribern would be the less lethal option. Would a pampered Ahn'hudin mogul hire a mated Urib berserker? And he had to hope that the Council Supreme did not set their sights on Ursula or Crow as traitors in collusion with Bran and Gil, but one could not count upon the sensibility of the ruling council members.

Ursula continued questioning him. "Why are we not riding the wyverns?"

"Their range is limited before they must rest."

"And after they rest?"

"Then they hunt. We did not carry meat for them."

"And we can't wait for them to hunt?"

"Not if they're going to hunt us."

"Hunt us?" She frowned. "Aren't they, like, domesticated?"

"No. Anyone who claims to have tamed a wyvern is lying. The beasts can be trained, but never tamed."

Ursula stopped asking questions.

By the time they reached the small box canyon Zul remembered from his decades of wandering, Suvesh was once again carrying the youngling. The castratus, although surprisingly tough, was nearing the end of his strength and endurance, too.

"We're here," Zul announced quietly as he scanned the space from where they stood at the canyon mouth.

High walls of jagged rock rose on either side of them. Out of sight around a corner, the music of falling water resounded. The small pool flowed into a rushing stream limned by a thin line of gravel and sand which gave way to a spread of wiry grass, rocks, scrubby trees, and brush before more walls of rock rose to tower heights.

"What is this place?" Ursula asked. "It looks like Box Canyon State Park in Idaho, but a lot smaller."

"It has no name that I've discovered," Zul replied. "But I have stayed here many times. It's a good place for a respite."

Suvesh glanced around and nodded. "Small game only. The wyverns would not be interested."

"And they prefer less enclosed spaces," Zul added.

Suvesh nodded. "They do." He glanced up at the craggy walls, noting the holes in the rock. "There may be an oryxis or two lurking in those caves."

Zul shook his head. "Oryxis can't climb that well. There are some smaller predators—kodos and yirklas—but they'll likely avoid us."

"What are kodos and yirklas?" Ursula asked.

"Yirklas are …" Zul's voice trailed off as he struggled to come up with a description his mate would understand.

"Yirklas are a bit like the wild dogs of Africa on Earth," Suvesh said.

"How do you know about the wild dogs of Africa?" Ursula asked.

"Crow's mother is from Earth, so Crow should know something of her home planet." He glanced at the youngling who had begun to wander off. "The wildlife of Earth interests him."

"Okay," Ursula said, frowning. "You do know that wild dogs are fierce hunters and *never get tired*. They tear their prey apart and begin eating it before it's dead." She shuddered.

"Much like yirklas," Suvesh replied. "Crow, return to me."

The boy sighed and obeyed.

"And what are kodos?" she asked Suvesh, as the castratus seemed to have knowledge that Zul did not.

"The name and form of a kodo is similar to that of your planet's komodo dragons," Zul answered. He felt proud for making that comparison. He'd spent a lot of time with Crow and Suvesh learning about Earth's wildlife from the many books Gil had imported from her homeland at Ursula's request.

"Oh, *hell* no!" Ursula shook her head. "I am *not* staying where komodo dragons roam freely—and neither is Crow."

"We will keep you and Crow safe from predation," he assured her. Suvesh nodded his commitment to their well-being.

Crow drew himself up to his full height which was still quite a bit shorter than his mother and said with solemn conviction, "I am not afraid."

Ursula opened her mouth to object again, then merely sighed and shook her head. She glared at Zul. "If the dragons or wild dogs eat us, then we're coming back to haunt you."

CHAPTER 30

Ursula watched as Crow and Suvesh scouted a somewhat level place and set up camp. She considered asking why two tents were set up, then decided against questioning the decision. *Doubtless they have valid reasons.* Besides, she was weary. *Sick and tired of arguing and losing, more like.*

The stinging candor came from her own conscience rather than one of her mates. Once the tents were erected, Zul set Suvesh to gathering firewood while he scraped out a shallow firepit.

"The fire will deter the predators from approaching," he said after she offered to assist in setting up camp and he declined that offer, telling her instead to keep a close eye on her son.

Ursula did that anyway. No one needed to remind her.

Suvesh soon returned with an armful of sticks, and Zul sent him out for more. "Best to build up a supply just in case we're out here longer than expected."

"And how long do we expect to be out here?" Ursula probed.

Zul did not answer her.

Finally, she sighed and repositioned herself on the boulder she sat upon. "Zul, we're entirely out of touch. We have no communication devices that I'm aware of. Why can't you tell me what's going on?"

He met her gaze and his hands stilled. "I do not know what is going on—"

Ursula scoffed. He frowned at her.

"—and Bran has cut off all communication."

She rolled her eyes. "So, talk to Gil."

He blinked in confusion. Did she not understand how the triad bond worked between bonded warriors? "I cannot."

Her head tilted to one side. "Why not?"

"That is not the way the triad bond works."

"Why not?"

Why was she asking questions like a child? Her persistence annoyed him, but he stifled that annoyance and returned his focus to laying sticks in the firepit.

"Do you think you must go through Bran to speak with Gil?" she asked, ignoring his refusal to discuss this triad bond further. "Bran's not a switchboard. You can communicate with Gil directly. After all, I can communicate with each of you directly without having to involve the other two if I want."

Zul went still. Raising his head, he asked in astonishment, "You can do that?"

"Well, duh! Yes, I can do that. I can have mental conversations with one of you without the other two overhearing. It's helpful when it comes to discussing things like holiday gifts." She shook her head. "That's how I managed to surprise Bran for Christmas last year."

"Christmas?" he echoed, wondering what that was. Then he shook his head and refocused. "You can speak mind-to-mind to any one of us without going through Bran?"

Ursula sighed. "Yes, Zul. That's what I just said." She paused and frowned. "Did you not realize that?"

Zul looked down at his hands because, no, he had not realized that was possible. The concept astonished him, as he'd always known that his former prime listened in on his every communication with their second and vice versa. He was simultaneously astonished at the trust Bran gave him and the freedom that trust offered.

Ursula interpreted his silence and his grim expression correctly. Heart breaking for him, she got down from the boulder and moved beside him, setting her hand on his arm. "I'm so sorry, Zul. I didn't realize you didn't know about... about..." She sighed in a moment of comprehensive forgiveness for not keeping her informed. "Anyway, I'll quit pestering. I'm sure not knowing aggravates you as much as it does me."

He looked at her hand on his arm.

Thinking about how micromanaging and controlling his former prime was, Ursula said, "You know, Zul, your former prime was a real asshole."

Zul shook his head and chuckled, his shoulders relaxing from the tension they'd carried. He ran the back of one knuckle down her cheek and said, "Yes, *elska'adir*, my former prime was a real asshole."

She gave him a smile and returned to her boulder. "Crow, you're wandering too far. Come closer!"

"Ah, Mama, do I have to?"

"Yes, you have to."

The youngling pouted as he dragged his feet in obedience to his mother's command.

Ursula looked at Zul and asked, "Will you ask Gil? Or at least try? The mate bond does not stretch so far."

Zul blinked, astonished again. He'd not realized that the bond between mates was weaker—or at least shorter—than the bond between triad warriors.

Once again, she interpreted his expression correctly. "I think the warrior bond is stronger because it's a matter of survival. If distance means a failure to communicate, then one of you dies which means that your mate cannot conceive young and perpetuate the species."

"You've given this some thought," he commented.

Ursula pointed to herself and simply repeated what she'd said before: "I'm female. That doesn't mean I'm stupid."

He dipped his chin in acknowledgement, beginning to understand how keeping her ignorant had both offended and insulted her. "I am sorry, *elska'adir*."

"For not keeping me informed?"

He nodded.

"I won't say it's okay, because it's not. However, I realize that you and my other two mates don't always understand that having information is *always* better than ignorance—even when I can't do anything to change the circumstances." Again, she tilted her head while keeping her wandering son in her peripheral vision. "How realistic is it that the Council Supreme would arrest me and torture me for information?"

Again, he was impressed by her insight. "Quite likely, actually. While females may not have political power, they are still governed by our laws and held accountable."

"You know that's not fair."

"Life's not fair," he muttered.

Ursula snorted. "Yeah, I've gathered that. But shouldn't the governed have a say in the governing?"

He looked at her, not quite understanding.

"I know you do research and look up the wildlife of Earth because you believe that Crow should know a bit about his mother's home planet—and I approve of it. I think it's wonderful. But perhaps you might want to do a little research on the women's suffrage movement on Earth. Remember what I told you about women's circumstances before the 1920s? They were much like females here on Uribern: legally chattel and ceasing to exist as distinct legal entities upon marriage—er, mating—but they were also held to the same legal accountability as men without having anything close to the same rights and privileges. For anyone remotely intelligent, that's offensive."

Zul blinked and listened.

"I've done a bit of research: not much, just a bit. I'm not a historian," she admitted. "But I cannot help drawing parallels between Urib society now and U.S. society before the 1920s. For a culture with such advanced technology that Earth would traffick women in exchange for access to some of that technology, Uribern is incredibly backward in its societal attitude toward women... er... females."

Slowly, he asked, "And what do you want on behalf of all females?"

"Well, Urib males elect their Council Supreme, don't they?"

Zul shook his head. "Retiring council members appoint their successors."

Her eyes widened. "Oh, that's not fair at all! The Council Supreme doesn't represent the people then, does it?"

"No, it doesn't. That is what Bran, Gil, and their co-conspirators are trying to change."

Ursula nodded, glad to have confirmation. "Then their revolution is long overdue."

"Do you really think so?"

She nodded, a decisive gesture. "Yes, I do." She took a breath and gazed into the distance, then shouted at her wandering son, "Crow, get back here!"

Zul glanced at the child and darted toward him, seeing what the child and his mother had not: a lurking predator. Claws extended, he roared and pounced on a kodo that stalked an easy meal. The kodo screeched. Crow cried out. Ursula screamed and dashed toward her son. She snatched him in her arms and raced away as Zul dispatched the ferocious lizard with brutal efficiency. Clutching her son, she saw the size of the kodo and shuddered. It was at least six feet long from snout to tail and had to weigh more than she did.

Lifting the dead animal in his right arm, Zul grinned and said, "We'll dine on fresh meat tonight."

CHAPTER 31

Ursula lost count of the days they spent in that box canyon. Zul noted the loss of her appetite and commented upon it. She brushed it off as a distaste for the monotony of their diet and took pains not to let him witness the occasional bout of nausea. The few times she could not conceal it, she passed it off as a human reaction to their diet because the hardship of camping, despite the supplies Zul and Suvesh brought, made every day seem longer than it really was. In addition and quite simply, maintaining an acceptably modern standard of cleanliness when camping just wasn't possible without a great deal of effort that none of the males were willing to accept. Crow, like most little boys, enjoyed being dirty.

At least the water in the stream flowing through the canyon was potable. Or maybe it wasn't, and that was the problem. There was nothing else to drink, so they drank what was available. The assumed potability of the water saved her hours and hours of needing to boil it before consumption to avoid dysentery, cholera, or whatever other nasty alien bacteria lurked in wait to cause diarrhea, belly cramps, fever, vomiting and other misery-inducing symptoms. Unfortunately, cold water simply wasn't effective at cleaning lizard grease off their limited cookware. Perhaps that grease had gone rancid? Ursula considered the time and effort of boiling water to clean the lizard grease.

And, ugh, she was sick and tired of eating game. Except for the small, carefully hoarded and sparingly consumed store of dried fruits and nuts brought along in satchels from the manor, their diet consisted of meat, meat, and more meat. If she'd brought her some of her jewelry, she would have traded it all for a handful of fruit and vegetables, but there was no trade to be made.

Privacy, in addition to fruits and vegetables and modern standards of hygiene, was another luxury she was forced to abandon, especially after nearly being attacked by a pack of hungry yirklas. Only her shriek of terror had caught both Zul and Suvesh's attention and saved her from being mauled to death. Zul, who had been hunting, somehow managed to move fast enough to put himself between the yirklas and his mate. Upon seeing his metamorphosis from the Zul she knew into the enraged berserker, Ursula understood why they'd assigned him to the duty of protecting her and Crow.

After that incident, Ursula wondered how Zul had managed to camp out there by himself without falling prey to the predators that called the box canyon home. Ursula resented not being able to perform necessary biological functions without someone standing guard over her—and that someone was almost always Zul. Zul did not want Suvesh performing that intimate duty, so Ursula did her best to wait until he returned from hunting.

She hated thinking that the box canyon with its primitive conditions, inconvenience, and dangerous predators was the safest place for them, but she did not challenge his decision to stay or demand to move elsewhere. Instead, she held her tongue, kept a watchful eye on her son when Suvesh wasn't otherwise occupied, and endured. Zul hunted, Suvesh cleaned the game and cooked it, and Ursula cleaned up afterward. After the first few meals, she enlisted Crow's help, although the boy protested.

"If you want to eat, then you help with the work," she said.

"Do as your mama says," Zul added.

She enlisted her son's assistance with other domestic chores, too. Both of them helped Suvesh gather wood and keep the fire burning. Ursula and Suvesh constantly hauled water in the two collapsible buckets they had. Ursula was surprised at the volume of water they used and looked for ways to minimize that consumption without further relinquishing cleanliness. Ursula even demanded Crow assist with washing their meager wardrobes in the stream. The lack of laundry soap meant their clothing remained stained even though they were rinsed clean.

Keeping their earlier conversation in mind, she asked Zul only once if he'd been able to communicate with Gil. He nodded and offered no further information. His reticence aggravated her, but she had no desire to argue with him again. Or was it still? She'd lost track and appreciated sleeping in the protective embrace of Zul's arms too much to maintain the frosty silence she'd treated him to back in Fangrys. Ursula liked to consider herself practical when need be—and sleeping safe and warm within her berserker's embrace was much better than lying cold and alone, separated from the hard ground by a mere blanket.

Zul watched as her cheeks lost fullness and her ribs became prominent despite the gentle roundness of her belly. She was losing weight, and he did not like it. However, he was unwilling to subject her to a trek across the desert to the nearest bastion of civilization where they could be identified and arrested.

One evening after a supper killed that day and cooked over the fire, she asked as Suvesh listened with ill-concealed interest, "How did you know to bring us here?"

"This is a place I stayed often enough during the years I wandered after my Prime and Second were killed," Zul replied.

She shook her head. "No, that's not what I meant. How did you know to leave Fangrys that night?"

"Ah." He nodded and decided to give her as much honesty as he dared. "Bran, Gil, and I made plans. If circumstances were such that it was prudent to flee to secure your safety, then they would order me to retreat. Gil relayed the order."

"And?" she prompted.

Zul shrugged. "He ordered me to retreat and cut off communication." He made no mention of Bran having cut off communication first.

Ursula rolled her lips between her teeth as she absorbed the information, sparse as it was. "And have you checked in with Gil since then?"

"Yes, you know I have." He did not mention how often; that wasn't important.

She closed her eyes, taking a moment to master her easily aroused temper. Composing herself, she asked in an even tone, "Is there any information you can give me? Any reassurance as to whether Bran even lives?"

"He lives," Zul replied. "How do you not sense this?"

She took a breath then explained again, trying to make him understand: "Remember, I told you that the mental connection of a mate bond disappears over great distances."

He nodded.

"I don't know how far we are from the capital, but I'm sure it's a lot further than a day or night's flight on a wyvern."

He nodded again.

"That distance doesn't make the connection go away," she rubbed her palm against her breastbone. "It's more like the connection goes quiet as if it were waiting to pick up the signal again." She shook her head, unsure whether her description made sense. "It's not an absence or void like I felt after Crow died. It's a... a... stillness, a *waiting*." She realized she was rubbing that spot over her heart raw and moved her hand to her lap. "I don't know how else to describe it."

"Bran lives," Zul said again, offering that small reassurance. Then he ripped it away because withholding the information likely did more harm than divulging it. "Gil told me he was tortured."

"*Tortured?*" she cried out.

"Bran did not reveal our location because he does not know it. He stayed strong."

"Oh, poor Bran! And Gil?"

"Gil is surrounded by his fellow rebels, and they are more than enough to intimidate the Guard Supreme." He paused. "In fact, Gil told me it was the Omari Prime who persuaded the commander of the Guard Supreme not to torture Bran to the extent the governing council wished. He managed to convince them that severing a limb or two or blinding him or something else fundamentally damaging would enrage the populace and backfire on them."

"Severing a limb? *Blinding* him?" Ursula echoed faintly. "That's *barbaric!*"

Zul agreed. "Gil informed me this afternoon that Bran was returned to his care."

"How is he?"

"Injured. Badly so. But he's alive and in possession of all his necessary parts."

She looked away in an effort to master her emotions, then she raised tear-filled eyes to him. "Zul, I need to return to him—them."

He nodded. "And they need you. But they also need you to be safe, and that is what Bran and Gil charged me to do: keep you and Crow safe. I will do that to my last breath."

"I know," she replied, her voice soft with acceptance. She looked away, eyes focused in the dark distance and not seeing anything beyond the orange flicker of fire in her peripheral vision. "I'm *so* ready for this to end."

Zul was, too, but he was determined never to lie to her again and refused to offer false comfort. "I will let you know the moment it is safe to return home."

She returned her gaze to his, solemn and steady. "I'll hold you to that."

CHAPTER 32

The meeting at the High Temple of the Suns had not gone well, and the council members who deigned to meet with the revolutionaries had reneged on their agreement to turn Bran over to them. The Supreme Council's perfidy resulted in violent backlash, and much of the capital city now lay in rubble. Victory was bittersweet, but what remained of the Guard Supreme finally delivered Bran to Gil's care. Yiis wasted no time summoning a physician.

Gil urged the physician to greater effort to save his Prime. Bran looked worse than Crow had after the berserker's last, fatal battle. He tried to console himself with the fact that the Guard Supreme had not lopped off any limbs, although no other part of Bran's body remained free of damage. Contusions, lacerations, and burns covered him from pate to tail tip to toenails, some of which had been pulled out. The council had not fed him well, either, if the protrusion of his ribs and general gauntness were any indication.

The physician withdrew the flexible tube which delivered both sustenance and healing agents directly into Bran's veins. He looked up and sighed. "That's all I can do for now. The rest is up to him."

Gil understood what the physician did not say: that Bran needed the full complement of his bonds. They would give him the connections of encouragement, love, mental and emotional strength, and support he needed to live. The physician could only tackle the physical damage.

His consciousness traveled up the triad bond which still remained silent. He paused at the barrier Bran had erected to keep his pain and suffering from flooding the connection and igniting Zul's berserker rage where that rage could not be relieved without hurting those whom they cared about. Gil wanted to think that Bran had sought to spare him, too. Bran was noble like that.

However, Bran was now weak and the barrier flimsy. Gil broke through it with ease, although it would have been more accurate to say he dismantled it. Dismantling involved guile and subtlety, not brute force. Sliding through the thin barrier to the core of the connection, he found the blood-red strand that led to Zul. With ghostly fingers, he plucked the strand.

Zul responded immediately. *Gil.*

Zul. It's time to return. Come to the capital.

There was a brief pause. *How is Bran?*

Bad. He needs all of us here—you, Ursula, and Crow.

We'll come as quickly as we can. There was another pause. *How goes the rebellion?*

Gil snorted. *I think we won, but it feels like a hollow victory. The populace is in an uproar. Two members of the Council Supreme were killed. The city is in ruins.*

Were they assassinated?

Gil snorted again. *They were challenged and they lost.* He paused, thinking how their ancient laws of right by combat had actually worked in their favor. He flexed his hands, relishing the memory of tearing out that smug council member's throat and watching his blood spill onto the arena's sandy floor. Too many assumed him weak because he was the Second, neither the dominant Prime nor the brawny berserker Third. It had been satisfying to prove them wrong and validate himself before his own people as a strong, skilled, and worthy warrior.

He continued his summary report: *Six more abandoned their positions and fled for safety before they, too, could be challenged. The three who remain in the capital cannot govern. The Council Supreme has effectively been defeated.* Gil made no mention of the deployment of troops against the people, the pitched battles within the capital and beyond, the toll of rage, resentment, and death upon Urib society. Zul would see and understand all that soon enough.

You acquitted yourself well, Zul complimented him, catching a mental whiff of Gil's memories of that duel. *Councilor Ur'uki was a skilled fighter.*

That's why he yielded to the council's urging to accept my challenge by combat, Gil replied.

He underestimated you.

Many do.

But they digressed, and Bran's mind grew restless sensing the intrusion of Gil's presence.

Zul, I must go. Come quickly. I will send transportation.

Zul relayed the coordinates for their location and terminated the connection. Knowing that arrival of the conveyance would take time, he added, *Alert us when our transportation is near.*

I will. Sitting at Bran's bedside, Gil returned his focus to his Prime. He took Bran's hand in his, hoping the physical touch would keep his Prime anchored to life. He spoke to Bran, oftentimes nothing more than nonsense, hoping the sound of his voice would draw him back.

As the days passed, Pako, Yiis, and Mosk, who recently arrived with Carmen and their children, took turns with Gil, sitting by Bran's bedside to ensure he knew he would never be left alone or abandoned.

One afternoon, the captain of the Guard Supreme visited the house where they were staying. Mosk greeted him with a blade leveled at his throat and snarled, "What do you want?"

The captain met his gaze with cool respect, but did not step back from the blade's lethal edge. "The Council Supreme has disbanded, and the senior member invites you and the new council to the palace."

Mosk's eyes narrowed with suspicion. "And why would he invite us?"

"The Council Supreme agreed upon a peaceful surrender."

"They do not wish to die," Mosk stated.

"No, they do not, and they understand they cannot refuse honorable challenge by combat," the captain replied, knowing the Fangrys and Omari Triads would decimate the remaining council members in trials by combat. "They also do not want to see Uribern governed by a council made solely of disgruntled warriors."

Overhearing the conversation, Yiis approached Mosk from behind and snorted. "They've finally figured out that a ruling council appointed from a single caste isn't in Uribern's best interests, hm?"

The captain's chin dipped once. Raising it, he replied, "They do care about our planet and its people."

"Not enough," Mosk snapped. He lowered his knife and glanced at Yiis. "What say you?"

Yiis' expression soured. "Brannal cen'Vyr hovers near death."

"I regret his injuries," the captain said, as much of an apology as they were going to get.

"You are responsible for those injuries," Yiis pointed out.

"The Council Supreme wanted worse."

"What's going on?" Gil asked, joining them. He looked drawn and weary. "I heard voices."

"We've been invited to the palace," Mosk explained. "Apparently, the senior member of the Council Supreme wishes to officially transfer power and authority from them to the new governing council."

"I'll need to get word out," Gil said. His lips peeled back from his pointed teeth as he said to the captain, "Guard the senior councilor well and let him know we will come when we are ready *and* when Brannal cen'Vyr is strong enough."

The captain nodded. "I will inform him myself."

"Yes," Mosk murmured. "We wouldn't want the senior councilor to die, would we?"

Yiis leaned forward. "Guard him well, for if that miscreant dies, I'll challenge you myself."

"My lords," the captain replied with a bow. He turned on his heel and walked away.

Before he'd gone three steps, the door closed behind him.

"What do you make of that?" Mosk asked.

"They're aiming for a bloodless hand-off," Yiis replied with a snort. The rebellion had not been bloodless in the least. He shrugged. "It will impart some legitimacy, and we won't be seen as usurpers—or at least not as much so."

Gil rolled his shoulders to ease the kinks of tight, sore muscles. "Each caste will have to elect its own leaders to represent them in the new governing council. That will take some time."

"And blood," Yiis murmured.

Mosk nodded and added, "We'll set a date by which time they must present the leaders they wish to represent them."

Gil shook his head and chuckled.

"What's so amusing?" Yiis asked.

"Our mates would be very proud of us right now."

The other two males paused to ponder that, then they began to laugh.

"And rights for females?" Mosk asked after their moment of mirth.

Gil shrugged. "Ursula once urged me to read her country's Constitution. The revolutionaries who founded her homeland were, indeed, *revolutionary*. But even so, they did not afford females rights: such rights were later added through amendments."

"Do you have a copy of this Constitution?" Mosk asked.

"I do. I'll send it to you to read."

"What right does Ursula expect?" Yiis asked.

"She wants the right to vote, to have a voice in determining the laws that govern her." Gil met their eyes. "After having been ruled by a corrupt Council Supreme for far too long, we want the same, do we not?"

Mosk grinned. "We do."

Yiis nodded. "Carmen will be pleased." He grinned. "And a pleased Carmen is eager to become a *satisfied* Carmen."

"I can't wait," Mosk said, rubbing his hands together. "It has been too long since we fucked our mate."

Gil agreed. It had been too long since he, Bran, and Zul fucked their mate. The next time the four of them joined in the bedchamber, perhaps they would be fortunate enough to impregnate Ursula. She glowed when she was pregnant, so round and ripe and beautiful.

Mosk slapped him on the back of the shoulder. "You look like shit. Get some rest. I'll sit with Bran while you sleep."

"And get something to eat first," Yiis added.

Gil nodded and rubbed the back of his neck. "After I alert the castes. They need to hold elections—and quickly."

CHAPTER 33

"We leave tomorrow," Zul announced as he set down a dead lizard and began to butcher it with efficient skill. Near their tents, Suvesh continued his instruction, teaching Crow about the flora, fauna, rocks, and soil. The boy soaked up such knowledge like a sponge.

Looking up from the stream where she was washing laundry, Ursula lifted up the sodden mass of cloth and wrung it. "What time tomorrow?"

He looked at the sky and his hands stilled during the pause to calculate the distance and travel time. "Afternoon."

Ursula's eyes lit up with hope. "You've heard from Bran?"

"No, from Gil." That light in her eyes dulled. Zul wanted to flinch at the pain he'd unintentionally caused and rushed to fix his error. "Bran lives, *elska'adir*. He *lives*."

She sighed, inferring from his emphasis on "lives" that Bran was in imminent danger of dying. "But he's not well."

Zul refused to lie because his mate was stronger than he'd originally assumed. She preferred truth, even if it hurt. "No, he is gravely injured."

He lifted a hand to give her a reassuring touch, but realized she probably wouldn't appreciate being smeared with lizard blood.

"He needs us," she said.

Zul agreed. "We are stronger together."

Ursula finished wringing the shirt she'd been washing. Rising to her feet, she snapped it free of the tight twist and draped it over a bit of scrub to dry. As she dunked the next piece of clothing in to soak it and begin scrubbing, she said, "How are we getting home? Can Suvesh somehow summon the wyverns?"

Zul looked at the carcass and peeled the scaly hide from the body. "We're going to the capital, not home. Gil is sending transportation. Not the wyverns." He rinsed the gutted and skinned carcass in the stream.

"A flying brick?"

Zul paused, giving her an incredulous look. Then he began to chuckle. "Flying brick indeed. Hah! That's an excellent description."

"How does he know where we are?" Ursula lifted Suvesh's shirt from the water and began to wring it out.

Zul pondered for a split second whether to give her the technical answer or the easy answer. Making his decision, he simply said, "Because I know where we are."

She scoffed. "Oh, that's not vague at all."

"Trust me, *elska'adir*."

"I do." She finished wringing out the shirt, flicked it free of the tight twist, and draped it close to the other shirt to dry. She looked at her hands roughened with the evidence of primitive living. "It will be nice to get back to civilization and modern amenities."

Zul lifted the dripping carcass. "I'll spit this and get it cooking."

She gave him a wry grin. "Mmm, more barbecued lizard. Yummy."

He shook his head and grinned at her sarcasm. He knew the comment was not an indictment of his culinary ability or his effectiveness as a provider, but merely an indication of tiredness. They were all weary of living in such primitive conditions and eating only what he could catch and kill. Luckily for them, Zul was an apex predator. Even the persistent and always-hungry yirklas had quickly learned to avoid him and those he protected. The kodos were not so wise.

He left Ursula kneeling beside the water and headed toward their small campsite where Suvesh had readied the spit with a freshly peeled and sharpened skewer. Glancing at the castratus, Zul admitted that he'd been impressed with Suvesh's resourcefulness and capability. Ursula's, too. She hadn't complained or whined about their circumstances. Instead, she'd risen to the occasion, showing a resilience and toughness he would never have expected from a delicate, pampered human hybrid, particularly a female.

The rest of the day passed as had the ones before. At supper, Zul announced their impending journey and added, "We'll be going to the capital, not home."

Ursula's hands immediately went to patting her hair, and she looked at her clothing which was definitely the worse for wear. "We look like savages."

Zul nodded. He hadn't considered a female's desire to look presentable. He reassured her, "A hot bath and appropriate garb will be available."

She nodded and did not question him as to how he could make that happen. She remembered the journey from the capital to Fangrys had taken days. She knew they were even further away from the city, but she had no way of knowing just how much. She sighed, silently remonstrating with herself for not better familiarizing herself with Uribern's geography.

As she lay in Zul's arms that night, he stroked her hair with a light touch and opened the triad bond. He found the insubstantial barrier weakened by Bran's own terribly weakened state and easily passed through it. He found the thin turquoise thread that represented the connection to Gil and plucked it.

What is it? Gil asked.

Ursula has questions.

Speak.

She worries she will not be presentable.

That's not a question, Zul.

Zul huffed silently, the puff of air ruffling his mate's hair. Gil knew what he meant. He waited rather than bicker. Gil did not disappoint him.

The manor at Fangrys was attacked. The castrati managed to secure the building, but it's damaged.

Is it structurally sound?

I believe so. The castrati were able to remove some of our belongings—

Zul cut him off. *I don't care about my stuff—or yours, for that matter. But our mate...*

Some of her garments were confiscated or destroyed, but the castrati were able to remove most of her clothing and jewelry to a safe location.

Where?

They will not disclose that location. The sheriff informed me that mercenaries hired by the Council Supreme still lurk in the village. It's safe to say that some will be keeping their eyes on the manor, too.

Our garb here is... worn, Zul admitted and dared not dwell on what might have happened to Ursula and Crow had he not gotten them to safety.

Of course, Gil replied, his tone prosaic. *I should have considered that. I will have appropriate garments for all of us shipped to the capital right away.*

Thank you. How are you getting word to the castrati?

The sheriff and mayor allow them access to their communication devices. The council's thugs destroyed ours.

Annoyance rippled through Zul's body and mind. *The Council Supreme has much to answer for.*

Aye, Gil replied and ended the conversation.

Before Zul slipped away from the triad bond, he lingered in Bran's mind and said, *Ursula, Crow, and I are coming. Remain strong. We need you.*

Exhausted by the effort of establishing and holding the connection over such a vast distance, he wasn't sure whether the small eddy of sensation he felt was Bran's wordless acknowledgment or just an insect crawling over his skin.

CHAPTER 34

Transportation sent by Gil waited for them just beyond the narrow entrance to the box canyon. They climbed into the conveyance, carrying their much-depleted packs with them. Zul entered first, ensuring the interior was clear of threats just in case an enemy had sent the transport in lieu of or before Gil's order.

"Wow, pretty luxurious," Ursula commented as she looked around, holding tightly to Crow's hand.

Zul noticed the crest emblazoned in a repeated pattern on the cornice and said nothing. Suvesh cast him a questioning glance, but made no mention of what they both realized: the transport belonged to the Council Supreme. Zul hoped they hadn't just walked into a trap. He was sure the loyal, resourceful castratus was already formulating plans for a quick escape, likely taking Crow with him.

When the door closed, the carriage rose smoothly and silently. After hovering a moment while the passengers secured themselves in their seats, the transport shot high into the air and streaked through the sky toward the nearest tunnel which happened to be even further away from the capital than the box canyon.

But Ursula didn't know that.

Whoever sent the luxuriously appointed carriage had supplied it well.

"Gil works quickly," Zul commented as he opened a chest stashed in one corner. He pulled out clean, new garments. "Suvesh, these looks like they will fit you."

He tossed the clothing to Suvesh who caught them. The castratus looked surprised to have been remembered by his master.

Ursula met the castratus' gaze and said gently, "Gil thinks of everything, doesn't he?"

Suvesh nodded, in awe of the warrior's kindness. In his experience, few masters would remember the welfare of their servants with such thoughtfulness. He closed his eyes in brief, thankful recollection of the memorial service Gil had swiftly organized and conducted for the castrati who had been killed by the rosvoi in defense of their Prima and her son. It had been more impressive than the one the Fangrys servants had organized at their Prima's request.

"And these are Crow's." Zul pulled out a small kilt, a shirt, socks, and shoes.

Zul tossed those to Suvesh, too. The castratus caught them and told the boy who demanded to put on his new clothes, "You must first bathe."

"Mama, do I gotta?"

Ursula grinned at her son's whining. The boy had vastly enjoyed the limited bathing and frequent rolling about in the dirt that seemed to be a hallmark of primitive camping. She supposed that was a trait universal to all young males, regardless of species. "Yes, you gotta."

"Come, Crow," Suvesh said with a gesture of his hand.

The child pouted, but demurred no further. Zul spied a spigot and metal bucket stamped with the Supreme Council's crest. He filled the bucket with warm water and found a cake of soap, washcloth, and towel. While he did that, Ursula spied a folded privacy screen and set it up in front of the grate where water would drip through. Crow didn't mind displaying his nudity, but Ursula had done her level best to maintain a respectable standard of modesty during their short exile, and she was determined to maintain it.

"Do we have enough water for four baths?" she asked.

Zul grinned at her obvious lust for cleanliness. "Yes, and plenty of soap."

Ursula smiled, relief making her shoulders sag. She spread her hands over her thighs and smoothed the worn fabric. "I'll be *so* glad to get out of these rags."

Zul thought she'd looked no more beautiful than when she'd worked alongside him in the box canyon, making them a complementary team of fugitives. "You have endured well."

"I used to go camping with my parents as a child." She shrugged. "They were outdoors enthusiasts, but me? Not so much. I like being outside, but in a tamed environment without poison ivy or chiggers."

Water splashed behind the privacy screen. Zul replied, "What are poison ivy and chiggers?"

"Leaves of three, let them be," Ursula recited the old warning in a sing-song voice. She took a breath. "Poison ivy is a plant—a vine, really—that has leaves coated with an oil… urisole… ursoil… whatever. Ugh. For most people who have the misfortune of coming into contact with it, that oil causes itchy rashes that take *forever* to heal. And chiggers are tiny, bloodsucking insects that burrow into skin and leave nasty, itchy bumps that also take forever to heal."

"I had not realized Earth was such a hostile planet."

Ursula shuddered. "It's not overly hostile—at least not where I lived. But anything that causes a rash or that sucks blood seems to be attracted to me or I to it. I learned in childhood that the wilderness was not my friend. I much prefer well-tended gardens and used to spend a lot of time at the local botanical garden. Admission to the outdoor gardens was free, so I'd spend many mornings or afternoons there sitting on a bench and reading."

Fascinated, Zul asked her to tell him more. Ursula smiled and obliged and asked him questions in kind, having the kind of personal conversation that deepened bonds of family and affection.

After Crow emerged from his bath, clean and garbed in his new clothing, he announced he was hungry.

"Suvesh," Ursula called out, "since I'm sure you've already been well-splashed, why don't you go ahead and bathe? Zul and I will make sure Crow's straight gut and hollow leg are filled."

The castratus poked his head out from behind the screen and looked to Zul for confirmation. The big warrior nodded, turning the Prima's suggestion into an order. He did not protest, knowing the futility of deterring the Prima from any decision she made, especially when any of her mates backed her up. He disappeared behind the screen.

"What is this 'straight gut and hollow leg?'" Zul asked, puzzled. Surely, his mate was not so unfamiliar with anatomy that she did not realize how incorrect that was?

She gave him a small, sad smile. "It's something my grandmother used to say before she died. It describes someone who is always hungry and consumes a lot of food."

Finding the food storage, Zul nodded, catching the visual in his imagination by thinking of his mate's ceramics: a figurine, hollow inside, with an empty belly leading directly into an empty leg, all needing to be filled. With deft efficiency, he assembled a hefty snack for the child and set the plate on a nearby table. Crow attacked the food as if he hadn't eaten in days.

After Suvesh finished bathing, Ursula demanded Zul bathe before she did. He argued that she should go first, but she convinced him by stating, "I plan to soak a good long while. There's no need for you to wait to get clean because I want to wallow in a bit of luxury."

Zul bowed to her reasoning and took a brief but thorough bath so as not to delay her the opportunity to wallow in a bit of luxury.

When Ursula emerged feeling fresh and clean and dressed in one of the floaty, filmy dresses she had previously complained about as being utterly impractical, she, too, availed herself of the food Zul put out for her to eat. All three males shook their heads, not understanding her happiness as she crunched through vegetables and fruits and ignored the meat.

"When we get home, I think I'm going to eat an entire block of cheese," she said with a sigh. "I do miss cheese."

Crow wrinkled his nose. "Cheese is yucky."

She chuckled. "Oh, son, cheese is often an acquired taste. I'm sure you'll like it when you're older."

Crow shook his head. "Nuh-uh."

Zul hoped the youngling his mate would eventually bear him would be just as carnivorous like all proper Uribs.

Soon the conveyance descended into a transportation tunnel and shot through the subterranean network spanning much of Uribern. It emerged to fly over four immense freshwater seas before again descending into the tunnels, connecting with trains when encountering other such carriages, and zipping through the tunnels alone when following its own programmed path. Zul, Ursula, Suvesh, and Crow used the six days of travel time to rest and relax and listen to the news broadcasts.

CHAPTER 35

Pako, Yiis, Mosk, and Carmen greeted them at the terminal. Zul and the Omari Triad watched with indulgent tolerance as the two women embraced and began chattering.

"Where are your boys?" Ursula eventually asked as they walked as a group toward the exit.

"Gil's watching them," Carmen answered, linking one arm with her friend's and resting her other hand on her baby bump. Zul eyed the bulge in suspicion. "You know, he's surprisingly good with children."

Ursula smiled. "I don't think it's all that surprising. Gil's good with people."

"A good Second is," Yiis commented.

"Stop listening, you big oaf. I wasn't talking to you," Carmen retorted with a smile.

"Then speak more softly," he whispered.

"Oh, you!" She smacked him on the arm, and he feigned injury just to make her smile.

Ursula's eyes were wide and her mouth gaped. Bending close to Carmen, she whispered, "Yiis made a joke? Who knew he had a sense of humor?"

"Yiis has hidden depths." Carmen giggled. "Now, Pako" — she used the Spanish pronunciation of "Paco"— "is more of a 'what you see is what you get' kind of man."

"Whizzy-wig," Ursula verbalized the abbreviation, WYSIWYG.

"I wasn't sure you knew that term. You are a generation younger than me."

"My folks used to use that and other terms," Ursula replied. "Hearing them brings back memories."

"Good memories, I hope."

"Yes, mostly."

A beast-drawn carriage picked them up at the curb. Ursula shook her head in disbelief after everyone climbed in and seated themselves. She commented, "I'll never get used to the weird combination of high tech and ancient tech used on this planet."

"I think it's the Urib way of preserving their history and culture," Carmen replied.

Ursula shrugged. "I don't recognize these beasties." She inhaled. "They don't stink like the numpties."

The driver slapped the reins over the beasts' backs, and the carriage, which hovered above the ground, eased forward. The six-legged animals were larger than the numpties, scaled (unlike the hairy numpties), and appeared to be of a similar phlegmatic temperament. Ursula wondered why they didn't use these strange beasts instead of numpties in Fangrys, and asked.

"They're not native to that part of the continent," Pako answered. "The capital is several thousand leagues north of Fangrys and Omari, so flora and fauna are adapted to the different climate here."

Ursula nodded, accepting the explanation, recalling that even in the USA, animals and plants at similar latitudes differed from East Coast to West Coast. Southern California didn't have alligators, but Georgia certainly did.

Ursula pressed her lips together at the widespread destruction and said nothing about it. The evidence of violent revolution needed no explanation. Instead, they discussed inconsequential topics during the ride to the large house where Gil and Bran and the Omari Triad were staying. It wouldn't have done for the driver or anyone else to overhear anything important or incriminating.

"Papa Gil!" Crow shouted when they arrived. Gil stood in the open doorway, Carmen's children peering from behind him.

Pako descended from the carriage first, then Yiis who handed Carmen to his Prime. Gil emerged from the house and nodded in greeting to them. Suvesh handed Crow to him then climbed down to again take charge of the youngling. Uncaring that Mosk and Zul were watching, Ursula flung herself into Gil's arms. He caught her with a low grunt and buried his nose in her hair, concealing his surprise when he noticed how thin she'd gotten.

"I missed you so much, *elska'adir*," he murmured, lips brushing against her hair. He raised his eyes to meet Zul's black gaze, conveying his gratitude for having taken good care of the two people most precious to him over those long weeks.

Mosk and Zul descended from the carriage and followed Gil and Ursula into the house.

"How is Bran?" Ursula asked, her lower lip trembling.

"He will be better now that you, Crow, and Zul are here," Gil assured her as much as he assured himself.

Ursula pressed a kiss to his palm then said, "Take me to him."

Gil did as she bade him, Zul following close behind.

Ursula gasped when she saw the Fangrys Prime lying in bed, swathed in bandages and looking disturbingly small and ashen. She kneeled beside the bed and took one of his big hands between her much smaller ones.

"Bran, I am here. I'm fine. Our son is fine. Come back to us," she pleaded. "Don't leave us like Crow did. I couldn't bear it. We all need you. *I* need you."

She continued to talk, begging him to hear her, to wake up, to come back to them until her voice grew hoarse. When her parched throat rasped every word, she switched to mental communication. The physical link of touch strengthened the bond between them. Bran's mental barriers dissolved into nothingness as she barreled through them to his consciousness buried deeply in a swirling well of pain, dark regret, and sorrow.

Zul and Gil joined her. Each of her males rested a hand on her shoulder and a hand on what small patches of Bran's hide the bandages did not cover. Thus connected by touch and mind, they forged a bright beckoning that burned away Bran's darkness, splintered his regret, and crushed his sorrow, replacing them with hope and love and their need for him. They remained that way late into the night, connected and urging Bran's return.

"Come back to us, Bran. Don't abandon us," she whispered, her voice hoarse. "Please, or our unborn child will never know you."

The other two males' eyes widened with surprise.

"You're pregnant?" Gil growled. "Why didn't you say anything?"

Zul gulped, wondering how he could have not known. "Why didn't you tell me?"

She looked over each shoulder in turn to meet each male's gaze. "It wouldn't have changed anything."

"But... but..." Zul spluttered.

"We would not have permitted you to fly on the wyvern," Gil said. "Or to live in such primitive conditions."

"Oh, you knew about that?" she responded. She pressed a hand over her belly, leaving one hand on Bran's broad chest.

"Yes, I knew about that. So did Bran. But we didn't know about the babe."

Zul squeezed her shoulder, not hard enough to hurt, but enough to let her know he meant business. "Do not keep secrets from us, Ursula. I will not have you risking our young."

She sighed because she knew she had risked her pregnancy. "And if I had told you? What then? What would you have done differently?"

"We would not have retreated to the box canyon."

"And you would have taken us somewhere civilized, I suppose?" she countered in an arch tone. "A place where it would have been easy to find us? Easy to take us into custody?"

Gil winced. Zul opened his mouth to protest, but Gil shook his head. "No, Ursula, we would have proceeded more cautiously."

"You mean you would have delayed the necessary action to effect the reforms that would keep mates together?"

"That 'reform' is not as important as you and our youngling," Zul snapped.

Ursula retorted, "No, it's *more* important. Rooting out a corrupt government and replacing it with honorable people is bigger than me, bigger than our children: it's important to all of Uribern."

"Not to us," Gil said, cupping her cheek with the hand that had rested on her shoulder. "To us, *you* are more important than the Council Supreme."

"Never to us. Family is more important than *anything*," Zul added. "I lived without family for too long. I know exactly how important family is—how important *you* are. You are *everything*."

"And Bran will feel the same way," Gil added.

Ursula looked at Bran again, eyes welling with tears that trickled down her cheeks. "Don't abandon us, Bran." She moved closer to him and held his limp hand over her belly. "Please."

Bran's eyelids flickered open, and his nostrils flared as he finally caught her scent, ripe and rich with life despite her gaunt figure. His golden eyes remained unfocused, but he turned his head toward his mate. *I will never abandon you.*

His eyes fluttered closed again and he sighed, a small smile curling the corners of his mouth. The others relaxed, for this was a natural, healing sleep rather than the oblivion of unconsciousness and despair. The three of them remained by his bedside for a good while longer. Suvesh brought Crow in to see his parents and bid them goodnight. Another servant brought in trays of food and drink. Exhausted, Ursula fell asleep in Gil's arms, her legs resting on Zul's lap.

"Is she safe?" Zul said when he was sure she was sound asleep. "If not, I will take her and Crow somewhere else, somewhere they are not endangered."

"We are safe," Gil assured him. "And we're now on the new Council Supreme. You and Mosk have been assigned to serve as the new joint commanders of the Guard Supreme."

Zul grimaced. "I never wanted that." He stroked Ursula's calf. "A mate is all I ever dreamed of, and she is *perfect*."

"Nor did I or Bran particularly want to serve on the new council," Gil admitted with a shrug. "But bonded and mated males from each caste have been elected to the new council—and we were *elected*." He stroked her hair, reveling in the fine, silky texture. "And, yes, she is perfect for us. She completes us."

"Elected?"

"Aye. And the warrior caste has two triads representing the honor of the new council and assuming the duty of enforcing our laws. The Primes will serve as the executive arm, Seconds as the highest and final arbiters of the law—the judicial arm, if you will—and Thirds as the highest enforcement of the law."

Zul nodded. "Fangrys and who else?"

"Omari. Pako will serve as chairman of the council and Bran as his chief advisor."

Zul was not surprised. "The people believe us honorable males."

"Yes, and we are. All Uribern knows this."

Zul shook his head. "I never wished to rule."

Gil shrugged. "We will support our Prime and ensure the council remains free of corruption."

Zul looked at their slumbering mate. "And our mate?"

"She and other adult females now have the right to vote for their castes' representatives. That was our first order of business." Gil smoothed the hair back from her forehead again. He determined that his next order of business would be to ensure their mate ate properly—all the fruits and vegetables and cheese she wanted. He'd have to see about importing more chocolate, too.

Zul nodded. "She'll appreciate that."

"For now," Gil said with a small grin. Their human hybrid mate would not be satisfied for long with that meager progress. "She'll start demanding more rights soon enough."

Zul smiled with a full display of sharp teeth as he'd learned from his mate. "That she will. And will we relent?"

Gil grinned at him. "Of course not. But we'll keep her happy nonetheless."

Zul nodded and looked forward to a lifetime of distracting their mate with a lifetime of orgasms.

THANK YOU!

Thank you for reading *Four Play*, the final book in the *Triune Alliance Brides* series. I hope you enjoyed it.

Like all independent authors, reader reviews mean the world to me. The success of today's authors depends on reader reviews, so I hope you will take a moment of your time to leave a review.

ABOUT THE AUTHOR

Holly Bargo is a pen name but really did exist in the form of a temperamental Appaloosa mare. That horse has long since crossed the fabled Rainbow Bridge, and the author still has horses. The love of horses, she asserts, is like malaria: once you're infected, there's no cure.

The author has been writing since childhood and has published over 30 books since 2014. In the intervening decades between childhood and publication, Holly grew up, graduated from university with a Bachelor of Arts in English, married, and had two children. She and her husband have been married 37 years and live on a hobby farm in southwestern Ohio. Her first grandchild was born on Christmas Eve in 2024.

If you'd like to contact Holly directly, use the contact form on her website: www.hollybargobooks.com. She loves to hear from readers.

BOOKS BY HOLLY BARGO

SERIES

The Bounty (published by 0-0-8 Studios)

Book 1: *The Bounty: Jones*
Book 2: *The Bounty: Gerlaugh*

Twin Moons Saga

Book 1: *Daughter of the Twin Moons*
Book 2: *Daughter of the Deepwood*
Book 3: *Daughter of the Dark Moon*
Book 4: *Knight of the Twin Moons*
Book 5: *Champion of the Twin Moons*
Book 6: *Light of the Twin Moons*

Triune Alliance Brides

Book 1: *Triple Burn*
Book 2: *Double Cut*
Book 3: *Single Stroke*
Book 4: *Four Play*

Russian Love

Book 1: *Russian Lullaby*
Book 2: *Russian Gold*
Book 3: *Russian Dawn*
Book 4: *Russian Pride*
Book 5: *Russian Revival*

Immortal Shifters
Books 1 & 2: *The Barbary Lion & Tiger in the Snow* (duet)
Book 3: *Bear of the Midnight Sun*
Book 4: *The Eagle at Dawn*

Tree of Life
Book 1: *Rowan*
Book 2: *Cassia*
Book 3: *Willow*

STAND-ALONE TITLES

FOCUS
Hogtied
Shot from the Hip
Satin Boots
The Falcon of Imenotash
Ulfbehrt's Legacy
The Diamond Gate
Pure Iron
The Mighty Finn
Six Shots Each Gun (with Russ Towne)
The Dragon Wore a Kilt

SHORT STORIES

Skeins of Gold: Rumpelstiltskin Retold
By Water Reborn